Shredded
by Karen Avivi

Shredded

ISBN 978-0-9918079-3-2

First edition, April 2013

Printed in the United States of America.

For everyone who lives each day like an adventure.

Chapter 1

I noticed the speed bump too late and hit it hard with my front tire, forcing tension up my arms and into my neck until my teeth rattled. Why did I have such a death grip on my handlebars? It's not like this was my first time on a bike. I tried to convince myself that today was no big deal, but that was a lie. Landing my back flip in front of the other BMX riders would prove to them I was serious. Only two of the guys in our group had ever done it. Once I did it, the rest of them would have to. Guys were like that. They hated being outdone by each other, or worse, by a girl.

Hopefully they'd also shut up about me and Sean going out. Their stupid little comments about me being his groupie fueled my drive to master the flip. As I rode to the skate park I pictured the looks I wanted to see on every one of their faces. They'd be sure I was going to wipe out, and then when I landed it, ha! I pedaled faster as I imagined their stunned looks. I loved letting people underestimate me and then showing them how wrong they were.

I turned onto a narrow, packed-dirt shortcut that was only accessible to bikes and pedestrians. I'd had my driver's license for over a year, but I still preferred riding whenever possible. The shortcut saved waiting at two lights that always seemed to take forever.

Even though it was only eight in the morning, the air was heating up. I unzipped my hoodie while riding no-handed. Early May could be cool, crisp, and perfect, or crazy, wet, and windy. The ice and snow that had lingered into April were gone, but I'd been caught in hailstorms before at the skate park and it wasn't fun. The only shelter was to get against the fence under your bike and let the storm pummel ice balls at you.

I rounded the final corner to get to the entrance and saw the familiar cluster of guys in black hoodies already there, including one with a Relentless logo. Sean. Good. We needed to talk. We'd been going out since February, but I hadn't seen him at all last week and we had to finalize our plans for prom. My mom was all over me for details and I had none. He wasn't good at talking on the phone or texting more than short responses so I wanted to see him in person.

Wait until he saw my new trick. Then he'd not only be able to say his girlfriend rode BMX, but that she could do a back flip, too. The rest of the guys would shut up, and Sean and I could make our prom plans.

I coasted to a stop at the top of the bowl, across from the guys. Miguel pointed to me, made a back-loop motion in the air and pointed to the ramp, then held up his video camera.

He was right. If I hesitated or stopped to talk I might get nervous. I gave him a thumbs-up.

Miguel and I had worked on my flips first in foam pits, then in a wood-floor indoor park, and now I was ready for the concrete outdoor skate park. Like he kept reminding me, if I didn't fall, it wouldn't matter what I was riding on.

He pointed to his eyes and then the group signaling he'd get everyone watching.

I pulled off my hoodie and chucked it on the fence that surrounded the skate park. I eased into the concrete bowl and rode up and down a few low ramps to get the feel, then climbed the stairs carrying my bike to the top of the quarter-pipe. I resisted the urge to check to see if Sean was watching. Miguel would make sure. I had to focus. This was it. I would either raise the bar or do an epic face-plant. I could do this. I had done it before. This time was no different.

I breathed in and visualized the flip, slightly moving my hands and leaning at the right times to simulate the whole thing. As I exhaled, I squeezed my eyes for a few seconds, burning in the image of the perfect flip. The hardest part was just pushing off and going for it.

With my next inhalation I dropped down the ledge onto the quarter-pipe, letting gravity hurtle me toward the tabletop ramp. When I maxed out my momentum I poured all my energy into pumping harder and faster to hit the ramp at full force. Push. Move. Breathe. Go! As the incline angled me closer to vertical, my body readjusted automatically like it had the million times I'd practiced.

Breathing deeper and faster, I moved higher and closer to the point of no return. My front tire spun off the top of the ramp and I shifted my weight back as I tilted my head and shoulders to lead my body into the flip. Gravity pulled my bike down, popping the front wheel up and transferring all that speed into a fast, tight spin. A glimpse of sky flashed. My entire world shrank down to the zone immediately surrounding me. It was like creating my own private pod in the middle of everything and escaping for a few seconds. Feeling both exhilarated and a little out of control I let myself go with the power of the rotation. When I saw the ramp I still had plenty of height to let my bike level and hit the top deck perfectly balanced. Yesss!

Excess adrenaline surged through me as I luxuriated in the fleeting moment of invincibility. I had no team, no opponent, just me, my bike and gravity. All mine. The wipeouts, workout and hours of practice were worth this victory.

To let the momentum run out I went up another quarter-pipe and then dragged my feet down to stop before pumping my right fist in the air. Miguel was whooping and yelling while the other guys stood there, stunned. Hah.

I rode up out of the bowl, but before I got to the group, Sean dropped his bike and walked away. What was that about?

When I got close enough, Miguel gave me a high five. "I knew you could pull it off! Way to go, Josie."

I slapped his hand back and undid my helmet strap. "Thanks. I had a great coach." I forced my voice to stay low and controlled, stifling the deep breaths my body wanted.

Two of the guys who hadn't yet tried to flip in the park gave me tight smiles. Now that I'd done it, they'd catch all kinds of crap until they both did it.

"What's with Sean?" I looked around the park, and a flash of pink caught my attention. I recognized a sophomore girl from school... was it Mary or Mandy? Yeah, she was definitely in the year behind me.

"Look!" Miguel flipped the viewer on his camera and replayed the landing. "I haven't used this camera much yet, but I think I kept you in frame."

The flip looked perfect on the replay. "You've got to send it to me!"

I looked for Sean but didn't see him anywhere in the park. What was going on with him?

The new girl was on her bike, trying to make her way across the grass and closer to the concrete bowl where we were. She was on a new bike, wearing dark jeans and a pink T-shirt, but not riding with much confidence. She'd better not be another groupie.

I hoped she wasn't after Miguel. His last "fan" had been really loud and irritating. Wait. I was getting as bad as the guys. Maybe this girl genuinely wanted to ride.

Having another girl to ride with would be awesome, but Mary-Mandy would need my help if she was going to survive with this gang. They were vicious toward people who looked flashy but couldn't ride. I'd learned to dress the same as them in mostly black and gray. A hot-pink shirt would only remind them that she wasn't in the testosterone club.

I rode over to her and pulled off my helmet.

"Hey." I moved closer to get a better look at her bike. "Nice ride."

She blinked and stammered. "Uhhh."

If I was making her that nervous, she had no chance with the guys.

"J!" Miguel called and waved me back over.

I rode away from Mary-Mandy and pulled up next to Miguel. "What's up with her?"

Miguel looked behind me and then at the ground. I turned back to see Sean ride up to Mary-Mandy with his entourage of four guys from his school. The tension in Mary-Mandy's body visibly released, and she reached over to tuck a lock of Sean's hair into his beanie. Great, some sophomore was hitting on my boyfriend. I headed back over there to help clarify the situation for her. When she ran her hand down his arm I envisioned knocking her right off that bike but Sean grabbed her hand. Good. Finally.

But Sean didn't push her away. He kissed her.

My body froze. I couldn't even blink to erase what I was seeing. Every insecurity and doubt I'd ever had about how much Sean liked me and whether or not he was cheating on me assaulted me in full force. Oh no. This was not happening.

"What the hell, Sean?" I yelled as I dropped my bike in the grass and marched up to him, stopping between him and whatsername.

Sean cracked his fingers one at a time. He always did that when he got nervous.

"Is this why you've been avoiding me?" I said, looking him in the eye. "What about us? What about prom?"

Mary-Mandy backed up to get around me but I kept moving, effectively cutting her off.

"Sean?" I said, moving closer, not letting my eyes drop from his. He couldn't look at me. Coward. I was going to make him say it out loud. Quietly scurrying away wasn't my style.

"The thing is, I'm, uhh, kind of with Mindy now."

Mindy. She'd managed to maneuver her way behind Sean. Her blond, shoulder-length hair was cut almost the same as mine, but she had blue eyes and mine were brown. She looked a lot like me, which was a little creepy.

"Kind of?" I repeated. He was such an idiot. But I was a bigger idiot for ever trusting him. I would have preferred handlebars in the gut. At least when that happened I saw it coming.

"So you're kind of not with me." I forced my fingernails into my palms until the pain helped me focus and temporarily avoid the agonizing hurt I felt boiling up. "Were you kind of planning on telling me?"

The others guys moved away, pretending to look for stuff in their backpacks or checking their bikes for loose screws.

"He's taking me to his prom," Mindy added, moving closer to Sean and putting her hand on his arm.

My shoulders pulled back as my body reflexively prepared for a fight. Even though I wanted to make Mindy eat some dirt, I forced myself to funnel my anger toward Sean. Girls fighting over him would just feed his ego.

I rotated my wrists and tilted my head to crack my neck. I looked up at Sean. "Can I talk to you for a minute—alone?"

He walked with me a few feet away, leaving Mindy watching us.

I couldn't believe he had dumped me. For a sophomore? He so deserved a kick in the balls, it took every ounce of self-control not to do it. "Sean. Look at me. What is going on?"

He ran his hands through his hair and then shook it back into his eyes. "Nothing. I'm with Mindy. It's easier." He pivoted away from me, obviously dying to get out of the conversation.

"Easier? What does that mean?" He made me sound like a math problem. I put my hands on my hips.

He met my eyes for a second, and I saw aggravation. "I dunno. Less pushy." He cracked two knuckles on his left hand. "I gotta go."

I let him walk away as I tried to figure out what happened. Was he seriously choosing some miscellaneous girl over me?

Sean's words kept replaying in my head. *Easier... Less pushy...*

Miguel and the guys from Sean's school were out of listening range but still close, watching a couple of other guys ride. I tried to catch Miguel's eye, but he wouldn't look at me. None of them would look at me, and none of them seemed surprised or particularly interested.

The reality of the situation hit me. No wonder Miguel wanted me to do the flip first. He knew about Mindy. All those "working with my dad" nights of Sean's had really been "spending time with my new girlfriend" nights, and I was the last to find out.

Without bothering to strap my helmet back on, I grabbed my bike and took off, riding hard to hit the low rails for the noisiest grind I could manage. Anything to drown out the roaring in my ears. Without hesitation or any shred of consideration for whose turn it was I hit ramp after ramp, gaining air, landing hard, making noise and taking up space. The guys stayed out of my way, leaving the park wide open for me to burn off the fury, even though it wasn't possible. After I'd exhausted myself, I went alone to the fence and grabbed my hoodie.

Miguel rode over. "Sorry. I thought you knew."

"Would I have been introducing…" My voice cracked and I swallowed. "…introducing myself to her if I knew?"

"Well, you knew he was kind of a player, didn't you?"

I didn't answer. Miguel was right. Sean had a reputation for going through girls, but that didn't mean what he had done was okay.

Miguel handed me a can of VaporTrail energy drink. "Forget about them."

I took a big swig to soothe the razor blades in my throat. "He said she's easier and less pushy. Am I pushy? What does that even mean?" I held the can out to give it back, but Miguel waved it off, motioning for me to finish it.

"I'll deny ever saying this, but I have a theory," he said.

Miguel was big on theories. I took another long swig.

"You're too good for him."

I finished the last drops and crumpled the can. "Come on, you sound like my mom."

"I mean as a rider. How does it look when his girlfriend can do a back flip and he can't?"

"Like he has a really cool girlfriend." I threw the crumpled can in the direction of the recycling bin and it went in.

"Not to him. It makes him look like a wuss. Didn't you notice him avoiding going to the foam pits with us? He's chickenshit and you make him look bad."

His theory made sense. My doing a back flip before him made Sean look a little bad, but he'd done a lot of power moves I'd never attempted. Flexibility moves were easier for me. The back flip wasn't so much power or flexibility as commitment. Not his specialty.

"I can't ride here anymore if it means seeing Sean with someone else." I tied my hoodie around my waist. "Would you mind going to Lakewood? I know it's kind of far, but they have a better park, and we could still train this summer for the Ultimate."

"About that," Miguel said.

"What? Is it your knee?"

Miguel had injured his right knee twice in the past year and had just taken six months off completely. We'd been counting down the days until he could start riding again so we could train hard all summer and take advantage of this year's Ultimate competition being held only forty minutes away in Chicago.

"The doctor said it was okay. It's my parents." He drew a curved line in the dirt with the toe of his shoe and then scuffed it out.

The relief I felt when he said the doctor cleared him was the complete opposite of the misery I saw on Miguel's face.

"What's the problem?" I asked in a low, quiet voice.

He exhaled and looked up, squinting at the sun. "They won't sign any waivers, so I can't compete until I turn eighteen next year."

"But you can ride?" I asked. He couldn't be this upset over the Ultimate.

"We got into an ugly argument about it being a waste of time and I insisted I was hanging around the park to film, and my stepdad said it was bull and I kept insisting and he kept pushing, and..."

Miguel lowered his head, took a breath, and paused.

I didn't say anything as I waited for him to finish.

He spoke again, more slowly and controlled. "I think we were both kind of bluffing at first, but it escalated and the bottom line is I have to go to film camp." He looked at me and tried to smile a little.

"I didn't know there was such a thing."

"Neither did I, but my stepdad found one. Probably just an excuse to have me out of the house half the summer. I leave right after school finishes and I'll be gone until the end of July."

No Miguel for half the summer? And Sean polluting the park with Mindy? The pain, hurt and anger I'd ignored burst through my earlier patch job, and I felt the girliest of reactions coming on with no way to stop it.

Chapter 2

I barely got the words out to tell Miguel I'd talk to him later before getting on my bike to leave. *Do not cry in front of the guys.* I willed myself to hold together until I turned the corner away from the park.

In all my years of riding, I'd broken my ankle, impaled my leg on a branch and torn my abdominal wall without crying, but getting dumped in front of everyone for a nobody sophomore was too much. I pedaled hard, forcing my way through the air to create enough wind resistance to rip the tears off my face.

The faster I rode the angrier I got. Who did Sean think he was? I'd been going to that park way before he showed up. I rode as well or better than the guys, and that had been enough to make me part of their group, until today.

I felt six years old again, with my brother Troy kicking me out after my mom had forced him to drag me along with his friends. The only way they'd let me play was if I could keep up, and I always did. Back then I towered over most of them, but they started transforming into giants one by one. Finally, my mom made me stop playing contact sports with them about the time Troy turned thirteen and I was twelve, but I kept riding BMX.

Trees, cars and side streets whizzed by in a blur as I furiously spun my legs, fighting for more speed without losing control. My bike hit its limit and no matter how hard I pushed it wasn't going to go any faster. I backed off and coasted, looking up to see how far I'd gone.

Wait a minute, had I missed a turn? These weren't Prairie Vista houses. I was in the wrong development. Crap. I'd made the trip from the park to home so many times it was automatic. I kept riding, looking for something I recognized. The mixture of confusion and familiarity felt odd, but more intriguing than scary. The streets snaked around in a maze, ensuring that I couldn't backtrack my way out. I was trapped into finding my way through.

After passing a forest-green house I was sure I'd already gone by, I turned another corner and instantly knew where I was. Maplewood Park. My favorite sledding hill was right there. I must have turned into Eagle Ridge Estates by mistake.

I glanced back, feeling a little silly. I guess I'd never gone to the park from this direction. I hopped the curb, rode onto the grass and across the park to get home.

After putting my bike in the garage and going in the house, I kicked off my shoes and headed straight for my room. Unfortunately I ran into Troy on my way through the kitchen, almost knocking him down, which wasn't easy to do anymore.

"Don't damage the merchandise, freak queen! How 'bout losing the hoodie so you can see a little?" He yanked my hood back, revealing my tear-stained face.

"Whoa, what happened to you?"

"Leave me alone!" I pushed his hand off me and shoved past him.

"Josie? What's wrong?" I heard my mom say from another room.

I kicked Troy in the shins. "Thanks a lot."

"Any time." He moved out of range so I couldn't kick him again.

"Just a minute!" I yelled in response to my mom and ran to the bathroom.

I splashed cold water on my face to hide some of the tears, but my red-rimmed eyes were a giveaway.

I found my mom in the living room sewing gold lion-head patches onto blue fabric squares. As president of the Booster Club she was forever doing school spirit stuff for Troy's teams.

She put her project down and walked over to me. "Honey, are you okay?" She brushed my hair off my face and turned my head from side to side.

"I had a small wipeout. It's nothing. Stung a little, that's all."

"Were you wearing your helmet?"

"Yes, Mom, I was wearing my helmet. It wasn't even a bad fall." I moved a pile of magazines off a cushioned chair and sat down.

She narrowed her eyes at me. "You know I don't like you riding with those daredevils. They don't all wear helmets."

Daredevils. What a joke. Only Miguel ever tried anything good. And Sean, but I didn't want to think about him. I gave her the response she wanted to hear. "I can think for myself, Mom. Just because they don't wear helmets doesn't mean I don't wear a helmet."

"Okay, honey. Be careful. I worry about you. You don't have to prove anything to them you know."

That's where she was wrong. I did have something to prove to them. Prove that I belonged there as much as they did whether I was someone's girlfriend or not.

"Stay right there," she said. "I have a surprise for you."

"Okay." I hoped it would be something quick. All I wanted was to be in my room alone.

My mom came back holding a prom dress I'd tried on three weeks ago and loved, but it was way too expensive. The reddish-coral shade practically burned with intensity. I brushed my fingers over the soft fabric.

"A colleague of mine went to an outlet last week and I asked her to look for it. Even there it was a little over our budget, but I told her to get it."

I couldn't tell her I wasn't going. It wasn't exactly a lie, just an omission. I didn't want her worrying about me, and I wanted that dress.

She removed the hanger and held the dress up, turning it to look at all sides. "I hope this one is true to size. We can't take it back, but we should be able to fix anything that's wrong. Try it on!"

She'd bought me a nonreturnable expensive prom dress. So it couldn't go back whether I had a boyfriend or not. I was destined to have it.

"Josie?" The smile started to melt off her face.

No way was I telling her Sean dumped me. I'd find a way to wear it.

"Sorry." I took the dress and went to my room. "Be right back!"

I lay the dress on a chair and flopped down on my bed. How had this happened?

Yesterday I had the perfect date and no dress, and today I had the perfect dress and no date.

I tried to think back to when I should have noticed Sean being less interested in me. The only thing I could think of was that when he'd mentioned getting a hotel room for after prom, I'd told him to forget it, there was no way my parents would let me stay out all night.

We'd done more than kiss, but not that much more. That might be because Troy had threatened to pummel anyone who tried anything with me. I couldn't wait for him to graduate and be gone. At least I'd have my senior year with no hovering older brother. The whole situation was making my head spin and all I could picture was Sean next to Mindy, and Mindy wearing my dress.

"Josie? Do you need help?"

I had to put that dress on before my mom burst into my room. She was so excited, I couldn't tell her about Sean. I'd have to figure something out.

"I'll be right out!" I peeled off my T-shirt and jeans and slid into the dress, but I couldn't zip it, so I walked out holding it against my chest.

She was so happy she practically bounced up and down. "Here. Stand on this," she said, pointing to the footstool she'd pulled into the middle of the living room.

She zipped me up and spun me around.

"Oh, Josie. It's perfect." She took a few steps back. "I'm going to go get the camera!"

I turned to look at myself in the mirror on the wall, and she was right. The dress was perfect for me. It hugged curves that didn't show in other clothes and made me look about five years older. Sean wasn't worthy of this dress.

"Take off those dirty socks!" she shouted as she retreated down the hall.

My white socks had a black grime outline above where my shoes had been.

I balanced on one foot to pull off the first sock, and when I put my bare foot down, I heard the house security system beep as the door from the back deck to the kitchen opened.

"Josie! Gianna is here," Troy shouted.

"Send her to the living room!" Gianna and I had been friends since we were little, and neither of us used the front door at each other's houses.

Gianna came into the living room with her boyfriend Bruce trailing behind her, checking messages on his phone. She clapped a hand over her mouth and walked around me.

"I love that dress! The color is gorgeous on you."

"Thanks." With her olive skin and long dark hair, Gianna could wear almost anything. She'd ordered a custom-made dress months ago.

"Where did you find it?"

"My mom got it, but…" I lifted the dress a few inches and let it resettle on my legs.

"We heard," Bruce said. "Dumped."

Why did Bruce and Gianna always have to be together? I knew she was happy to have a boyfriend, but I missed having my best friend to myself sometimes. Like now.

"How could you possibly know that already?" I asked.

"Min…" Gianna stopped when she saw the look I was giving her and then she started over. "I mean that sophomore slut…" She looked at me for approval and I nodded.

She continued "…changed her online status already and so did your evil ex."

Perfect. Just perfect

"You should change yours, cuz it looks kinda pathetic." Bruce didn't look up from his phone.

"I only found out I was single like, an hour ago."

"Got it!" I heard my mom say from down the hall.

"Don't tell my mom." I pulled off my other sock, stepped back up onto the footstool and put an *I'm a happy girl with a non-jerk boyfriend and a gorgeous prom dress* smile on my face.

My mom walked in with the camera. "Gianna, it's so nice to see you." Gianna and I used to be together almost every day, but lately we only saw each other outside of school maybe once a month.

"We were out finalizing the details for Bruce's tux, and I wanted to stop by."

Bruce looked up from his phone. "The cummerbund selection is complete."

"He's said that word like a hundred times since we left the rental place. It's making me crazy."

"Cummerbund." Bruce hugged Gianna around the waist and then busied himself with his phone again.

"We need to get going. I just wanted to say hi." Gianna unzipped her purse and pulled out sunglasses.

"Let me get some pictures."

Before I could figure out a way to stop her, my mom made the three of us pose for pictures. It was completely ridiculous. Why would we want pictures of me in my new dress with Gianna and Bruce?

She finally lowered the camera. "You should drop by more often, Gianna. We miss you."

Ohmigod, this was so embarrassing.

Gianna tugged on the side of her skirt. "Me too. It's been busy."

"I'm going to go take this off. Can you unzip it a little?" I moved my ponytail so Gianna could start the zipper. "I'll walk you guys out."

Gianna and Bruce said goodbye to my mom and I went with them on the back deck.

"Don't worry," Gianna said. "We'll find you someone to go to prom with, right?" She elbowed Bruce.

"Huh?" He looked at her and then at me. "Yeah, sure."

"I can't promise he'll be as good as Bruce, but we'll try." Gianna hugged me goodbye.

I watched as they left. I didn't want a Bruce. Bruce was too... too... I didn't know exactly. Predictable? Boring? Maybe that's the kind of guy I should have wanted. Someone who wore khaki pants and collared shirts and gelled his hair. My

preference for an unpredictable boyfriend had left me alone
with a dress and a bike.

Chapter 3

Even though I didn't want to think about Sean, prom, and everything else, my online status had to be updated right away. I was forced to use the family computer in the kitchen because my parents wouldn't let us have computers in our rooms. I logged on to my HeadSpace profile and removed relationship status completely because none of the choices worked for me. Complicated? No. Getting dumped was pretty simple. Looking for? A little revenge might be nice, but definitely not a Sean replacement.

I scanned my messages, not reading most of them until I ran across an update from Exquisite, the girls-only BMX group. It said "We're on the move!" and gave their new website address with images of different girls riding over the words *Gearing up for the best summer of BMX ever.*

A couple of girls I met at an indoor BMX event in January told me about Exquisite. I'd created a basic profile online, but then I got together with Sean, and I never updated my information or followed up with anyone. On the Exquisite site I scanned through the forum looking for any posts about the Ultimate contest or anyone in the area I could ride with over the summer. I could enter the Ultimate without Miguel, Sean and the guys, but I couldn't show up there alone like the world's biggest loser. Plus I needed to train. I could train by myself a lot, I had a half-pipe in my backyard, but it definitely helped to have someone watch me and to see what other people were doing.

The online forum at Exquisite had a handful of posts about people planning to make the trip to the Ultimate from all over the country. I clicked on one from someone called A1 with the subject "Road-trippin' 'n trainin'" and saw it was from Alexis Jacobs, a girl I knew from gymnastics years ago. She was pretty obnoxious then, flashy and loud. I went to her profile and it looked like she'd only gotten worse. There were at least twelve videos of her posing and talking, plus dozens of head shots of her. Alexis's videos and pictures had tons of anonymous comments like "Lookin' good, Lexie!" and "Nice ride." Ugh.

Her friends list included the name Lauryn Jax. I remembered seeing her at the event in January, but we hadn't talked. Lauryn's profile was professional-looking, with two videos where she pulled off some nice tricks and one still shot of her with her bike. She'd blocked comments. Lauryn always looked serious, never smiling. I couldn't picture her and Alexis riding together.

In the forums, Lauryn had posted a few things, but not much. Alexis was all over the forums, but she ran the whole site so it made sense she was keeping the conversations going. I couldn't find much information about her actually riding, but she was the only one who lived near me and openly invited people to contact her about getting together for training.

My profile needed to be fixed before I sent a message. I'd never changed the default icon or posted any good shots of me riding. I went back to my HeadSpace account to see if there was anything in my albums I could use.

One new message.

Sean.

An apology for being such an idiot?

"Hey, J. Can I get my Ambiguous Pluto shirt back?"

Was he kidding? First, he couldn't call me J anymore. That was for friends only. Second, since he dumped me in such a dickhead move, everything he ever gave me was fair game for abuse, sacrifice, and revenge.

Wants his shirt back. Should have thought of that before.

"No. I'm using it to clean my bike." I posted it as a reply to his comment on my wall where everyone could see it. Hah. I'd definitely get some "thumbs-up" for that.

The only action pictures I could find were a couple of old cell-phone shots, and Sean was in the best ones. I managed to use a paint program to replace his head with a black rectangle, making him look like a criminal. Perfect.

I posted my new photos on Exquisite and then wrote a message to Alexis, telling her I was in Oakton and maybe we could get together to ride. I read it over about eight times, making sure I sounded casual and not desperate before hitting send.

Staying home alone on a Saturday night was a choice. Gianna had tried to get me to go out and get back in the game. But that would have involved just *happening* to bump into one of Bruce's single friends like the time we met Jared, described to me as "sporty." Yeah, in a psycho obsessive-compulsive way. Jared had rattled off football statistics endlessly.

When I suggested that someone a little edgier might be more my type, Gianna found Liam. He played guitar in a popular band and at first seemed cool, but any time I tried to bluff my way through a conversation about indie bands I liked, he'd keep drilling "Which song?"

"Uhh, Coco Loco."

"The album version, the one they did online with their replacement drummer or the live version they recorded on tour last spring?"

I didn't know. I had no idea. I didn't even like the band that much. I was trying to be nice and see where it got me.

That's why Sean should have been perfect. We already shared a common interest, but we didn't spend hours obsessively discussing bike frames and forks and pegs. It wasn't that interesting even to us. So what was it about Sean? Well, he was good-looking. So I might be shallow, but he was exactly my type: athletic without being bulky and attractive without being all hair-gelled and fashion-forward. He looked great in a T-shirt and jeans. I had to stop thinking about him.

I approached my closet, slid open the mirrored door and looked at the mess. This was the perfect opportunity to purge old stuff I never wore anymore. The problem was I still liked most of it. Like my entwined vines T-shirt. I remember finding it on sale and Gianna and I both wanted it so she got the blue one and I got the red one. I hadn't seen hers in a while.

She probably got rid of it a long time ago.

I pulled it off the hanger, but then put it back and slid the door closed.

Doing my closet was too ambitious to start. I surveyed the books, magazines and clothes piled everywhere and then flopped on my bed to think of a plan.

The ceiling fan was spinning on low and I realized I'd never paid much attention to it. The edges of the blades looked kind of dusty. I could turn it off, get the vacuum and clean it.

Maybe it would be better to do a workout. Miguel had been bugging me to strengthen my core. Yes. Good idea. I lay there, thinking about it, but moving seemed like too much effort.

I could feel inertia and leadenness settling in for the night. Maybe I should have forced myself to go out. Miguel had invited me to hang out with him, but he went to the same school as Sean so the risk of bumping into Sean and Mindy was too high.

I pulled a pillow over my head to try to block out the Sean thoughts. If I could get through the rest of the school year I could focus on the summer. The summer of having nothing to do and no one to hang out with. Last summer was bad enough with Gianna meeting Bruce and transforming herself from my best friend into Bruce's girlfriend.

At first I was happy for her because he seemed nice, and he was nice. I figured they would fizzle when school started up, but instead they became the class couple. Gianna and I still talked, but our friendship was a distant second to her relationship with Bruce.

Miguel was the one who saved me. We had always been friends, and we started hanging out a lot more after Gianna ditched me. When he was recovering from his first injury last August, he spent a lot of time coaching me.

The ceiling fan was making me cold so I crawled under the comforter. Oh no. This was how it would start. I was in bed at nine thirty on a Saturday night.

After counting to three, I forced myself to get up. I went to the family computer and logged on. My messages showed no replies from Alexis yet.

I wasn't sure which was making me more anxious, being dumped or not being able to go back to the park to ride. Out of my list of two hundred friends on HeadSpace, none of them were people I could ride with or hang out with all summer.

I searched through online coverage of recent BMX competitions hoping to find videos of girls, but all the highlight clips featured the same handful of guys, in particular R.T. Torres. I bookmarked a link to the double back flip he did at the recent Xcite contest in Argentina.

Before logging off I checked my messages again and saw one from Alexis. *"OMG!!! Josie Peters from gymnastics??!! CALL ME!!!"* and she included her cell number.

She'd sent the message at ten thirty. It was eleven. She was probably still up. I could call. Or wait until tomorrow. I didn't want to look overly eager. Her message was pretty eager, though. Maybe I didn't have to worry about looking eager to her.

I punched in her number and she answered instantly as if she'd been holding her phone.

Loud conversation surrounded her. "Who is this?" Her tone was accusatory as if I'd broken a restraining order by calling.

"Josie Peters. You gave me your number."

"Josieeee!" Her tone changed to that of a kindergarten pal. "Where are you?"

"Oakton." Hopefully she wouldn't drill down to the fact that I was home.

She let out a long dramatic sigh. "You're so far." Her tone had changed again to extreme sadness. What was with her? Was she drunk? Maybe this was a bad idea.

"Stooop!" She let out a high-pitched squeal.

"You sound busy. I'll call back tomorrow."

"Wait. Hang on a minute." I heard a muffled sound as if she'd put her hand over her phone. The background noise dropped. "Let's make plans for next weekend." Finally she sounded almost coherent.

"Lauryn and I want to ride with you. She said she saw you at the Indoor Jam in January."

Even though Alexis seemed a little crazy, I couldn't afford to be picky. I needed people to train with. "Why don't you both come over here Saturday afternoon? I have a half-pipe in my backyard."

"Lauryn will love that! Send me the deets."

After I hung up, my phone prompted me to add her to my contacts. I hesitated, but added her. If it turned out to be a mistake I could always delete her later.

Chapter 4

For school Monday I had to hit the right balance of looking like I could have a boyfriend, but didn't desperately need one. If I could get through the first day, my dumping would be old news and I could move on.

Gianna made me promise to meet her early before school. I found her on the benches by the tennis courts where Bruce and the team had an early morning practice.

"I found a prom date for you." She sat up straight and turned to face me. "It's only weeks away, so you can't be picky."

Uh oh. If she wasn't even trying to build him up as my perfect life partner, he was hopeless.

"Let me at least try to find one myself before you go slumming for me. Give me until the end of the week."

"Too late. I already talked to him. He's not that bad." She gave me an obviously fake smile.

Not that bad? Not that bad was not good.

"No way. I'm not going with some loser." I stared her down so she'd know this wasn't a joke to me.

"He's not a loser. He's… misunderstood. You don't want that dress to go to waste, do you?"

She was right. I didn't have much choice. I closed my eyes and braced myself to find out who she'd asked. "Fine. Tell me."

"Connor Knight."

"Ha, ha. Very funny." Connor Knight was probably a genius, but borderline criminal.

"Come on—who?"

"Seriously, Connor."

"He's not even in school." Rumors said he was the one who managed to access the ventilation system and make the boys' locker room smell like buck urine last Wednesday. But there was no actual evidence, so he was only suspended on a technicality over ditched study halls.

"He'll be back today."

"How would you know that?"

"He's Bruce's cousin, remember?" She glanced at the courts and then looked back at me. "I saw him yesterday at a family party. Connor lost at Truth or Dare Monopoly and his brother dared him to go to prom. I told him I'd set it all up."

"Truth or Dare Monopoly?"

"Don't ask. The point is, it's him or no one."

I squeezed my eyes shut and pictured my dress. I could beg Miguel to go with me. If he felt sorry for me he might say yes. But I couldn't do that to him. He hated school events. Plus, then my parents would start raising their eyebrows every time I hung out with him, like *mmm hmm, just friends, sure…* If we were ever going to be more than friends it would have happened by now.

I tilted my head from side to side to crack my neck and then tried to stretch my shoulders. My whole body felt tight and uncomfortable. I stood and turned away from Gianna.

"I'm trying to help you."

I walked to the end of the row of bleachers and paused before turning back. She was right. I had no choice.

I slumped down onto the bench. "Fine. I'll go with Connor."

"Be nice."

"I'm nice." I dug through my backpack to get out my phone. Miguel and I usually checked in with each other before school.

"To Connor. When he asks you."

Great. So I had that awkward conversation to look forward to. And our lockers were only two apart, so as soon as I went to my locker, my fate would be sealed. The psycho's date.

Miguel texted that he'd seen my Exquisite profile and wanted to shoot more video of me. I told him to pick a day, then powered my phone off and slipped it into my backpack.

The tennis team finished their practice and Bruce came over to talk to Gianna.

Bruce punched me in the arm. "So you and Connor, huh?" He laughed and then ran into the school.

"You'll see," Gianna said. "It'll be fun. He's funny."

We went inside and of course, there was Connor, at our lockers.

Gianna shoved me. "Go."

I already had everything I needed for my first class but I went to my locker anyway. Amazing how something I'd done five or six times a day all year suddenly felt so uncomfortable.

I should say hi. I opened my mouth at the exact moment he bent down to pull something from the bottom. Had he seen me and ducked?

I shut my mouth, feeling ridiculous as I turned the combination dial on my lock, acutely aware of him next to me. I swung the door open exactly ninety degrees. It opened more and I grabbed it, but it resisted. I looked up to face Connor holding my locker door.

"Are you Josie?" he asked.

I didn't answer. We had classes together. He knew who I was.

"Gianna's friend?"

What was he doing? Asking me practice questions? We stood there looking at each other. I could *kill* Gianna, *kill* her. He seemed to be waiting for *me* to say something.

We stood there in a silent face-off. I played back my conversation with Gianna. I was sure she said he would ask me.

Wait, this was Connor. He was probably purposely trying to weird me out.

"Are you doing some sort of experiment on awkward social situations?" I asked him.

He grinned. "I'm always on the lookout for interesting data."

I closed my locker and started to turn away, but he put his hand on my elbow.

"Wait. Have you talked to Gianna since yesterday?"

"Yes." I turned to face him again. He actually wasn't bad-looking. His hair had a not-gelled, casual thing going, and he was built like a distance runner, lean and wiry. It was his eyes that got me. I was usually good at staring contests, but with Connor, I felt uncomfortable after a few seconds.

"So you'll go to prom with me."

"Yes." I forced myself to look right at him and hold steady.

Surprise and relief flashed in his brown, almost-black eyes before he blinked. "Excellent. But if you don't mind my asking, why aren't you already going?"

"She didn't tell you?"

"I didn't ask her." A spray-paint can fell out of his locker and rolled across the linoleum floor.

Connor let go of my elbow and retrieved the can.

I shifted my books closer to my body. "I got dumped Saturday. My ex is now going out with some sophomore."

He shook the can, causing the mixing beads to rattle against each other. "His loss." He chucked the empty-sounding can into the mess of books and papers in the bottom of his locker and pulled a smart phone out of his pocket. Getting caught using a phone in the building meant having it confiscated for a month.

"Peters, Josie. Prom date." He kept punching in data without looking up. "Eyes, brown. Hair, blond. Height, five foot four.

He was starting to creep me out.

"Weight..."

"Don't even go there." I tore off a scrap of paper and wrote my phone number on it. "Here's my number. That's all you need."

He looked up at me. "Blood type?"

"Why would you need my blood type?"

"Any history of motion sickness?"

"Just take my phone number." I handed him the scrap.

"I like to have comprehensive profile information."

Mindy and three of her sophomore henchwomen walked by. She was wearing one of Sean's T-shirts.

I swore under my breath.

"What?" Connor looked up.

"Not you. My replacement just paraded by in one of my ex's T-shirts."

He craned his neck to see behind him. "Which one?"

"Red shirt. Blond."

"Ahh. Want her to have a little trouble this afternoon? No permanent scarring. Mainly inconvenience and humiliation. It can be arranged."

"Let me think about it." I was tempted.

He entered my number in his phone, then flipped the scrap of paper and wrote his number on the back in neat, perfectly even handwriting.

"There. You can call in a strike any time. I'm running a last-minute prom- date special."

As he handed me the paper, the warning bell rang. Connor shut his locker, grinned at me and took off down the hall.

Chapter 5

I woke up early Saturday even though I hadn't set my alarm. I was so used to getting up and going riding that it was automatic. Stupid Sean. Because of him I was stuck auditioning potential new friends I found online. I purposely dug around my T-shirt drawer to find the bright blue MadKapp shirt I hadn't been wearing lately because Sean hated it. Hah. It fit perfectly.

An hour before Alexis and Lauryn were going to show up I got my bike out of the garage. I'd spent all Friday night doing a big spring cleaning, including taking the chain completely off and soaking it in degreaser, then readjusting everything to be in perfect condition. I arranged my helmet and gloves on the ground next to my bike, and I swept all the leaves and debris off the half-pipe.

After rechecking my bike, the half-pipe, my helmet and gloves, I went inside to check the time again. They should be arriving any minute. I couldn't expect too much. I'd been burned before by people who said they wanted to ride, but really only wanted to hang around with their bikes and talk. I understood that the social stuff was what it was all about for some people, but not me.

I rode to not think about anything.

When I was into it on a good day, it was almost like being disconnected from the rest of my life. I loved it and I needed to get it back.

I checked my phone. No messages. I couldn't sit around waiting. I got a piece of paper, drew an arrow on it, and wrote, "I'm in back—Josie." As I taped it to the front door, a burgundy Mazda3 pulled into the driveway, and a girl with a long brown ponytail got out.

"Lauryn?" I said.

She nodded. In person, she was much taller than I expected and super-skinny.

"You said you have a half-pipe?" she asked.

No chitchat. Perfect. I liked Lauryn already. "Yeah, in back. Should we wait for Alexis?"

"Do you like waiting?"

"Not really."

"Then we should start."

A tiny bubble of hope pushed its way into my thoughts, saying *See? It's all going to work out.* I allowed the bubble to stay, but not expand. I still had to see how she acted riding, giving and taking suggestions, and wiping out.

Lauryn got her bike out and I saw that she had a similar frame to mine, plus she'd swapped a few components and added front and rear stunt pegs to the axles on both sides of her wheels, exactly like me. She noticed the similarities between our bikes, too and asked me if I did most of the work on it myself.

I told her yes and showed her the big bar I'd added so I could do tailwhips. I explained that I'd been doing mostly street and park riding lately, but I still liked doing vert tricks on the half-pipe.

We carried our bikes up the steps to the half-pipe deck on the side closest to the garage.

I hoped I hadn't over-described my setup. I mean it was a nice half-pipe, but it wasn't like I lived in a mansion on acres of land. It was a pretty standard middle-class suburban house with a decent-sized yard and enough space so you couldn't see into the neighbors' windows, but the two facing ramps and trough of the half-pipe took up the whole yard. When we'd moved in Troy was only two and I was a baby and my mom had the old aboveground pool removed. They put the half-pipe up for Troy when he got into skateboarding and then upgraded it with metal coping along the lip when I started using it for BMX.

"Want to go first?" I asked.

She shook her head. "You go."

I'd spent countless hours riding that half-pipe and was comfortable with tricks I didn't try anywhere else. I started by riding down one side, up the other and doing a basic double-peg grind, turning my bike at the top of the curve so I landed sideways on my wheel pegs before dropping back down.

I kept riding from side to side doing different grinds each time I hit the upper lip. I tried one involving my rear peg plus a 180-degree turn but I lost control and landed on my left hip under my bike. I stood up, shook my legs out, and climbed out of the trough.

Looking down from the deck, Lauryn said, "Nice," then dropped in and did a 360-degree air turn at the top of the opposite side, landing in a fakie so she was riding backward down the ramp. Not an easy trick. She was good.

Each time she reached the top of the curve she did an air trick, and she missed a lot of them, but she'd jump right back on her bike and go again. Her riding style reminded me of Miguel's. No fear.

She kept doing different tricks, some I recognized but didn't know what they were called and others I'm sure I'd never seen before. She was landing badly, tumbling with her bike rolling over her until she reached the trough of the half-pipe.

Each time she got up she'd check her bike, climb back up and go again. Stopping wasn't an option for her.

My hands and feet started moving with hers, and adrenaline flowed through my body as if I were the one riding nonstop. I mouthed silent instructions to her when I could see what she needed to do. *Push down, hop up, shoulders back, lean forward, yes!*

Something wet and cold touched my right forearm.

"Aaaah," I yelled, snatching my arm away.

"Mesmerizing, isn't she?" said a girl with spiky black hair and a nose stud, clutching three slushie drinks together. Was this Alexis? Online she had sandy brown hair with chunky, light-blond streaks.

I jumped up so she wasn't towering over me and was happy to see she was my height or possibly shorter, but not taller. What was with the drastic change in her appearance? I couldn't ask without it sounding like I didn't like her new look, which I didn't.

"Lemon okay?" she asked as she put the drinks down.

"Alexis?"

She nodded and handed me the yellow slushie cup.

"We need some tunes." She pulled a set of expensive battery-powered speakers out of her purse and connected them to her digital music player. An Ambiguous Pluto song blasted into the yard.

Lauryn turned to us when the music started. "Hey!"

"Take a break already!" Alexis said.

When Lauryn rode over, Alexis handed her a blue slushie.

"Did you bring your bike or just all this crap?" Lauryn asked.

"If you don't want it, give it back," Alexis said, reaching to take the drink away.

Lauryn held it over Alexis's head. "Forget it, shorty."

All three of us took our drinks to the driveway so Alexis could get her bike out of one of those sporty topless SUVs that could make a trip to the grocery store fun. I watched as she lifted her bike out of the back with one hand and I tried not to think about how I always had to wrestle my bike in and out of the trunk of my mom's car.

"So, how's it going? Lauryn's good, huh?" she said to me.

"Yeah, impressive."

"Did you see Josie ride yet?" she asked Lauryn.

Lauryn nodded.

"And?"

"Not bad."

Not bad? Not bad? I hadn't done anything super-impressive, but I should have ranked more than "not bad."

"Don't worry," Alexis said. "That's high praise coming from her."

"Looks like I'm up." Alexis changed the song, turned up the volume, and hit the half-pipe.

At the top of the rise, she stopped on her back wheel and held it, paused, completely still. It was a trademark move to show control. I counted off silently like I did when I was trying to balance like that, one Mississippi, two Mississippi, three Mississippi. After six Mississippis I stopped counting and stared, afraid to blink. I couldn't see her moving or twitching at all, it was as if she'd managed to freeze herself. Finally, when I couldn't stand it anymore, she spun around and dropped back. She popped up on her front wheel on the other side, dropped back, popped up high on her back wheel, and kept dropping and popping without ever breaking her flow or showing any loss of control. It was truly incredible. I wished the guys could see these two ride; they'd never make fun of girl riders again.

I thought of the hours I'd wasted that week mooning over Sean and wished I'd spent them practicing instead. Alexis and Lauryn obviously trained hard.

Alexis had been riding for what felt like twenty minutes nonstop and she didn't look tired. The sun blasted heat down as if it were mid-July instead of early May. Even though I was only sitting there watching, droplets of sweat ran down my spine. I'd already finished my slushie and was dying for another cool drink.

When Alexis finished, I stood up and clapped and so did Lauryn. I heard a long, loud series of whistles from behind us and I turned to look.

Troy.

"Aren't you going to introduce me?" he asked, walking up in a pair of cutoff sweatpant shorts and no shirt.

"Alexis, Lauryn, Troy. Bye."

He straightened himself up to a full muscular flex, showing off the physique he obsessively worked on with year-round training. He couldn't have been more obvious if he were a male gorilla pounding on his chest.

Lauryn took a step back, but Alexis blatantly looked Troy over from head to toe.

"Troy, *bye*!" I made a shooing motion with my hands as if I were trying to move cattle. "Go put a shirt on."

He swaggered away slowly, knowing that Alexis was watching him.

"Sorry about that, I said. "He's..."

"Would he be going to watch you compete?" she asked.

Troy hadn't shown much interest in anything I did for years, but my parents might force him to watch me at the Ultimate, so I answered, "Sure."

"Ohhh," she said, looking past me to see if he was still parading around half-dressed.

As much as Troy irritated me, I wasn't above using his questionable appeal to help me get in this group.

I started to put my helmet back on so I could go again and take my riding up a notch when another car pulled in the driveway, a sporty Nissan. Miguel got out and waved to me.

"What is this, hot-guy central?" Alexis asked.

Miguel walked over and leaned on the fence to the backyard. "I'm glad you're home," he said to me. "Are you busy Thursday afternoon? I can do your video then if you have time."

I shook my head at him. He could have called or texted. He dropped by to see what Alexis and Lauryn were like.

I opened the gate so he could come in the backyard. "Thursday works for me."

"You're doing a video?" Alexis looked at me and then at Miguel.

"Would you film all of us, like a team video?" she asked him.

"Alexis!" Lauryn said.

"Arrange it with Josie," Miguel told her.

I couldn't tell if he was serious about filming everyone or trying to shake Alexis off. I pulled him aside so we could talk without Alexis hearing me. "Are you sure about the group video?" I asked.

"Once I do the setup it's no big deal. How's it going? Okay?"

"Yeah. Better than okay. Too bad you missed seeing them ride. They're good."

I brought him over and introduced him to Lauryn and Alexis. He said something about liking Lauryn's bike before leaving and telling me to call him later.

"So, what's the story there?" Alexis asked after he left.

"Story?"

"Is he another brother?"

"He's a friend."

"Are you guys...?" She gave me a look and a suggestive grin.

"Friends," I told her.

"Just friends? Is he gay?"

"What? No!"

"So why just friends?"

"Can we inventory Josie's hot guy friends inside with cold-drink refills?" Lauryn asked.

"Good idea." I told them to leave their bikes against the house in back, and we went inside. While I was getting out lemonade, Alexis wandered around the living room looking at family photos.

"Why didn't you tell me your brother was so hot?" Alexis asked.

"Because he's smelly and irritating."

Lauryn laughed and helped pour the lemonade while Alexis leaned forward on the kitchen island. "So what's his deal?"

"He got a baseball scholarship to Michigan State and he starts there in the fall." I slid a glass to her.

"That's not what I meant. Does he have a girlfriend?"

"He has tons of girlfriends." I opened a container of oatmeal chocolate chip cookies that miraculously weren't gone yet.

"I mean *girlfriend* girlfriend."

"He has companions for the evening," I said, wondering if she was the same way with guys. "Take a number."

I passed the cookie container to Lauryn, who took one, but Alexis acted like it was invisible and sat back in her chair, somewhat deflated.

Scaring her off would be a mistake. Much as I detested Troy, if he could help me win over Alexis, I'd encourage her a little.

"But you're definitely his type."

She instantly brightened and took a cookie.

Lauryn looked at me and rolled her eyes.

"Since we're doing inventory, who is that guy whose head you blocked out in your profile pictures?" Lauryn asked.

"My ex. Sean." I explained about Mindy at the park and not wanting to go back.

Lauryn shook her head. "That sucks."

"You need to meet some new guys and you'll forget about him." Alexis raised her glass to her mouth, but then tilted it away and kept talking. "I know you said you want to train and do the Ultimate, but why not do all the summer events with us? We need to get more girls signed up so more competitions add a girls' category. Tell her, Lauryn."

All the summer events? Just doing the Ultimate seemed close to impossible.

Lauryn drew watery circles on the kitchen island. "Competing is good training."

"We're doing every event that's drivable starting with the Titanic BMX Throwdown," Alexis said. "There's the Outrageous Jam in Ohio in June, Explosion in Milwaukee in July and then the Ultimate in August. It's going to be awesome."

Lauryn ate a cookie while Alexis continued. "We're getting as many girls to go as we can. MadKapp has been expanding their girls' team, and I heard they're looking for US BMX riders."

I choked down a bite of cookie. "Where did you hear that?"

"Lauryn, tell her while I run to the bathroom." Alexis got up and I pointed her in the right direction.

"One of my friends is sponsored by MadKapp. They're talking about the US, but the girls' scene here has been getting smaller instead of bigger so they're not sure. We need people at the summer events," Lauryn said.

I put the empty cookie container in the sink. Riding at different parks, getting sponsored by MadKapp—it all sounded incredible.

Chapter 6

After Lauryn and Alexis left I went back to the kitchen and put Alexis's glass in the dishwasher.

Being able to train and ride with Lauryn might make putting up with Alexis worthwhile.

The door to the garage swung open and my mom pushed her way in, her arms loaded with groceries.

I grabbed three bags. "Mom, you don't have to bring everything in at once."

She dropped the rest on the floor. "It's my workout."

"It would be more cardio if you carried one bag at a time."

"True." She pushed her hair off her face. "Is your brother home?"

"He left a while ago, and I haven't heard him come back yet." I closed the door to the garage and helped her unload the bags, half-listening as she told me about everyone she bumped in to at the store. She got my attention when she mentioned a girl from my school going on a summer trip.

"You know Bianca, Lucie's daughter?" She didn't wait for a response as she put two boxes of oven-ready lasagna noodles on the counter.

"She was turned down by Habitat for Humanity so she and her friends created their own plan. They're going to El Salvador to help set up a counseling clinic for women. That girl has gumption. She doesn't let anyone stand in her way when she wants to do something."

She kept talking about other kids in my school, but most of those stories were the usual house-party fiasco or surprisingly current makeup and breakup information. By now she probably knew about me and Sean, but thankfully she hadn't mentioned anything. The speed and accuracy of the mom circuit scared me sometimes.

When we finished putting groceries away, she told me to go do homework so she could start dinner. I knew it was code for get out of the kitchen and keep out. She hated having anyone underfoot when she cooked. She wouldn't even allow my dad in the kitchen to help.

I went to the computer and checked for messages. A long, rambling text from Alexis repeated what she'd already told me about really, really, really needing more girls to sign up for the Midwest events and included links to all the competitions they planned to do over the summer and a reminder about Miguel filming the three of us on Thursday. Lauryn sent a bulleted list of strategies, video links, and tricks from previous years.

If Bianca could get her parents to let her work in a clinic in Central America, then I should be able to convince my parents to let me travel to neighboring states. I needed to know exactly what kind of time and money I was looking at, so I prepared a detailed itinerary for the entire summer. My plan included a complete breakdown of costs, mileage, stopping points, and local emergency contacts. Doing all the contests wasn't cheap because of entry fees, hotels, food and gas. I'd definitely need some financial assistance, but it had to be cheaper than flying to El Salvador.

I wrote back to Lauryn and Alexis telling them it looked good and I'd finalize our filming plan for Thursday. After printing out my final version of the itinerary and logging off the computer I went to my room to strategize.

I'd bring up what my mom told me about Bianca at dinner and then mention that I wanted to do something this summer. The competitions made my plan look serious, not fun, and my itinerary showed...

Troy stuck his head in my room. "Dinner in ten," he said.

"Okay," I told him without looking up.

My parents always let Troy go to football, baseball and basketball camp in the summer. Me going to different BMX events should be the same thing. Plus it would show everyone that I wasn't just riding a bike around. BMX was a serious sport with big-name sponsors.

My floorboards creaked, and I looked up to see Troy walking into my room. "How is that Alexis chick so hot? I thought all BMX chicks were dogs."

"Go away, Troy. She's not interested."

"Of course she's interested," he said flexing. "Why don't you and that Alexis chick switch to a girl sport?"

I looked back at my itinerary. "Get out."

"What's that?" he asked and grabbed at the papers.

I pulled them out of his reach and stuffed them under a pillow.

He turned, leaned over to aim at me, and gassed my whole room with a vile rotting stink.

"Gross! Get out!" I grabbed a stapler and whipped it at the source of the stink, throwing as hard as I could.

Troy turned as I threw and the stapler hit him right in the crotch.

"Ow!" He dropped to the floor clutching himself.

I jumped over his thrashing legs "Oh, sorry. Does that hurt? I wouldn't know—being a girl."

"Troy! Josie! What is going on in there?" my dad yelled down the hall.

"Nothing!" I answered. "Troy tripped."

"It's time for dinner."

Troy staggered upright and made a move to hit me but I ducked and faux-kneed him as I bolted out of my room ahead of him.

I couldn't be sure if I'd actually injured Troy or if he was putting on a performance to get me in trouble, but he made a big production about holding an ice pack to his crotch and moaning every time he shifted in his chair at the dinner table.

"No wonder the only person who will go to prom with you is that psycho, Connor."

I glared at Troy and he smirked back.

My mom tilted her head to the side and looked at me. "Connor? Connor Knight? Wasn't he suspended?"

Sometimes I hated having a mom so heavily involved in the booster club.

"Wait a minute," my dad said. "Someone better fill me in on what's going on around here. What happened to that Sean kid?"

"He dumped her," Troy said.

"That's not helpful." My mom turned to Troy. "Can't you fix Josie up with one of your friends?"

"No!" Troy and I both rejected that idea.

"Connor is harmless. It was a stink bomb. He likes bending rules is all." I speared salad with my fork and ate a bite.

My dad didn't look convinced.

"It will be fine," I insisted. "He's Bruce's cousin. We'll go with Gianna."

"It is nice to see you with Gianna again," my mom said. "Such a nice girl." She sighed. "Apparently Connor's parents practically let him run wild. Did you know he spent last summer traipsing around Europe unsupervised?"

My parents exchanged a *we'll talk later, away from the kids* look.

If they were this nervous about me going to prom with Connor, how was I going to convince them to let me spend nights in hotel rooms in other cities with Lauryn and Alexis over the summer?

Chapter 7

Sunday I still didn't have any great ideas. If Troy hadn't brought up Connor at dinner... I couldn't get caught up thinking how much better my life would be without Troy. He'd ruined so many other things, why would this be any different? There were still 116 days to endure before he left for college.

Four phone messages had come in while I'd been sleeping. Lauryn and Alexis had both signed up for the Titanic BMX Throwdown in St. Louis, Miguel was scouting locations for filming on Thursday, and Gianna wanted to come over to show me something on her way to the mall.

I texted Gianna that I was up and she could come over any time.

I was barely showered and still finishing breakfast when Gianna showed up, knocking at the sliding door connecting the kitchen to the backyard. I waved her in while I drank my orange juice.

After sliding the door closed behind her, she turned to me and lifted her chin. "Look! Notice anything?"

Crap. I was bad at this game. Her hair was the same; she was wearing jeans and a shirt that wasn't particularly remarkable. No visible tattoos or piercings, but that would be pretty shocking for Gianna.

"Um, no."

She moved closer. "My necklace."

Her silver chain with several purple—amethyst, I think— stones on it was pretty. "Nice. Is it new?"

"Bruce gave it to me for our one-year anniversary. It's going to look perfect with my prom dress."

"Congratulations!" I hoped Gianna didn't pick up on the false note of fake enthusiasm in my voice.

"I know. I can't believe it's been a year already." She fingered the stones, smoothing them down on her throat. The "Bruce" ring sounded on her phone, and she reached for it.

A dreamy look emerged on her face and I felt a monstrous, ugly reaction. What was wrong with me? Couldn't I be happy for my friend? Why was I so jealous?

I didn't want a Bruce. I swear, I didn't. It wasn't Bruce. It was... Why couldn't I have a real prom date? Why did Sean have to be a loser cheater? Why was I stuck going with a guy who'd lost a bet?

"I'm sorry." She put her phone down. "I should be helping you, not showing off."

"You're not showing off." Well, she was a little. "Helping me what?"

"Have you picked out the jewelry and shoes you're going to wear?"

"No." I'd been so preoccupied thinking about Lauryn and Alexis and the road trip I hadn't had time to think about it.

"We'll go shopping together." The Bruce ring tone sounded again and she glanced at her phone. "I have to go. We'll shop tomorrow after school. Okay?"

I told her yes and slid the door open so she could get out.

As she left, my mom came in the kitchen.

"Was that Gianna?"

"Yeah, we're going shopping tomorrow for jewelry and shoes."

"Oh, honey!" She stood back, put her hands on my shoulders and kissed me on my forehead.

"Mom, what?"

"It's… You and Gianna shopping for… I'm so happy." She looked at me longer and then turned away.

Was she crying?

She picked up her purse off the counter, pulled out a stack of bills, and handed it to me.

Whoa. There was more money there than she'd ever given me for a school-clothes shopping excursion. Ever.

"Mom? What is this?"

"I want you to have fun shopping. It's so nice to see you like this."

"Thanks." I looked at the cash in my hands. Prom was making my mom crazy. This might work to my advantage.

The Monday shopping trip stretched into Tuesday and Wednesday. My mom made me try on the whole ensemble each time I bought something new until finally she agreed that everything was perfect.

Gianna and Bruce had worked out the logistics for the pre-party and transportation to the hotel. All I needed to do was arrange the last details with Connor. He'd been suspiciously quiet all week, but he assured me he had a tux and a car, and he was aware that prom was Saturday. If he could get through two more days without getting himself in trouble we'd be all set.

Thursday morning he wasn't at his locker when I got to school. I texted him, asking him to meet me at lunch. Then I read messages from Alexis, Lauryn, and Miguel finalizing our plans for filming after school. Miguel had scouted a location that was forty minutes away from us, but an hour-and-a-half drive for Alexis and Lauryn. He said we could fit in a quick video of me alone before we met them.

I texted back, *"Sounds good. Cya."*

As I turned my phone off, Connor came running up wearing a fur hat with earflaps and frantically spun the combination on his lock. "Abort. Abort. Operation Zephyr is a no-go." He spoke in a low, urgent voice. "Repeat. Operation Zephyr is a no-go. Dragon Two, do you copy?"

His head was bent down, but I could see wires and a microphone peeking out of the right earflap. I looked up and down the hall, but didn't see anyone else in a fur hat. Dragon Two must have been in a remote location.

"Rendezvous at the safe house. Sixteen hundred." He lifted his head and looked down the hall. "Copy that. Over."

Connor took off the fur hat and dangled it from the back hook in his locker, then whistled *Pop Goes the Weasel* as he pulled a notebook from the top shelf.

"Connor?" I closed my locker and waited for him to look up. "I have the final details figured out for Saturday. If you could come by my house at..."

Static blasted from his locker and a frantic voice called out *CODE RED, CODE RED.*

"Crap." Connor grabbed the hat and slammed his locker shut. He took a step and then turned to me. "Sorry. I'm sure your plan is fine. Send it to me."

I watched him run off again. Whatever he was doing, I hoped it wouldn't get him suspended or on the booster moms' blacklist before Saturday.

No stink bombs, fire alarms, or other mayhem erupted and I didn't hear anything about Connor being hauled down to the dean's office, so I assumed Operation Zephyr had been stopped in time. I was relieved to not have to think about potential prom disasters so I could focus on getting some good video footage. Lauryn and Alexis both had lots of clips. Thanks to Miguel, I had one good one of my back flip, but I needed more.

Miguel picked me up after school and we drove to an apartment building that had the perfect outside handrail to film. He parked a couple of blocks away so we could get my bike and his camera out without the people in the building seeing us. Their rail was popular with BMXers, but BMXers were not popular with the people who lived there.

"Let me know when to go," I whispered as Miguel adjusted his setup.

The building had an iron hand railing that followed a ramp into the parking garage. The railing had two tight turns before the steepest part. It was tricky but doable.

Miguel turned his camera on and walked backward a few steps in front of me, then gave me a thumbs-up sign to go.

I moved as quietly as possible riding my bike up the ramp, but angry knocking came from inside one of the apartments, warning that someone in the building saw me and wasn't happy. This happened a lot, and I knew I'd still have time for one attempt before security or police arrived. I hurried to the top of the ramp, no longer trying to keep quiet.

At the top, about ten feet off the ground, I took a deep breath and visualized the perfect ride and landing. Committing myself to that picture, I rolled a few feet and hopped my bike up onto the railing so the stunt pegs sticking out from the center of my front and back wheels balanced on the metal rail.

The grinding sound of metal on metal increased as I scraped my way down. I shifted my weight to navigate the first turn, held on through the next curve, and tightened my grip as I hurtled toward the bottom. The end of the rail launched me in the air, and I landed with no bobbles. Perfect. Exactly as I'd pictured it.

My execution of a beautiful double-peg rail grind went unappreciated at first. The back door of the apartment building flew open and an obese man shuffled out shaking his fist. "You kids! Get out of here before I call the cops!"

"Go!" Miguel ran, clutching his video equipment to his chest.

With luck the angry man hadn't spotted the blond ponytail hanging out of my helmet. I'd dressed in a black T-shirt and jeans, making me look like any of the guy riders in the neighborhood. I sped down the street to Miguel's car, jumped off my bike, stuffed it in the back and barely made it into the passenger seat before he took off.

I turned to look behind us.

"Anyone following us?"

"Nah. I've been chased by way better. If we go down, it won't be a guy like that who catches us."

"Did you get me on video?"

"I think so. We'll check when we stop."

The drive to meet Lauryn and Alexis almost killed me, I was so anxious to see how the film turned out. When we got to the location, they were already there.

I told them about being chased away while Miguel queued up the footage.

"Riding the summer circuit will be so much better," Alexis said. "Soon we'll hit every good spot in the Midwest."

I'd been avoiding the subject of the road trip. I needed to score some prom points with my parents before I could bring it up.

"Only seventeen more days until Titanic," Lauryn said while balancing on one wheel.

Miguel called us over. "Oh yeah, the sparks are flying. You've got to see it!"

We crowded around the viewer, and he replayed it for us three times.

Lauryn gave me a high five. "Impressive! I love how the sparks show up on the video. You can use it in the caption: Sparks fly when Josie Peters rides."

"So, Mr. Director," Alexis asked, "where do you want us?"

Miguel had chosen a gravel road with rolling dirt mounds that had been set up by dirt-bike riders. He explained how he wanted to see us in a line bobbing up and down.

"You can do tricks, but try to stay upright, and take turns getting in front."

I pedaled away with Lauryn and Alexis, riding three across. Like many freestylers, we'd stripped the brakes off our bikes, and we picked up speed as we went flying down the first hill.

Alexis pulled in front on the first set of rollers. Then I pedaled harder to go faster. I hit the next uphill first and was in front when I launched airborne off the top. I flung my arms straight out for a huge no-hander. I sailed high, flying up and forward in an arc. I watched to anticipate the landing, but the ground in front was higher than I expected, and my front wheel hit before I had my hands back in position. My bike slowed but my body kept going and I pitched forward, smashing my face on the handlebars as the momentum forced me over the front of the bike.

As I twisted awkwardly in the air I could feel it going much worse than other times I'd gone over the bars. I tried to gauge what was going to hurt most, hitting the ground, my bike landing on me, or Alexis and Lauryn mowing me down from behind. I curled into a protective ball a second before my left side hit the ground, dragging me to a stop on the gravel.

My bike crashed down next to my shoulders and I felt my hair getting pulled as someone—Lauryn?—rode past my head. I heard yelling as another bike whizzed behind me.

I uncurled and pushed to get up. Pain shot through my left wrist as I staggered upright. Something thick flooded the back of my throat. Ugh, was that blood? The more I tried to breathe the more I swallowed and choked. Gross. I leaned forward as coughs racked my body. Each spasm hurt worse and increased the spray pattern of red spreading across the gravel.

Chapter 8

I remember dropping down to my hands and knees and thinking maybe I shouldn't have stood up. Then I could sort of picture Alexis freaking out, Lauryn taking charge, and Miguel filming everything. The rest was a blur of an ambulance ride, x-rays, and my mom showing up at the hospital.

The doctor kept telling her it looked worse than it was. Just a sprained wrist. Three weeks of no riding. I needed rest but not bed rest. No reason to stay home from school more than a day. She seemed to be more traumatized than I was. The doctor had to keep asking her if she was okay and reassuring her that I was fine.

It felt good to sleep in Friday morning but by afternoon I was restless and no one would give me a straight answer about what happened to my bike. Miguel said something vague about looking at it later and asked if he could put my wipeout video online. I told him to go ahead.

I called Connor and explained the deal I'd worked out with my parents. I could go to prom for a few hours. No pre-or post-parties and no dancing. It wasn't ideal, but I was going.

By Saturday I felt like I'd been trampled by an elephant. Over-the-counter pain-killers dulled the misery to a low throb for sleeping, but I didn't want to be woozy for prom so I didn't take any pills after the morning. By the time I had to go to the hairdresser I was getting better at acting as though I wasn't miserable. Once she recovered from the shock of seeing my face, my hairdresser managed to do a good job changing my usual ponytail by pulling my hair up high in back with curls tumbling down.

At home, sitting in front of the mirror in my room, I leaned back and squeezed my makeup bag between my knees so I could unzip it. Unfortunately, there wasn't enough concealer in the world to make me look even close to presentable. Lip gloss was the only makeup I could wear. This was not the way I'd envisioned myself getting ready for my junior prom. The other girls prepared by getting facials and manicures while I'd given myself two black eyes.

At least my parents had agreed to let me go.

The doorbell rang.

"Josie?" my dad called. "Connor is here. Do you need help?"

"No! I'll be right there." I managed to put both earrings in, but the necklace was impossible.

I stood up and mistakenly put weight on my wrist, sending a blast of pain up through my elbow.

Nothing felt comfortable: the bulky wrap on my wrist, the itchy sling, tight dress, or strappy shoes. I hoped I could pull this off. Sore spots all over my body begged for rest, and I wasn't even out of my room yet. I had to hide how bad I felt or my parents wouldn't let me out of the house.

I wasn't the only one who looked different. Connor was transformed. His custom-fitted tux showed off his perfect proportions, and his hair had a casually grown-out yet freshly cut look.

One of my heels snagged on the carpet and I almost fell.

"Any news about my bike?" I asked after regaining my balance. I hadn't seen it since the crash. All anyone had told me was it didn't look good.

"Forget about the bike for a minute." My dad tightened his grip on the camera. "Are you sure this is a good idea? Can you walk in those shoes?"

"I'm fine. Are we sure we want pictures?"

"Everything that happens makes us who we are," my mom said, taking the necklace out of my hand to help me put it on.

"Whoa!" Connor blatantly stared at me. "You look amazing."

"Thank you. The dress matches my bruises, doesn't it?"

"I've got to get a picture of this." He pulled out his phone and took a couple of shots. "I've never seen so many bruises on one person."

My mom brushed a piece of hair off my face and sighed. "Are you sure you're okay?"

She smiled, but she probably wished she had the kind of daughter who didn't wipe out doing a bike trick two days before prom.

"Maybe we can retouch the pictures," I said in a lame effort to cheer her up.

"We might as well capture the moment. Hopefully there won't be another one like it," my dad said.

"There's always senior prom," I said.

My mom shook her head as my dad had Connor and me stand in different poses.

After a few pictures we finally left the house.

In the driveway was a silver-grey Porsche Boxter.

"Is that your car?" my dad asked Connor.

"It's my dad's." Connor grinned until he saw how unhappy my dad looked. "Don't worry. I've been ordered under penalty of death to not exceed sixty-five miles an hour."

"So I don't even need to mention the no-drinking part."

"Dad! We need to go," I said. We'd missed the pre-parties so we needed to go straight to the prom at the Palmeri Towers in downtown Chicago.

Connor walked me around to the passenger side and opened the door. "I've already been threatened with a slow, painful tortuous death."

"Remember," my mom said, "no dancing. You're only dropping in and leaving."

"I know, Mom. We're good."

From the outside, the car was all grace and elegance, but it wasn't exactly designed for allowing passengers to easily get in wearing a form-fitting dress. I couldn't maneuver myself low enough to slide in, and not being able to put any weight on my left wrist wasn't helping. By hiking up my dress I was able to squat and drop down into the seat which pulled my dress up even more.

Connor slid his hands over my hips to help ease my dress down. The more his hands brushed my thighs, the more I squirmed and twisted the fabric.

"Josie, hold still. Lift up a little."

I had to lean back and push down with my feet to bridge my butt off the seat so Connor could angle my dress into place. Could I possibly look any less graceful?

"Sorry we had to miss the pre-party," I said as he walked over to the driver's side.

Connor straightened the rearview mirror and settled into his seat. "The parties were of no interest to me. This was strictly a recon mission. Investigating opportunities for future operations. You've already made it much more interesting than I could have hoped."

As he pulled out of the driveway, I saw my reflection in the side mirror. I looked awful. "Interesting, huh?"

"I have to say I'm impressed."

"That I can't stay on my bike?"

"It rocks that you're going to prom anyway. Most girls would threaten to stay home if they even had a zit. But I don't get it."

"Get what?"

"Why are you going?"

I smoothed the soft fabric of my dress on my legs. When my parents asked I'd told them it was because I didn't want to miss out on my junior prom, but that wasn't the truth.

I closed my eyes for a second, glanced at Connor, and then looked at the road in front of us. "Everyone assumed I wouldn't go. Not because I was injured so badly, but because I look terrible. If a guy had sprained his wrist and had two black eyes no one would expect him to stay home."

I paused, but Connor didn't say anything, so I continued. "I guess I don't like being treated differently because I'm a girl. It makes me want to prove everyone wrong. If they'd been pressuring me to go I probably would have stayed home. I know that sounds crazy."

"Makes perfect sense to me."

I hadn't been to school on Friday, so apart from my family, no one had seen what I looked like. People in the hotel lobby stared at me, and I knew the stares would only get worse from people I knew.

Connor and I followed the signs to the ballroom, and the music and buzz of conversation got louder.

At the ticket table outside the doors, a teacher I'd never had looked at me in horror as I handed her our tickets.

"My God, what happened?" she asked.

"A little wipeout on my bike. It looks worse than it is."

I purposely added extra bounce and enthusiasm as I walked to prove my point.

"Ready to go in?" Connor asked.

I nodded. The initial shock would be the worst, like dropping down on a ramp. After that it all went easier. Usually.

Inside the ballroom, the lights were low, and people were already sitting down eating salad.

Two empty seats were available at Gianna's table in a prime location right by the dance floor.

"You look great!" Gianna said as we sat down.

The other girls joined in commenting on my dress, my jewelry, my hair, everything except my bruised, scraped-up face and wrist in a sling.

"What's going on?" I asked.

"What do you mean?" Gianna made big, fake-innocent eyes.

"Gianna warned everyone that you were a little messed up, and threatened bodily harm to anyone who said anything about you looking less than spectacular." Bruce said.

I smiled at her. "I'd go over there and hug you if it wouldn't hurt so much. I appreciate being treated like nothing happened, but you're allowed to ask me questions."

I re-explained what had happened while eating as much salad as I could with only a fork, but I had to leave the big pieces of tomato on my plate.

As soon as my salad plate was cleared one of the guys at the table said, "My little sister is dying to ride BMX but my parents won't let her."

"Why not?" I asked.

"Because they don't want her to wind up looking like you. No offense."

"Is BMX those little bikes?" one of the girls asked.

"Yes it's on smaller bikes than road bikes or mountain bikes. There's BMX racing in the Olympics, but that's not the kind I do. I do freestyle tricks and park riding, kind of like skateboarders. You must have seen the skateboarding competitions on TV?"

"Yeah," her boyfriend said. He moved aside to let the server put down our main-course plates.

The giant hunk of chicken dared me to find a way to eat it one-handed. I wedged my fork into my left hand and picked up my knife with my right hand when Connor reached over and cut up the chicken for me.

"This is ridiculous," I said. "But thank you."

Luckily dessert was chocolate mousse—easy to eat one-handed. When I dug my spoon in to scrape out the last bite the ballroom lights lowered and the principal took the stage for the prom court announcements.

Not surprisingly, Troy was crowned king and I faux-applauded with my right hand on the table, glad it was almost over. A popular dance song blasted, and the people who were still at the table got up to dance.

One of the Saturday BMX regulars at the park moved in front of me on the dance floor, and his eyes widened when he saw me.

He stopped and walked over. "Holy shit!"

The rest of the BMX guys from my school crowded around, leaving the girls dancing.

"Anything serious?" one asked.

"Sprained wrist. It'll heal, but my bike is trashed."

"Your video is insane," one of the guys said. "I can't believe you got up after that fall. You've got like fifty hits on it already." He pulled out his phone, stood next to me and took our picture. The rest of the guys scrambled to get pictures of me and of them with me.

I blinked and turned my head to refocus my eyes after a flash. No. It couldn't be.

Sean.

With Mindy.

My eyes squeezed shut and I reopened them slowly.

He saw me and walked over, staring. My arm throbbed and I swallowed repeatedly to fight the feeling that my throat was closing.

He stopped when he was about a foot away from me and said, "Ouch."

"Thanks," I told him. "You look nice too."

Mindy trailed a half step behind him, her pearl-white perfection making me feel even more beastly.

"No, I mean..."

I cut him off. "What are you doing here? You don't even go to this school." I looked past him to Mindy, who stood glued to Sean's side, glaring at me.

Mindy was only a sophomore, She couldn't get tickets. You had to be a junior or senior.

Sean shrugged and then mumbled, "She arranged it so we were both on other people's tickets. I didn't think you'd be here."

"Well it is *my* prom" I said.

He hadn't stopped staring at my face. "Sorry. I uhh…"

"Just go," I said.

Mindy tugged on his arm and they moved away from me, disappearing onto the dance floor.

Yay, me—I'd won. I was right and he was wrong and here I was by myself. The truth was, no one cared. I was a gossip tidbit at best. Whether or not I could fall and get up again or stand up to my ex and his new girlfriend didn't matter to anyone but me.

I went to the lobby outside the ballroom and found Connor peering out from a cluster of pillars in a darkened corner.

He waved me over. "I heard about your ex showing up. Thought I'd give you some space."

I thanked him and asked if he was ready to leave.

"One more thing." He held up a black lacy corset sideways so the front flapped open. "I found this female undergarment. What's it called?"

"A corset or bustier. Pushes everything up and out. It's usually worn under a strapless dress." Who was in black strapless?

"Right. And is your ex's date in black?"

Mindy's dress was all white. No way would she be wearing black under it. "No."

"So if she were to find this wedged in next to the passenger seat of his car, it might make for some interesting conversation on the way home."

I had to admire the way his mind worked. "Do it." I told him which car was Sean's and the license-plate number.

Connor nodded once. "Meet me by the valet in ten minutes."

I peeked back in the ballroom to see if I could find Gianna, but a slow song was playing which meant she was immersed in her Bruce bubble on the dance floor. Slow songs were either the best or the worst. All the actual couples danced, but the people who were only together to go to prom sat at their tables looking bored and uncomfortable. What would it be like to slow dance with Connor? Not so bad.

I slunk out of the ballroom and texted Gianna that we were leaving.

Connor was already at the valet when I got there. "I don't even want to know how you got into his car."

He shrugged. "It's easier than people think."

Even if he was a little devious, Connor was basically a nice guy. "I appreciate you doing this. I mean not just the Sean thing. Going to prom even though we missed most of it and not caring that I'm all bruised."

Connor tilted his head and looked at me for a second. "I actually had some fun, and minimizing my time spent in this ridiculous ritual met one of my objectives."

"Why do you enjoy causing so much mayhem?"

"In situations where you can't beat other people at their game, if you can at least screw them up, it's immensely satisfying."

Chapter 9

My body felt racked. I'd been shifting all night trying to find a comfortable position but always hit a sore spot. Hopefully I'd loosen up once I got moving. Even my feet were throbbing. At least with prom done I wouldn't have to wear those crazy shoes again.

Funny how the only people who weren't surprised to see me show up were the BMX guys. Except Sean. It hurt me that after we'd spent three months together he didn't know me very well. But then I had no idea he was cheating on me so maybe we didn't know each other at all.

I needed to check my wipeout video online. I'd watched it once after Miguel sent it to me, but the fact that it was getting so many hits had me intrigued. A wave of cinnamon scent propelled me out of bed.

At the kitchen table, Troy and my parents were finishing scrambled eggs and cinnamon-streusel coffee cake. The microwave clock said ten fifteen. I'd slept for ten hours. No wonder I was so hungry. An enormous corner piece of coffee cake with lots of extra icing would fix that.

"You can't only eat cake for breakfast," my mom said when she saw my plate. "Have some eggs."

"Please pass the eggs," I said to Troy who as usual had all the food near him.

"You may call me Your Majesty," he said, handing over the platter.

"What?"

"Prom king," my dad said.

Great. It had already gone to his head. Like his ego needed another boost.

Troy pushed back from the table and asked to be excused.

"Your Majesty, before you leave again, don't forget to mow the lawn," my dad said.

Troy scowled at me. Usually I did it, but with my wrist not usable, the lawn was now his job.

"How long before that Band-Aid comes off?" he asked.

"Three weeks," I told him. I would have gladly mowed the lawn if it meant I could ride again.

"We'll see what the doctor says," my mom answered. "We go back in three weeks to have it checked." She aimed her statement at me.

"I know, yes. No riding until I get the official okay."

Since last night I had new messages from Alexis, Sean, Miguel, Connor, and Gianna. Sean's message had a bunch of picture attachments. "The guys wanted me to send you some pics." He must have managed to get them all without Mindy noticing, or maybe they ended up having a huge fight over the bustier. I smiled, thinking of Connor's plan. My phone had a low battery so I downloaded the images to the computer.

I opened Connor's next. "Hope you're feeling okay today. Thanks for last night." He had turned out to be the perfect date. His revenge on Mindy and Sean had been exactly what I needed and felt much better than a pep talk. When he dropped me off I found myself wondering what it would be like if he kissed me, but of course he didn't.

Miguel asked how I was and when he could visit. "About your bike... I have a connection. Don't tell anyone—call me for info."

I would definitely call him. Fixing my bike wasn't going to be easy and I'd need help.

Gianna's message made me smile. "I can't believe SHE showed up with HIM. She's going DOWN." Hah. If Mindy was dumb enough to bring Sean to the same prom picnic as Gianna, it was going to get ugly.

When the pictures finished downloading, I clicked on the first one. My eyes looked weird, like I was wearing a mask. My favorite was one where I stood with my right hand on my hip, looking straight at the camera while the guys were disorganized and moving around behind me out of focus. I didn't remember posing for it or why I would have been standing that way, but it kind of looked cool.

Alexis's message gave a link to my video and said she'd never had so much traffic on Exquisite. "We're famous! Put a prom pic of you on your profile to show people you're okay. They're flooding me asking about you."

I pulled up the video so I could see how many views it had. Over one hundred!

Most of the comments were simple one-liners like "Sick!" "Insane!" and "Ouch!"

Some of the early anonymous comments had been deleted, but a newer one from this morning caught my attention "That whut happenz when girls ride. She shud be topless n make me a snack."

Was that a joke? I checked the name of the commenter. Anonymous. Of course. Idiot. Wouldn't even use his name.

I forced myself to loosen my grip on the mouse so I could scroll down. How many stupid anonymous comments were there? The majority were supportive, but the nasty ones were bad. I needed to get Miguel to delete them or give me access to delete them. My phone beeped a no-power warning so I ran to my room to get my charger. On my way back to the computer I heard clicking. Crap. The last thing I needed was for Troy to see those comments.

"Troy. Get out. I was using…"

As I turned the corner from the hallway I saw that it wasn't Troy. It was my mom. And she was reading the comments.

"Mom! Stop."

She didn't even look up as she kept scrolling. "Some of the worst ones from last night have been deleted. That's good. These aren't so bad."

What? Last night? I moved so I was next to her and could see what she was looking at.

"You already knew?"

She turned to face me. "I received no fewer than six phone calls last night telling me about your video. I would have preferred that you tell me you were putting a video of yourself online. We've talked about this."

Whoever said that the older generation couldn't figure out computers had never met my mom and her network of mom spies. To them, the internet was a gold mine of information about us.

"I'm sorry. I didn't think a bike-crash video was a big deal. I had no idea that many people would look at it. I'm texting Miguel to block the comments. I feel sick reading them."

She moved back in the chair and looked me in the eyes. "There are a lot of unstable people in the world. You can't take those negative comments personally. They say more about the person who wrote them than they do about you."

"Even the ones admiring the blood gushing down my face?"

"No. The ones like this R.T. Torres person. Does he go to your school?"

R.T. Torres? The double-back flip guy in all the videos? I hadn't seen any comments from R.T. Torres.

"What?" I leaned over her shoulder to see the monitor better.

"R.T. Torres defended you." She scrolled through the comments to find it. "All these wussy anon haters shud shut up, they'd be crying to their mamas, taking a fall like that. This chick has balls."

Hearing my mom read about wussy haters and me having balls would have been funny if I had felt at all like laughing.

She stopped reading and said, "He could use some help with his spelling, but his heart is in the right place."

"Can I see the rest?" I asked and reached for the mouse.

She held it out of my reach. "You need to develop a thicker skin."

"What do you mean?" I shifted to face her.

"You didn't cry when you landed face-first, but when you put a video of yourself online without telling your parents and anonymous crazy people posted rude comments, you got upset."

"I'm not upset!" Too late I realized I was talking too loud to not be upset.

She gave me a mom look. "If you want to put videos of yourself on the internet, you need to be able to delete those kinds of comments and forget about it."

"The fact that people purposely take the time to post garbage about me makes me sick."

"And?" she asked

"And?" I asked back.

"What are you going to do about it?"

Chapter 10

The first thing I was going to do about it was send a friend request to R.T. Torres on HeadSpace. A positive comment from him meant way more than all the anonymous crap.

I called Alexis to see if she'd noticed his comment and the others and to see if she got a lot of anti-girl stuff on Exquisite she had to delete.

She sighed before answering. "I may as well pull down the whole Exquisite site. It was stupid."

That was not the reaction I was expecting. "What's going on?"

"They cancelled the girls' category in the Ultimate."

"What?" I got up from my bed, fighting stiffness in my back. "Can they do that?"

"Their official statement says it's because of scheduling conflicts, but the forums say it's because they think with so few girls the quality of the riding will be bad and tricks will be lame. They had a lot of guys sign up already and not so many girls so they cut it."

Cut it. Cut it? I started walking in a slow circle, not able to process what she was saying.

"So what, we're out?"

She gave another long sigh. "They kept five slots at the beginning of each amateur guys' event for girls."

"That's it? Five total?"

"Five. And it gets worse. All girls have to qualify with scores from May to July. Pro girls are being treated like amateurs."

"Do they not want girls there?"

"They say we can ride Exhibition."

"Well, we still have to go." I told her. "We'll do Exhibition."

"I don't want to be in stupid Exhibition that no one watches," she said, her voice lifeless. "No one cares."

If Alexis was that deflated and unmotivated, lots of other girl riders were probably feeling the same way. We had to do something.

"We'll make them care and make them watch."

"You sound like Lauryn. She's out training right now she's so pissed."

"Don't do anything to Exquisite. Keep it up until we come up with a plan."

We hung up and I tossed the phone in the corner of my bed. Getting cut from the competition sucked. No wonder more girls weren't riding. With the stupid comments people made at prom, plus the nasty posts on my video, and now getting kicked out of the Ultimate, it was obvious we weren't wanted.

No. That wasn't true.

Just like the video comments, it was probably a few idiots who were causing all the trouble. The question was, how to beat them?

I had to get outside. Even though I couldn't ride, I went to the garage and tried not to look at the twisted metal wreck that used to be my bike. I grabbed an old soccer ball and kicked it against the half-pipe. The ball made a satisfying *bam* as it collided with the wooden ramp and I had to duck so it wouldn't hit me on the way back.

Bam I kicked it for stupid Sean and his stupid games.

Bam, bam for all the moronic comments people posted on my video.

I hauled my leg back to kick in retaliation for the cancellation of the Ultimate.

"Josie?" A female voice called me.

Behind the fence by the yard, Lauryn sat on her bike, her T-shirt drenched in sweat. Without her saying anything, I knew. She was even more pissed off than I was.

I didn't know Lauryn that well, but I doubted that she liked being told she couldn't do something for no good reason any more than I did. I walked a few steps closer to her and let my soccer ball roll by and bounce off the ramp behind me.

"How's the wrist?" She used the bottom of her shirt to wipe sweat off her face.

"Three weeks." I wiggled the fingers on my left hand as if to check that it was healing.

"You heard?" There was an edge to her voice. She was angry but not defeated.

"About Ultimate? Yeah." I matched her tone. What was she here for? I had the impression that she hadn't made up her mind about something and was testing me.

With her feet resting on her bike pedals, Lauryn held on to the fence for balance. "I was at that park by your house and I started riding and I didn't know where I was going, but..." She paused and I waited. It was the most she'd ever said to me.

She put her feet on the ground and looked me in the eyes as if she'd finally decided to say whatever it was she came here for. "With a little training you have a chance at making one of those five slots."

I blinked rapidly. *Me?* Before, she'd said my riding was *not bad*. Now I was in a league with the pros?

I gave up trying to match her control and let myself babble in an emotional Alexis-like fashion. "Pro girls from all over the world will be at those contests, competing to get in."

"I didn't say it would be easy." Her eyes were on me, challenging me. "I said it was doable if you decide to go for it. We need you at those qualifiers."

I had no bike, my wrist was unusable, my savings would barely cover the costs of the qualifying contests, and I hadn't worked up the nerve to ask my parents, but something else, something far removed and protected from all that logic told me I could do it, that I needed to do it or I'd regret it forever.

"I'm in."

She nodded. "Good."

"Why do the guys dominate BMX?" I asked her. I didn't expect a response, so I kept talking, more to myself than to her. "It could be because more girls aren't encouraged to even try. If I didn't have an older brother with a bike I probably wouldn't have tried."

"Yeah, me too," she said. "We need to reach all those girls without older brothers."

I thought about what I would have liked when I was learning. "We should do a girls-only intro-to-BMX clinic. We'd be helping them get used to the bikes, showing them that girls do ride, and starting them on basic tricks. We'd have to find a couple of bikes for them to use. All we'd need would be a little space."

"Sponsors love that stuff," she said.

I expected her to ride off, but she hesitated.

"You know..." For once I did know what she wanted to say, so I saved her from having to finish.

"Yeah, it pisses me off, too. We'll show them."

She nodded and left, kicking up a cloud of dirt behind her.

Chapter 11

Sunday family dinners usually involved Troy inhaling massive quantities of food and my mom acting surprised, as if he didn't do it every night. She'd go over his crazy baseball practice and game schedule for the week, trying to figure out when she'd go watch and when my dad would go. I always ate quietly and commented occasionally so I wouldn't be accused of being sullen or asked what was wrong.

But this time, when my dad started with his customary "So, what's new?" I went for it.

"You know those comments on my video about how girls shouldn't ride BMX?"

"Yes," my mom said looking up from her salad.

"I'd like to go out there and shut them up."

"How?" my dad asked, giving my mom a *what's this?* look. My mom shrugged and mouthed *I don't know* and then she looked at me.

I told them about the Ultimate and the cancellation of the girls' category. "The main argument against girls is that we can't ride well and that we don't have enough muscle to take falls like the guys. Thanks to that video, I've become known as the girl who got back up, so I'd like do two nearby contests this summer and hopefully qualify to compete in the Ultimate where I can either ride really well or fall in a spectacularly bloody fashion and stand back up."

When I finally paused, I expected my mom to launch into a female-equality tirade and instantly take my side.

"Honey, why not let your wrist heal and then we'll see."

I recognized the look she was giving me. She was picturing me as a little kid. *We'll see* was basically *no*. How could she not even consider it?

"What do you mean?"

"Maybe you need to take a little rest from riding."

I wanted to jump out of my chair and do nonstop jumping jacks to prove I was in shape, but I forced myself to take a deep breath before responding so I couldn't be accused of being overdramatic.

"A little rest? You make me sound like a Victorian lady with the vapors. When Troy broke two ribs you let him sign up for football camp. You're treating me different."

"Josie, watch your tone," my dad said.

I chewed the inside of my cheek to try to dissipate some of the irritation I felt building. They were already ganged up against me. I couldn't let it go.

I kept my tone flat and even. "Sorry, but it's true and it's not fair. It's discrimination."

Troy was taking full advantage of not being asked questions to eat more and more roast beef, as if he hadn't been fed all weekend.

My mom looked down at her plate and moved her fork around in her potatoes. "She's right."

"What?" my dad asked.

"I was treating Josie different. I don't like seeing either one of our kids hurt, but somehow Josie's black-and-blue face is worse than Troy's cracked ribs."

Yessss, yesss! I was still in the running.

My dad looked over at Troy and noticed his plate was almost clean. "Troy!" he said. "Slow down."

Troy kept eating, oblivious.

"Josie…," my dad started.

I braced myself for a final no from him.

"We want you to stay in one piece. We're not saying no." He held up his hand in a wait gesture to prevent anyone from interrupting him and gave my mother a look "But we need more information about where you're going and with whom before we can make a decision."

I excused myself to get a printout of my itinerary and handed it to him.

He glanced at it, quickly flipping the pages. "I can see you put some time into this. Give us a chance to look it over, okay?"

"We still need to meet these girls and their parents," my mom said, giving my dad a *we need to talk about this* look.

Tension released from my neck and shoulders. This was a huge improvement over *we'll see.* "Sure, no problem."

Troy stopped eating, leaned back and let rip a huge burp.

"Troy!" Both my parents yelled at him.

"Sorry," he said.

"Do you have anything to contribute to the conversation?" my mom asked.

"That Alexis chick is smokin' hot."

Chapter 12

At school Monday, people who hadn't seen me at prom stared and asked what happened and if I was all right. I was feeling awkward enough carrying books one-handed without having people staring and whispering. I'd be happy when my wipeout was old news.

Gianna left me a note before study hall, and I opened it before starting my homework. *OMG. PP = crazy. M = crying. S = bored. Could not find out deets of what happened except rumor that M accused S of cheating with your brother's date. As if. You n C were cute. Did u have fun? More than fun? Tell me all l8r.*

I folded the paper and put it in a zippered part of my backpack. So Sean and Mindy were fighting at prom picnic. Excellent. Did I have fun with Connor? Sure. More than fun? More than I expected. As much as she was asking? No. I didn't get a romantic vibe from him. He felt like a friend, like Miguel. Oops. I'd meant to message Miguel this morning about his bike shop connection. I wanted to set that up as soon as possible.

I finished my trig homework and still had ten minutes left, so I made a list of everything I needed to get done. Why couldn't school teach me anything useful like how to speed up the healing process? It was like a word problem with no easy solution. If Josie has to let her wrist heal for three weeks, but needs to be in peak condition for a contest in five weeks, what can she do to train?

Essay question: Suggest three ways Josie can get a good-quality competition-worthy bike without spending any money or stealing it. List the pros and cons for each. And for extra points, explain how Josie can convince her parents to let her travel to competitions this summer and sign the waivers.

The bell rang before I could even begin to try to answer any of my questions.

Three more people stopped to ask me what happened before I got to my locker. I leaned my forehead against the cool metal to relax for a minute while I dialed my combination. The door stuck and as I yanked it harder, my notebook slid out from my right arm.

Connor picked it up and handed it to me. "Trouble functioning with only one hand?"

"Thanks." I stuffed the notebook in my locker. "And thanks for prom. It looks like our plan worked. My ex and his new girlfriend are fighting."

"Huh?" He closed his locker. "Oh, that. Good. It was productive for me, too. I got lots of good intel for future planning. Keep me in mind for next year. It may get interesting."

He grabbed a book that was about to tumble out of the bottom of my locker and crammed it back in, stabilizing the pile at the same time. "Are you sure you're okay? You look like you haven't slept in days."

I pulled a pen off the top shelf. "Do you ever feel like your life is much more complicated than the trivial problems they have us working on in class?"

"All the time." He grinned. "Anything I can help with?"

"Not unless you have a way to make time simultaneously speed up and slow down, and to get people to do your bidding."

"Ahh. I haven't tackled time travel, but I have looked into hypnosis. It appears promising, but I wouldn't attempt it for any practical application yet. I'll let you know when my technique improves."

A noise like a duck quacking sounded from down the hall.

Connor glanced over his shoulder and turned to me. "I've got to go. Let me know if you need anything. No request too strange."

"Thanks, Connor. I appreciate it."

I pulled my lunch and phone out of my locker and went outside to check for messages from Lauryn and Alexis. I'd asked them about going to dinner, explaining that my parents insisted on meeting them and their parents. Alexis confirmed that she and her mom could come Wednesday. Lauryn said it didn't matter what day we chose, her parents wouldn't come. She said maybe, possibly if my parents absolutely insisted, she might be able to arrange a quick phone call, but to try to not go there.

By Wednesday I'd I set everything up, sent reminders to Alexis and Lauryn and reconfirmed the reservation, but at five my dad wasn't home.

"Do you think he forgot?" I asked my mom.

"I saw him schedule you in his agenda. You will have his full attention. I promise."

At five fifteen he pulled in the driveway. I yelled to my mom that he was home. "Come on! Let's go. This is your idea. We need to be there first."

"Josie, relax! My God. You're acting so nervous."

I dragged my mom out the front door.

"Hold on. Don't lock up yet," she told me. "He may want to get out of his suit and tie. Give him a minute."

I followed her to my dad's car. He held up a hand and pointed to his earpiece.

My mom tugged on her Oakton Lions long-sleeved shirt and mouthed, *change?* My dad shook his head no so she went back to close and lock the house.

We got in the car while he kept talking.

"Yes,... Yes, absolutely. You're one hundred percent... Okay, I've got it. I'll have it for you first thing... Yes... Yes."

I wasn't sure he knew where we were going, but he headed in the direction of the highway so I stayed quiet. After he agreed some more with whomever he was talking to, he finally pulled the earpiece out, clicked his phone off and said hello.

"I'm all yours. Last call of the day, Josie Peters. A tough customer."

"Did you actually put me in your agenda?"

"I did. Where are we going?"

"Pomadoro at Deerplain Mall."

"Chain Italian food it is."

"The point isn't to have the best meal ever. They live two hours from us. I had to pick somewhere in the middle."

"So. We're meeting your friends Lauryn and Alexis and Alexis's mother."

"Yes."

"Are these girls your age?"

"Alexis is a junior like me. Lauryn graduates this year."

"And her parents are okay with this road-trip plan?"

"I guess so."

My mom turned to my dad, and I could picture the *told you so* look she was giving him.

"You've never met their parents?" my mom asked.

"No. Lauryn and Alexis have come over, but I haven't been to their houses."

She twisted in her seat to look at me over her shoulder. "So you don't know them well at all. Not like Gianna."

Enough with me and Gianna. We weren't best friends anymore. Why couldn't she move past it?

My mom turned back, pausing to give my dad another look before facing the road.

"We ride bikes together. Have you guys met the extended families of your golf and tennis partners?"

"No." My dad looked at me in the rear view mirror. "But we're not seventeen-year-olds going on overnight trips with strangers."

Lauryn and Alexis weren't *strangers*.

"Ask me what tricks they're good at. I can tell you that."

"Go ahead."

"Lauryn is really good at air tricks on the half-pipe. Alexis is good at flatland. I want to ride with them this summer."

"I'd like to know a little more about the kind of people they are." My dad reached over and squeezed my mom's knee.

"Please don't grill them." I was lucky Alexis and Lauryn agreed to go to this stupid dinner. This was even worse than when my parents insisted on meeting Sean. At least that had been quick. Dinner was going to take hours.

"What's the point if we can't ask questions?" my mom asked.

This was going to be so embarrassing. It was already bad enough that both my parents insisted on meeting everybody.

My dad turned on the radio and my parents listened to the news while I checked messages and texted Lauryn and Alexis. When we pulled in to the massive Deerplain Mall parking lot, shared by MegaLots and Bob's Toy Barn, I quickly logged in to my HeadSpace account. I'd still have a few minutes before we got to the Pomadoro.

I had one new post. "Saw your video. Nice wipe. Hurt bad?" R.T. Torres.

I froze, not breathing, not moving. Was this real? The red letters of his name fuzzed as I stared at the screen.

Oh. My. God. R.T. Torres had not only accepted my friend request, he had posted on my wall. Maybe being one of the few girls in this sport was finally going to work to my advantage if it meant a guy like R.T. Torres would notice me. My fingers fumbled as I clicked his name to see more.

"Turn that off and don't even think about having it on at the table." My mom hovered outside her open car door. I opened my mouth to beg for another minute, saw the look on her face, and clicked my phone off. Crap. I should have checked HeadSpace first. R.T. Torres! I had to write something back.

As my parents and I settled at our table for six, Alexis, her mom, and Lauryn walked up.

My parents weren't going to like Alexis's short skirt and tight T-shirt, but luckily her mom's charcoal-grey suit and buttoned-up shirt made her look like a lawyer or accountant or some kind of professional. Good. This was a good start.

My dad started the introductions and Alexis's mom returned his handshake. "Jasmine Jacobs." She turned to me. "It's nice to finally meet the famous Josie with the half-pipe in her backyard and the cute older brother."

Troy's little sister. That was me. I shook her hand and she insisted that I call her Jasmine, not Mrs. Jacobs.

After sitting down, the adults did the dull small-talk thing about weather, traffic and work. Jasmine nodded with the same glazed look most people got when my dad explained that he sold carbon composites to the aviation industry. No one was completely sure what that meant. Airplane parts? Basically he was gone most of the time.

"Susan, that must be hard on you, having Mike on the road so much," Jasmine said to my mom.

I needed to escape this conversation and reread R.T.'s message. I tried to get Lauryn's attention but she was engrossed in the menu. Alexis was fiddling with her bracelets and I couldn't reach either of them under the table.

"I'm used to it now," my mom said. "I taught elementary school before my oldest, Troy, was born, but since then running the household has been more than a full-time job."

Jasmine leaned her clasped hands on the table. "I deal with burnout cases all the time in my practice. As a counseling psychologist, I see far too many people trying to do too much."

This was going to be the longest dinner ever. I willed Alexis to look at me, but she wasn't paying attention.

Our waitress showed up with our drinks and did a double-take when she got to me, losing her place in her rehearsed daily-specials speech.

"I fell off my bike but I'm fine," I told her.

"So, what's good here?" my dad asked her as she finished handing out drinks.

She paused for several seconds before answering. "Uhhh, the linguini special is popular tonight."

I closed my menu and put it down. "I usually get the tortellini alfredo."

"Spaghetti and meatballs," Lauryn said. She was all in black, making her skin look even paler than I remembered.

"Ahh to have your metabolism," Alexis's mom said. "Alexis and I have to stick to salads."

The waitress left with our orders and I seized my chance.

"Can you excuse me for a minute? I need to wash my hands." I elbowed Alexis as I walked by her and gave her a *come with me* look.

Alexis slid her chair away from the table. "Me too. Be right back."

As soon as we were away from the table I pulled my phone out. "I have to show you something but we can't leave Lauryn alone with my parents for too long. My dad is going to interrogate her."

Alexis waved her hand, dismissing my concern. "Your dad is Mr. Rogers compared to Lauryn's dad. She'll be fine. What's up?"

"R.T. Torres sent me a message on my wall!"

"What? Let me see!" She reached for my phone. "So, R.T. Torres, huh?" She squeezed my good arm. "He wants to know if you're okay. Put up a picture of you and that guy from prom!"

"What? I'm not showing him a picture of me and Connor. I wouldn't want him showing me a picture of him and his prom date."

"But imagine if he did. How would you feel?"

"Insanely jealous."

"Exactly," she said, not looking up from the screen as she clicked through the pictures in my online album.

She had a point.

"Put this one up!" She picked one that showed my bruises and my bandaged wrist, and Connor had his arm around my waist and we were both laughing. If it hadn't been for my face, it would have been the perfect prom photo.

Alexis and I carefully crafted a response that was longer than I wanted and less flirty than she wanted. She posted the compromise we agreed on with the prom picture. "A couple of bruises—see pic, but my bike is totaled. Won't be competing at T. Throwdown—you?"

"We better go." I stashed my phone and we hurried back.

My dad stood up as we approached the table. "We were about to send in a search party."

"Sorry," I mumbled, putting my napkin back on my lap. "Did we miss anything?"

"We learned that Lauryn plans on going to Illinois State in the fall, and Jasmine assured us that Alexis is an excellent driver with highway experience. Her SUV is well-maintained, and she has a Triple-A Plus card in case of a roadside emergency," he said. "And your ginger ale is here."

Those were the questions he needed to ask in person? I could have texted all that, but whatever.

"I'm not too concerned about their road safety," Jasmine said. "The drives can be done in daylight and taking multi-day solo trips is a natural progression for Alexis. It's important to give teenagers independence in increments. We can't shelter them or they'll be living in the basement when they're thirty-five, and if we turn them loose at eighteen with no preparation, they wind up starring in Girls Gone Wild videos."

My mom's eyes widened.

Great. Just what she needed. More things to worry about.

Jasmine nodded. "It happens."

My mom sipped her iced tea and took a deep breath before talking. "I'm not comfortable with unsupervised teenagers in hotel rooms. If one of us or a coach or an adult we knew was there, I'd feel much better about it."

What? Was she considering going with us? She hadn't even gone to watch when I did a competition before.

Alexis looked at me in panic.

"Our food is here," I announced as our waitress set up a tray full of plates next to our table.

After we'd eaten a few bites, Jasmine said, "I share your concern, Susan. I told Alexis she has to call every night to check in, but honestly, even with an adult there, unless you tie the kids to a leash, they'll find a way to do what they want. We can't let ourselves be ruled by fear. We'd never get anywhere."

"Yes, exactly," Lauryn said in the loudest voice I'd ever heard her use. Everyone waited for her to say more, but she let silence stretch over the table.

Finally, Jasmine cleared her throat. "I think they'd choose somewhere with a beach, not fairgrounds in the Midwest if meeting boys was their primary objective."

"What is your primary objective?" my dad asked.

I stopped pushing the tortellini around my plate and looked up. "I told you. We want to compete in the Ultimate and we have to qualify at the earlier events."

"I'd like to hear Lauryn's answer," he said.

"Sponsorship." She picked up her knife. "I'd like to get sponsored. All the big ones will be at the Ultimate."

"What do your parents think about this trip?"

Lauryn sliced a meatball into quarters. "They're fine with it."

Lauryn held a piece of meatball on her fork but hesitated to put it in her mouth, probably waiting to see if she was going to be asked more questions.

"Alexis? Are you hoping to get sponsored?" my mom asked.

"The odds of me being sponsored are small. I'd actually love to spend the summer at a beach."

"Forget it," Jasmine said.

Alexis speared a tomato on her fork. "Anyway, Josie already reserved the best guy."

"What?" I sputtered, choking on a mouthful of tortellini.

"R.T."

She *did not* just say that in front of my parents. I shot her a look, but she ate her salad, oblivious to the damage she was doing to my cause.

"Is he the boy who defended you in those video comments?" my mom asked. "I thought you didn't know him."

"I don't."

My dad raised his eyebrows.

"I don't know him. I have no idea if he'll be at any of those contests."

"He will be," Lauryn said. "He's everywhere. R.T. Torres is officially on the UnnUsual team, but he travels with what's known as Team Torres. His whole family is there for every contest. His dad is his manager, his mom coordinates his bookings, and his sisters, brothers cousins, whatever are there helping out."

How did Lauryn know so much about R.T.? "You've seen him compete?"

"Yeah. I went to the Ultimate in Austin last summer. That's part of what made me want to do it this year."

I had to find out more of what she knew, but later—away from my parents.

My dad asked Alexis a bunch of questions and luckily she stayed on topic and didn't bring up R.T. or any other guy any of us supposedly had a crush on.

When the waitress came to clear our plates, Alexis's mom looked at her watch. "This has been lovely, but we should be going."

Lauryn excused herself to go to the bathroom and Alexis and I followed.

"Meet us outside the front door, and don't take too long," my mom told me.

"So how do you think it went? Did we pass?" Alexis asked.

"Hard to say. We were doing okay until you made it sound like I was chasing after R.T. What was that?"

"So what if you have a little fling this summer? Do your parents think you're some kind of nun?"

"Do not say anything about R.T. in front of my parents. I need them to think we are going as serious sports competitors, not to chase guys around."

"We *are* going as serious competitors," Lauryn called from inside her bathroom stall. "We won't be chasing anyone anywhere, right Alexis?"

Jasmine swung the door open and called out, "Girls, come on. Josie's parents are already in their car out front. We need to get going!"

I quickly said goodbye to everyone and got in the car.

My dad turned to face me from the passenger seat while my mom drove.

"So." He tilted his head to look down at me.

"So?" I asked.

"While we agree with what Jasmine said about independence, and Lauryn and Alexis seem like perfectly nice girls, *we*…" He put too much extra emphasis on the *we*. That meant they'd agreed to stand together on something. Not good.

He glanced at my mom, looked back at me, and continued, "*We'd* be more comfortable with these road trips if an adult went with you. We'll check our schedules and see what we can come up with, okay?"

I had no choice but to agree. "Okay. Thanks for dinner."

"No problem." He turned back and settled in the passenger seat, and then turned the radio to a classic station.

Great. My only chance at making the Ultimate depended on one of my parents driving me to qualifying events. But there was no way my dad would spend his few days at home driving me around, and my mom would never leave Troy at home alone.

Oh no.

She couldn't be considering bringing Troy, could she?

No.

He'd never agree.

Do not panic. There had to be another way.

By Friday R.T. hadn't written back yet. But what did I expect? He was probably out training, not obsessively checking for messages.

My phone rang while I was holding it, wishing a message from R.T. would appear.

It was Miguel. "Hey peg arm. Any word yet on the Peters family road trip?"

"Not yet. The Outrageous Jam is only four weeks away. If I'm doing that one I need to know so I can train."

"Act like they're going to say yes. Are you watching those videos I told you about?"

"No, not yet."

"Do it . Seriously. It's been proven that athletes who keep training mentally lose less conditioning than those who don't do anything."

"Fine. I'll train mentally."

I hated not being able to ride. I'd been using a spinning bike in the basement to keep my legs and cardio in shape, but it wasn't the same as the feel of the road or ramps.

"I can't believe you'll be gone soon. How long is that film camp?"

"Six weeks. I'm hoping to do some riding while I'm there. They've got to have some sweet spots."

I wished Connor would invent some sort of time manipulator. I'd stretch it so my wrist was healed and then stretch it again so Miguel would be back from his film camp.

"Speaking of riding, what's happening tomorrow? You gave me like zero details." Miguel and I had salvaged what we could from my wreck and figured out what we could fix, find, or replace, leaving me minus one bike frame.

"You'll be meeting Leo at Spoked. He's a friend of my mom's. His new girlfriend is working for him from one to closing, and with her there keeping an eye on the shop he'll be able to take a break to talk to you."

"Does his girlfriend ride BMX?" I asked.

"No, she's some hard-core mountain-bike chick. Leo's crazy about her. He'll be in a good mood while she's in the shop."

"Josie! Troy, dinner!" my mom's voice echoed down the hallway.

I hung up with Miguel and went to the dinner table.

Troy paraded in wearing one of his baseball shirts. "Say hello to the last-ever Oakton Central Lions baseball player to wear number five." He turned so we could see the number on his back, bowed, and then pulled the shirt off and draped it over a chair.

My mom ran over and gave him a huge hug. "I'm so proud of you. When did you find out?"

"Coach told me today. They'll do a little ceremony after the last game next weekend."

I had to congratulate him. "Way to go, Troy."

He nodded in my direction. "Thanks. Is Dad out?"

My mom bustled around, serving heaping portions of shepherd's pie and salad to Troy. "He's supposed to be here any minute."

She slopped some food on a plate for me and for her and sat down. "You should have called me when you found out, Troy. I would have had a bigger celebration. We'll go all out after your last game."

My dad joined us when we were halfway done eating. "Sorry I'm late."

After Troy finished talking about himself and left the table, I decided to ask my dad for some help. "I'm glad you're here. I need your expertise on charming people into doing my bidding."

"I resemble that comment." He leaned his forearms on the table and faced me. "What's going on?"

I went to my room and grabbed the sponsorship package I'd prepared. I showed my dad the schedule of the summer competitions I was doing, my bio with action shots, statistics on the traffic for my video, and then explained the bike situation and how I needed to convince Leo to give me a frame. Ideally I'd get it for free, but even at cost would be great.

"You're serious about this, aren't you?"

"Well, yeah." I wasn't sure what he was so surprised about.

"Susan, have you seen this?"

"What is it?" My mom dried her hands on a dishtowel and opened up my presentation, then gave me a funny look. "I never saw this. You didn't ask for *my* help. And you've written this as if you're definitely going to all these events this summer."

Uh oh. Trouble. I needed to skate out of this. "I'm being positive and proactive." That was the advice she always gave us whenever we whined or complained, but she didn't look convinced. "I can change the heading to Planned Events, so it won't seem so definite."

She read through more of the pages.

"You've been barely maintaining a B average in school and you did this on your own?" my dad asked.

"Yeah."

My mom sat down next to my dad. "Don't say yeah. Say yes, and what we're asking is where did all this motivation come from?"

"I want to ride and compete, and I need a bike and your approval to go on the trip. You spent a lot of extra money on my prom dress, so I couldn't ask you for a bike frame on top of it. There's no school BMX team or BMX booster club. If I don't organize everything myself, it won't happen."

My parents exchanged a *we need to talk* look.

"This package you've prepared is certainly professional-looking." My dad put the papers back in order and looked me in the eyes. "So, we know what you want. What does this bike shop manager want?"

"What do you mean?"

"What you need to do is to go in there and tell him how you can help him get what he wants."

"He wants to make money."

"Someone who wants to make a lot of money probably doesn't open a local bike shop," he said. "I'm guessing he wants to make enough money to lead a comfortable existence and keep the shop open."

"It's Leo at Spokes, right?" my mom asked. "I see him riding his bike all over town. What else do you know about him?"

"Well, he has a new girlfriend who was a bigwig on the mountain-bike circuit."

"Bingo!" My dad slapped his hand on the table.

Bingo? My dad was such a dork, but I needed his help, so I didn't laugh.

"Impressing a new girlfriend is your ticket in. Tell him you have a way for him to reach out to more female riders like yourself. Try to do it when his girlfriend is in the shop."

"And what's my way to reach out to new female riders?"

"Going to those competitions," my mom said quietly, more to herself than to me.

"I did have an idea about giving a free clinic to introduce girls to BMX," I told them.

"There you go—that's perfect." My dad leaned back and put his arm around the back of my mom's chair. "Start with the offer of the bike clinic and then close with the request for a frame. But remember, the economy is bad. You may not get anything but his time."

After dinner I checked for messages from R.T. (none) and outlined my bike clinic idea.

I visualized Leo telling me he had just received a new demo bike and didn't have space for it in the store. Yeah, right. I'd be lucky to get a free water bottle.

Chapter 13

Saturday morning I couldn't decide which look to go for: girly Josie or sporty Josie? This was one of those times when the advice *be yourself* didn't work. I decided to go for conservative and responsible Josie with khaki pants, a white blouse and low-heeled shoes. The bruises on my face had changed from purple to green and brown. I had no choice about how they looked.

Miguel picked me up, but I hesitated before getting in his car. "Do I look too business-y? Should I change into jeans?"

"You're fine. It's Leo."

I'd bought a few things at Spoked, but I couldn't remember meeting Leo in particular. I ordered most of the components on my bike online, so it's not like I was in there buying new stuff all the time.

Miguel dropped me off and said he'd be back in a half hour.

A bell sounded when I stepped on the mat inside the door to the shop. A tall woman with short brown hair who must have been Leo's girlfriend stopped putting new cycling jerseys on a rack by the front door. She wore jeans and a V-neck technical shirt I'd seen online that cost seventy dollars.

"Hi," I said. "I'm Josie Peters. I have an appointment to talk to Leo."

She stood up and shouted "Leo!" to the back of the store, then turned to face me.

"Sandra," she said. "So you're Miguel's friend, the BMX girl."

"That's me."

"Looks like you had a bad fall."

"Only a sprain," I said holding up my left hand as if to prove I could still use it.

"Once I impaled myself on a branch. Missed my lung by a quarter of an inch."

"Did you keep riding after that?" I asked.

"Sure," she said. "Statistically I'm more likely to get injured driving on the highway to get here than on my bike."

She went back to hanging shirts, so I wandered around the store. Leo only had a small selection of older model BMX bikes, all discounted. Apparently BMX wasn't a huge part of his sales.

A stocky guy wearing a tight black T-shirt with a brand name of insanely expensive Italian road bikes walked up, wiping his hands on a rag. He looked old, thirty at least.

"Finished my fourth tune-up today. It's the season. No one thinks to bring their bikes in during February." He shook my hand and introduced himself as Leo. "So Josie, are you one of the people who waits for nice weather to get a tune-up?"

"I do my own tune-ups and repairs."

"Good. Good for you, bad for me." He smiled. "Come on, we'll sit behind the counter. It usually doesn't get busy until a little later."

I followed him to the area behind the cash register. He pulled out a chair and said, "You can sit here. Wait, hold on. Don't want you to get your outfit dirty."

A serious rider should look like she can get dirty. I'd overdressed.

He came back with a towel and draped it over the chair, making me feel like a princess.

I launched into my rehearsed speech about helping bring girls into the store, wanting to qualify for the Ultimate, and the bike clinic.

He was watching me talk, but I didn't think he was listening.

"Did you fall on your face?"

He couldn't be that concerned about my bruises. He must have seen tons of injuries. "I hit the bars. It's not that bad."

"But you want to keep riding."

Was he worried I'd be too scared of falling to get back on? "As soon as it's healed and I get a bike put back together, yes."

He shook his head. "I know guys who would be scared off permanently after a fall like that."

I didn't like his implication that if guys were scared, a girl should be more scared.

"It looks worse than it is." I forced a smile and tried to act as if it was nothing.

He waited for me to stop smiling and look him in the eyes. "I've taken falls; I know what it feels like."

I didn't want to talk about the fall or my face. I needed a frame.

"So what do you think of the clinic as a way to get girls into the store?" I asked.

"Cute idea," he said.

Cute? *Cute?*

"Miguel mentioned you needed a frame. I have something in back that should work for you. Wait one minute."

He didn't care about anything I'd told him or the presentation package I'd apparently wasted hours putting together. But if he wanted to give me a free bike frame because I was bruised and knew a friend of a friend, then great. I'd take it for whatever reason.

When I saw him emerge from the back room, I stood up to see the frame.

Oh no. No way.

He held out the most hideous, ridiculous-looking frame I'd ever seen. Pastel shades of blue, lavender, yellow, and pink swirled in a psychotic pattern, like a baby nightmare. It had to be a joke.

"What do you think?" he said.

He must have been using it to test paint. I could paint over it.

"The size looks good," I said.

"No—the paint."

He turned it around to show that he'd painted my name on it in fuchsia with stars around it. He'd customized it for me! I couldn't tell him it was hideous.

"Is this a tester?" I asked.

"Exactly. We're testing a new line of custom-painted bikes. This is one of my first, and it's yours. No charge."

"Thanks," I said.

Sandra came over and looked at the bike and then at me.

"See," Leo said. "She likes it."

"Are you sure?" Sandra asked. "I told him it was too girly. I think he needs to tone it down."

"Well you could," I said, seizing the opportunity to admit I didn't love it.

"She's just being nice," he said. "She really liked it when I first showed it to her. You should have seen the expression on her face."

"I bet," Sandra said.

"When people see her riding it they'll all want one," Leo said.

I could *not* be seen riding that thing all summer, but my only other option was no frame. I'd have to deal with it.

"Hey!" Miguel walked in and leaned over the counter.

"Whoa, what's that?" he asked.

"My new frame," I said, plastering a huge smile on my face. "Isn't it great?"

"You can't..." he started to say.

I made a shhh! motion to Miguel so he wouldn't say anything else and asked him to carry the frame to his car.

I thanked Leo and went outside where Miguel was looking at the frame from different angles.

"You can't ride it like this. We'll paint over it."

"We can't—he's proud of his new custom painting. Here, give me your keys so I can open the trunk."

Miguel held his keys away from me. "J, seriously, you *can't* ride this. I'll talk to him."

"No. I need this bike. If he gets mad and takes it back I'll be screwed. Please, just help me put it together."

He looked at me, looked at the frame, sighed and put it in the trunk. "Okay, but don't tell anyone I had anything to do with it."

After we drove away I asked, "It's even worse than Mindy's bike, isn't it?"

"Sean painted it black for her."

Of course he did.

Miguel tightened the crank arms and shook his head. "I was hoping once it all got put together it wouldn't look so ridiculous."

"You said to act as if everything would work out. This frame has to work out; my parents have to approve."

Miguel stood back to look at it. "You know..." he said. "Under the paint, it isn't a bad frame."

"That's better. We need to focus on how it performs."

I got on so he could make some final adjustment to the fit.

"Josie Peters, you get off that bike this instant!" My mom stormed out of the house and marched into the yard next to me and Miguel.

Miguel dropped a wrench and it clattered on the cement. What was she screaming about? I was just sitting.

"I'm not riding. This is the frame I got from Spoked. We're adjusting the fit."

"You're on the verge of riding. Fitting that bike is not more important than having a functioning wrist. Honestly! What are you thinking?"

She couldn't say *wow, nice frame.* Or *hey, I know how much you wanted to get that,* or *congratulations on your first sponsorship.* No. It was *you can't be trusted.* Nice. But of course I couldn't say anything. I still needed their approval for the trip, so I had to suck it up and act like I was wrong.

I slowly climbed off the bike.

Miguel stood and wiped his hands on his jeans. "I can test it. Okay?"

"Sure." I couldn't even look at my mother.

Miguel rode back and forth in the trough of the half-pipe and then got off the bike and walked it over to us. "Feels solid. We can tighten it up once you can ride it for real."

My mom still stood there with her arms folded, as though if she took her eyes off me for a minute I'd start riding.

"Hey!" My dad walked up. "Why is everyone in the backyard?"

"We're adjusting the frame I got." I told him.

My dad raised his eyebrows. "So your meeting was a success. That's great!" He stood next to my mom and put his arm around her waist.

She pulled away from him. "It's not great. You weren't here to get a call from the hospital about her hitting her head and needing x-rays."

"Mom, I'm fine," I said. "I won't ride until the doctor says okay."

My dad whispered something to my mom and she stopped scowling.

"It's time to put it away," she said. "Miguel, will you be joining us for dinner?"

"No, thanks. I need to get going. Where do you want the bike?"

"I've got it." My dad took the bike from Miguel. "That's quite the paint job," he said. "Is that your name? With stars?"

"Put it out of reach. She was almost riding it." My mom stomped back into the house and yanked the sliding door shut behind her.

"I wasn't riding." I told him. "We were fitting it."

"Give your mom a break, honey. It's hard to look at you with all those bruises."

I walked Miguel to his car. "Thanks for all your help, but even with the bike it doesn't look good for me going on that trip. Did you see my mom freak out?"

"Yeah, she's definitely not cool with you getting back in the game. Maybe they'll send you to film camp with me."

My calendar had so many countdowns on it I had to use different colored pens to keep track. Six days until the doctor said I could ride again. Eleven days until school finished and twenty-six days until the Outrageous Jam.

Lauryn and Alexis begged me to go with them to St. Louis for the weekend to watch the Titanic Throwdown, and even Miguel was going, but I couldn't. I desperately wanted to, but I knew my attendance at Troy's final game and number retirement hoopla was mandatory. If I'd even asked my parents about the possibility of not being there, it would have been a huge black mark. I made Alexis and Miguel swear to send me updates every time anything happened that I was missing.

To make the *good Josie* package complete, I told Gianna I'd hang out with her while she watched Bruce's tennis match Saturday morning. When she picked me up at eight it was already getting hot. Zero clouds, no wind. The perfect day to be riding. My wrist felt one hundred percent healed, and it killed me to be picked up and driven around instead of riding, but I had to hold out.

Gianna and I settled into two spots in the center of the stands by the tennis courts.

We talked about school and summer and I told her about my parents approving my road-trip plan.

"My mom finally agreed that I could go with Bruce's family to the cottage they rented on some lake in Wisconsin." She fanned herself with the tennis schedule. "They're into water-skiing and wind surfing."

"But you don't even like swimming." I tried fanning myself, but the warm air wasn't soothing.

"I'm getting better." She opened her schedule and checked the time. "It's going to be so hard next year with him away at college."

She could hang out with me, but I could see that wasn't what she wanted anymore.

My phone buzzed with a text message from Alexis. *R.T.T. is here. He's even hotter in person. DROOL!*

I was missing *everything*. Being here as one of the player's girlfriend's friends was completely pathetic. I looked around the stands at other players' girlfriends and girls who were probably their friends. If this was a girls' tennis match, would their boyfriends and their boyfriends' friends be there? Maybe a few, but not as many.

"What?" Gianna asked.

"What?"

"You're mumbling something and you sound mad."

Oops. "Getting hot. I'm going to go get a drink. Want something?"

I got us both slushies to keep us cool while we watched the next match, but it was a blowout of ace serves and not very interesting. Lauryn was probably riding. Miguel promised to text me her results as soon as he could. I kept checking my phone, but no messages. I went to my HeadSpace wall, and I had a reply from R.T.

Nice dress. Really pretty.

He was commenting on my dress? I reread his message, looking for subtext, but stopped when a new message came in from Miguel: *Lauryn 2nd place in vert! Got video. Wish u were here.*

Alexis texted next: *R.T.T asked about you. Gave him your number and told him to text. U can thank me l8r.*

He was asking about me? Asking what? I texted her back, demanding details.

"What are you reading?" Gianna asked.

"What?"

"What?" She imitated me and I felt myself blush.

"Come on, it's me. Who is he?"

"A BMX guy."

"Not Sean." She pushed her sunglasses on top of her head to give me her *I'm serious* look.

"No. Not Sean. He's not from here. I've actually never met him."

"So you're internet dating?"

"No we're... I'll see him at the next event. He's nothing serious."

Alexis didn't write back, and I had nothing from R.T.

As the announcer called out Bruce's match, Gianna focused her attention on the court.

I forced myself to put my phone away and watch with her.

Gianna was on the edge of her seat, and Bruce played a good game against a tough opponent.

When he won I was happy not only for him but that the game didn't go into a tie breaker.

After congratulating Bruce and saying goodbye to Gianna, I pulled my phone out as I headed over to the baseball field to find my parents.

R.T. Torres: *You're not here! Thought you would be. See you in CLE? Did you get your bike figured out?*

I stopped walking so I could reread it. He definitely sounded disappointed that I wasn't there. Why, why couldn't I be there?

I kept my reply friendly but short: *6 days before doctor says I'm ok to ride. Can't wait.*

I didn't mention anything about my bike. Letting my wrist heal was one thing. Getting used to riding the pastel JOSIE star bike in public was another.

My mom waved me over. I had to stop texting or she'd take my phone away.

Troy won his game and my parents joined him on the pitcher's mound when they announced his number retirement. My mom was practically crying and my dad had the biggest smile I'd ever seen.

If I did well at the Ultimate and my parents saw the crowds, the media, and all the attention, then maybe it could be me who made them look that way for once.

I took a bunch of pictures with my mom's camera and then waited as people crowded around Troy and my parents, congratulating them.

When my doctor's appointment finally arrived, I assured him and my mother I'd followed his instructions perfectly—icing, resting and doing mobility exercises. My wrist still felt a little stiff but there was no numbness.

He prodded at it, did a few flexibility tests, and gave me the okay to ride.

As soon as we got home I ran straight to the garage and pulled my bike down.

"We're eating dinner in twenty minutes," my mom reminded me.

"I'll be done in fifteen," I promised.

"Wear your helmet."

I threw my helmet on, jumped on my bike, and pedaled over to the half-pipe. It felt odd. Not only my wrist, but the bike, too. I knew it was normal after a fall and a new bike, but a momentary flash of panic ran through me. What if I wavered? What if I? No. Stop it. I was fine. It healed fine. This was exactly why I had to get back on.

I rode up and down a few times, and started to get in a groove when Troy yelled for me to come eat dinner.

I got up early to ride Friday before school and rode again after school. I felt pretty good on the half-pipe, but the true test would be a full park.

No way was I going to the Sean and Mindy park. I decided to go to Lakewood even though it was forty minutes away. At least I wouldn't have to worry about running into any of Sean's gang.

Alexis, Lauryn, and Miguel offered to go with me, but I wanted to do my first test ride by myself so I could see how it felt without them watching.

I left early Saturday morning to get there in plenty of time. BMXers were only allowed in the park for an hour. Outside the park, skateboarders crisscrossed the parking lot, waiting to go back in after the BMXers were out. One of the reasons I liked this park was that people respected the different hours posted for BMX and skateboarding even though it wasn't officially enforced. Some parks had everyone riding at once and it was a mess. The two factions grudgingly acknowledged each other but also resented each other, claiming the other had the best hours or too much time. A few people rode both skateboards and BMX bikes, but for most of us, it was one or the other.

The skateboarders would definitely rip into me about my pastel bike, but if I wanted to ride, taking verbal abuse couldn't be avoided. Getting used to riding again after an injury was only part of what I had to do today. I had to also get used to riding on a swirly pastel bike with my name on it in fuchsia with stars.

Don't think. Just grab the bike and go. They can sense hesitation and fear.

"Nice bike!" One of the guys walking around carrying his skateboard moved in closer to look. "Check it out!"

I didn't stop or look at him or his friends who came over to point and laugh. I could do this. Once I started riding I'd be okay. The bike was solid. It was a good frame. That's what mattered. Not the paint.

A guy on a black bike rode on the low rails, working on peg grinds while a bunch of other guys did air tricks on the half-pipe. Normally I would wait and watch more before riding, but in this case, standing around with my bike would make me an easy target.

I secured my helmet and rode up and down a couple of ramps, getting the feel of the bike, then did an easy rail grind. The vibration in the handles and the air circulating around me made me realize how much I'd missed riding. The bike felt stiff and unfamiliar, like I was borrowing a bike instead of riding my own.

The back flip would be a bit much on my first day back, so I stuck to some easier tricks, like barspins. The next time I went airborne, I spun the handlebars clockwise, moving the entire front wheel. Grabbing the grips on the way back, I wobbled and barely landed it. I rode around to let my shakiness wear off. The first day back was sure to be the worst.

I needed to practice. After doing the same rail again and landing it better, I felt good. I kept testing my bike and wrist until the skateboarders poured back into the park, yelling at us to get out.

After finishing my last grind, I walked my bike into the parking lot.

A guy on a black bike with blue rims looked at my bike. "Jesus Christ!"

"No, she's Josie," a guy on a green bike said. "Can't you read?"

I'd been so close to getting out. If I acted like I didn't care, they'd get bored.

The green-bike guy looked at me, looked at my helmet and did a double-take. "You're that wipeout chick!"

I pulled off my helmet. The Exquisite sticker on it was pretty noticeable. Miguel had panned in on my face in the wipeout film and you could see the big sticker on my old helmet. I liked how the logo looked in front so I'd put a replacement sticker in the same place on my new helmet.

"It's the wipeout chick!" he shouted.

Of all the things I could have been known for, why was it my epic wipeout?

Five other guys came toward me.

I stood tall and looked each of them in the eye as they approached. No reaction. No fear.

"No shit," one of them said.

"Are you sure she wiped out?" black-bike guy asked. "Maybe she got beat up for having such a lame bike."

A couple of the other guys burst out laughing.

I was still a good fifty feet from my car. I'd have to endure some harassing before I could get away without looking like I was running away. They'd get bored eventually.

"There are stars around her name," black-bike guy said, laughing and pointing. "Did you see it?"

"Back off," said a guy in a VaporTrail T-shirt with no bike. "It's a good idea. I'm painting my next bike to look like shit with my name all over it. Maybe then it won't get jacked." He looked at me. "Is that why you did it?"

"Yeah." There was no point explaining the real story. "I can leave it unlocked anywhere and no one touches it."

"Shit, man," green-bike guy said. "They need to keep whoever did that away from paint guns."

I left them arguing about the pros and cons of my bike-theft-prevention strategy. Maybe Leo was on to something—custom-painted bikes too ugly to steal.

The last week of school flew by in an exhausting whirlwind of final exams and training. I should have been thrilled on the first morning of summer vacation, but I was dreading saying goodbye to Miguel.

When I got to his house, his mom led me to his room and knocked on the door.

"Josie's here." She gave me a tight smile and left.

When the door opened I looked in and stopped. "Whoa. I didn't know your carpet was blue." I'd never seen enough of a clean patch to know the color before.

"Very funny." He flopped down on his bed next to a stuffed backpack.

Two black suitcases sat on the floor next to a pile of boxes. All his posters and pictures were off the walls, leaving white scars and dirty outlines on the beige paint.

"Are you moving out?"

"They're decorating while I'm gone. New paint, new carpet. Maybe it's a hint they want a new me." He heaved the backpack over his shoulder. "They won't bother actually weighing this, will they? It's about fifteen pounds over the carry-on weight limit."

"I've been on a plane exactly once, so you're asking the wrong person." I sat on the chair by his desk. "Are you sure there's no way your stepdad will change his mind at the last minute?"

"No, and I did my best to piss him off. I tried using reverse psychology, but it backfired." He let the backpack slide onto the bed and sat down on the floor. "I decided to act as if I was looking forward to film camp. I ordered a bunch of books the professor wrote on photography and film and when they got here I made a point of reading them in the living room in front of everyone. Since I actually ended up reading the books, I discovered that the guy is kind of a genius. I'm pretty lucky I get to study under him. Anyway, you'll be too busy on your wild road-trip adventure to miss me."

"*If* I get to go. Are you going to ride at all when you're over there?" I swiveled on his chair, pushing right, then left.

"There are a couple of interesting parks I'll definitely visit, but I'm not bringing a bike. I'm kind of looking forward to being film guy instead of injured BMX guy for a change."

"You're not injured BMX guy, and you sound like you don't plan on coming back." Even his closet was empty.

"If someone offered me a truckload of money to stay I can't say I'd turn it down, but my plan is to go to camp and be back in six weeks. I'll be back in time to film you in the Ultimate, and by then I won't be cutting off your head or screwing up the lighting."

"*If* I qualify."

"Not *if, when.* Remember, picture that perfect ride. Feel it and make it happen."

I pictured myself at the top of a ramp with the Ultimate logo on it. He'd given me the "picture it" advice about a million times last summer. We'd spent practically every day together by the end. I felt lost already and he wasn't even gone yet.

"Stop looking so sad," he said. "You're going on my dream trip. You're going to have to live it for both of us."

I was almost relieved when his mom said dinner was ready and I had to go. Miguel's stark room and packed bags were too depressing to look at anymore.

On Saturday Lauryn and Alexis had invited me to meet them at Lakewood Park to ride, but it was Troy's graduation and my attendance was mandatory. I forced myself to look on the bright side. My days of being known as his younger sister were winding down. I'd be the only Peters at school for one glorious year.

Even though it was overcast, it didn't look like rain, so they held the ceremony outside. We got there early enough to get a decent seat on the top row of the bleachers so we could lean back. I wedged myself into the corner and pulled out my phone. R.T. and I had been texting each other back and forth a lot, plus he was writing on my HeadSpace wall.

"*Sessioning at Cantcope. U riding 2day?*"

"*Stuck at bro grad,*" I wrote back.

"*U have bro?*"

I'd linked to Troy as my brother on my HeadSpace wall, but maybe R.T. hadn't drilled down on the minutiae of my profile like I'd done to his.

Everyone I met this summer would get to know me first and then, maybe, find out about Troy, instead of the other way around. *If* my parents let me go. Or as Miguel would say *when* they let me go.

When the ceremony started, my mom gave me her *put your phone away* look so I settled in to act enthralled as they called off the six hundred plus names in Troy's graduating class. One of the first people I recognized going up to get her diploma was Mindy's older sister. I scanned the crowd, looking where the applause was the loudest and saw Mindy, but no Sean. Had they broken up? Had he come up with some lame excuse why he couldn't go to a family thing with her? Maybe her parents were even less impressed with Sean than my parents had been.

Bruce was up next. I clapped and saw Gianna sitting with his family. She'd invited me to Bruce's graduation party later.

Next year it would be me and Gianna graduating. A long way off.

Halfway through the L's the sky cleared up and the sun beat on us, heating the metal bleachers way past uncomfortable. Sweat was dripping down my back by the N's. I thought I'd die before they got to P.

When Troy's name was finally called, he took his time standing up, swaggered to the podium, and then paused. He changed his stance to hold an invisible bat, swung and watched as if he'd hit another home run. The crowd went wild, cheering and applauding louder as Troy raised his arms in victory.

After he finally took his diploma and headed back to his seat, my mom lost it and sobbed. "I remember his first day of kindergarten."

My dad held her around the shoulders and talked to her in a low voice until she finally laughed. I snuck a peek at my phone. One message from Alexis: "*Lauryn has 360s dialed!*" Nothing from R.T.

I zoned out and visualized as many tricks as I could as the ceremony slogged through the end of the alphabet. When Brenda Zav finally got back to her seat, we applauded the whole class for the last time and left.

Troy had his choice of any restaurant for dinner, but instead of choosing somewhere nice where we never got to go, he insisted on going to Hog Heaven so he could get a ridiculously big full rack of ribs. I think he purposely took forever eating it, basking in the glow of my parents' admiration plus extra congratulations from a handful of people in the restaurant who recognized him from his games. I escaped to the bathroom to send text messages three times before my dad told me that was enough.

When Troy was about three-quarters of the way through his ribs, a skateboarder I recognized from the park I used to go to with Sean's gang stopped by to talk to Troy. "You going to finish that whole rack? I only got two-thirds of the way through it."

Troy introduced Rick and told my mom, "This is the guy I was telling you about. Got into Northern because of skateboarding."

"That's impressive," my mom said. "Congratulations."

"Thanks," Rick said. "I wrote my application essay on competing in the Ultimate last summer, and I guess it was what the admissions people wanted." He turned to me. "Haven't seen you around the park lately. Heard you got hurt. Are you coming back?"

I cleared my throat. It was the first time anyone had asked me a question all night. "I just got the okay to ride again. I've been going to Lakewood, and I hope to do some competitions this summer to qualify for the Ultimate."

"You definitely should. A girl who does extreme sports. Golden." He looked toward the exit. "My parents are waiting for me. I gotta go."

After he left, my dad asked how Troy knew about Rick's acceptance at Northern.

"A guy from there came to talk to us at one of those create-your-future talks. He said something about being in extreme sports showing initiative and out-of-the box thinking."

I thought about the gang of guys I rode with. Some of them were innovative, some were show-offs. Miguel was the only one other than me who would probably even bother applying to college. He was definitely an innovator.

"He got an actual scholarship?" my dad asked.

"Better deal than I got, at a better school."

My dad leaned back in his chair. "So Josie's BMX riding is now considered a sign of innovation?"

Troy shrugged as he picked up his fork to dig in to his molten lava cake "I doubt anyone will give her a scholarship for doing extreme sports in the backyard."

Ohmigod, had Troy actually *helped* me? Only because he didn't realize what he was saying. I had to strike right then while I had an opening. I swallowed my bite of lava cake. "I'll have to get into college the old-fashioned way, working for minimum wage and paying for it myself." I looked around the restaurant. "I should ask for an application. Maybe I could be a Hog Heaven waitress this summer."

My parents didn't take the bait. They didn't even exchange a look that said *we've been so wrong about Josie, we should tell her right now she can go on her trip.*

They sat there making small talk.

When Troy eventually finished his dessert, my parents let me go to Bruce's graduation party to meet Gianna.

The street in front of Bruce's house was crammed with cars parked along both sides. I had to find a spot two blocks down and walk. The backyard was packed and I didn't see Gianna anywhere. I texted her that I was there and considered leaving when a familiar voice called me.

"Josie! Finally someone who's not an annoying relative." Connor made his way next to me.

Someone jostled me from behind. I regained my balance and stepped back. "These are all relatives?"

"Pretty much. Lots of cousins. Four of them are my sisters. If people think you're my girlfriend, play along, okay? It would be a huge favor—it's easier than explaining the truth, and it'll save me from being set up on blind dates."

"Sure."

"Perfect. Are you hungry?" he asked.

I told him I'd just been to Hog Heaven and couldn't stuff any more food in if I had to. Another person bumped me, spilling something sticky on my arm.

"Follow me." Connor took my hand and pulled me after him toward the back of Bruce's yard. "I found a spot earlier that will keep us out of the mob."

He stopped at a low cement ledge around a flowerbed in the corner of the yard. I looked for Gianna and checked my messages before sitting.

"Was that you who did the demotivation posters?" I asked.

He grinned but didn't answer.

It had to have been Connor. He'd done an amazing job on the last day of school replacing the real motivation posters with fake demotivation posters that used the same image and title, but with a different message. "My favorite was PERSISTENCE, showing one person running way behind the other, and the message *She's gone man, get over it.* I can't even remember what it used to say."

"I can't confirm or deny any such activity."

"They looked professional."

Connor shrugged. "Demotivation isn't exactly new, but it's not as old as the lame trick the seniors pulled. Chairs and desks on the lawn? Total lack of imagination."

"So next year's senior prank is already in the works?"

"Those planning it might be tossing some ideas around, but they don't want to limit themselves to their current skill sets."

I didn't know how to respond to that so I changed the subject. "Any summer plans?" I shifted so I was sitting further back on the ledge. With Connor around, maybe spending the summer here wouldn't be so bad.

"I've got a full load of camps lined up to refine my knowledge of artificial intelligence, blacksmithing, and survival tactics."

Connor would be gone, too. Any hope I'd had of possibly having one friend around disappeared.

A guy I didn't know and a middle-aged man walked by us, then the guy stopped and turned to face me. "Aren't you Troy Peters's sister?"

"This is Josie Peters." Connor introduced me to one of his uncles and a cousin.

The uncle staggered toward me, spilling his beer on his already stained shirt. "Helluva year for Troy. Helluva year." He took a long sip of his beer before continuing. "Had a good run. Good for him. He'll always have those memories. Best days, high school. Best days."

Connor's cousin got the uncle moving and Connor turned to me after watching them go. "Promise you'll bludgeon me with a heavy object if you run into me ten years from now and I'm babbling about high school being the best time of my life."

"I promise to end your misery, but only if you'll do the same for me."

"Agreed."

"How depressing, to be an adult and looking back on high school," I said. "I can't make a move without my parents signing a waiver, and this is supposed to be the time of my life?"

"You don't have to tell me about restrictions." Connor's watch beeped and he smiled.

"What's that? Explosion alert?"

"Rescue mission. My brother is trapped with an aunt determined to pair him up with the girl of his dreams. I promised I'd save him if he hit the alarm."

We both stood. "I should get going, too. If you see Gianna…"

"I'll tell her you spent the last hour looking for her and finally gave up."

"Thanks, Connor. Enjoy your summer."

I took a last long look at the party before going to my car. I felt bad leaving without finding Gianna, but odds were she was with Bruce or one of his sisters, planning their summer vacation. I couldn't listen to any more about everyone else's amazing summer plans that involved leaving me stuck here alone.

I spent Sunday going around town filling out applications. Even though my parents hadn't officially said no, I couldn't wait or I'd end up with a leftover job or no job, which would make me a house slave for the summer with no money.

I got back from WrapIt just in time for another Peters family dinner.

Troy was already at the table with a thick envelope next to his plate. "Got my schedule for the summer."

My mom pulled the family calendar off the refrigerator and started mapping his camps and practices onto June. I watched as she drew a line through the dates of the Outrageous Jam, which wasn't on the family calendar, not even in pencil.

"Speaking of summer schedules…," my dad said.

This was the part where he'd tell us he was going to be gone for six weeks somewhere on the other side of the world, and my mom would be busy, and I couldn't stress her out by being gone. I kept my head down and nibbled on my hamburger.

"Josie?" My dad made sure he had everyone's attention and then looked at my mom.

She put her pen down, took a deep breath, and put a fake happy face on. "We've decided."

I braced myself.

"To let you go on your trip on your own."

I froze, unable to swallow or blink. She said yes? How was that possible?

My mom rattled off her conditions, *call as soon as I got to any location, call every day. Promise no drugs…* I didn't care what she made me agree to, I was going! I pushed my chair back, got up and gave her a huge hug. "Thank you! Thank you! You're the best!"

I hugged my dad too and then ran to my room to get the waivers before they changed their minds. I started to run back, remembered I was supposed to be recuperating and forced myself to amble the rest of the way to the dining room.

Finally, finally they were taking BMX seriously and seeing it as a real sport.

My mom signed the first waiver and slid it to me. "It will be good for you to get this out of your system this summer."

What? Get what out of my system? I didn't say anything. I couldn't pick a fight now.

My dad picked up my plate and stacked it on top of his. "Nothing wrong with wanting a little adventure. Can't blame you for wanting a last summer of fun. Next year you'll have to get a job over the summer." He cleared the rest of the plates and I sat silently as my mom finished signing my waivers and got back to her Troy calendar.

Chapter 14

My dad was only home for a few days after Troy's graduation. The day before he was supposed to leave on his trip he came in my room, sat on my bed, and asked if I had a minute.

I sensed a lecture coming. My dad never hung out in my room.

"Your mother thinks I'll scare you by telling you these things, but I think you need to be aware that there are a lot of dangerous people out there and a group of teenage girls traveling alone is a prime target. You need to be defensive to keep out of trouble."

I assured him that I was aware of evil in the world, but he insisted on giving me his full speech. "You need to question the intentions of any stranger who approaches you. No one should be asking a group of teenage girls for directions or help with a flat tire. If anyone comes up to you, be wary."

His speech reminded me of the stranger-danger stuff we learned in kindergarten, but I told him I was listening and that I would be wary.

He headed toward the door, paused and turned back. "One more thing."

More? Please not a *teenage boys are only after one thing* speech.

"Please try to give your mom a break."

"I haven't done anything..."

He held up his hand to stop me. "You've heard of empty-nest syndrome? Troy leaving is hard on her, so make sure she knows you need her and not just for laundry and food. Go to her for the big stuff, okay?"

He had never said anything like that to me before. I promised I would do my best, and he left my room.

If I went to her about how scared I was to screw up in competition and about Lauryn and Alexis replacing me and about being stuck at home alone with no friends, she wouldn't be able to help. She was stuck here so I couldn't tell her it was my worst nightmare. Maybe I could ask her to help me figure out which clothes to pack.

Gianna left the Saturday before I was scheduled to go. Even though we hadn't been spending much time together, it felt weird to know I wouldn't see her all summer. Luckily there were zero rain days in the week leading up to the Outrageous Jam, so I got in a ton of training until I decided to take a break so my body could recover. My wrist felt one hundred percent and all the tricks I had were pretty solid. The question was could I pull them off when it counted in front of people and judges?

An hour before Lauryn and Alexis were supposed to pick me up to leave, I'd already checked my bike, unpacked and repacked my repair kit, gone over the registration information, and reviewed the route map with my mom even though we were using a GPS.

When Alexis and Lauryn finally pulled in a half hour later I put my bike in the back of the SUV and crammed my suitcase next to the three already there. I almost asked why there were three bags but the two matching cheetah-print bags with matching A.J. tags answered my question.

After I re-promised not to take drugs and to call as soon as we got there, we finally left.

I leaned forward from the backseat so I was between Alexis and Lauryn. "Alexis, you have a bag for each day of the competition."

"One is filled with condoms."

"What?" Lauryn asked as she maneuvered out of my subdivision.

"Okay, not filled, but Jasmine gave me the longest lecture ever on safe sex and the responsibility of fertility and she made me take an enormous box even though I'm already on the pill. Ask me anything about any sexually transmitted disease."

"Herpes?" Lauryn said.

Alexis started to share what she knew but Lauryn cut her off. "Change subject!"

Alexis reached for a tote bag at her feet. "I did manage to get something potentially useful. I grabbed a couple of books about technique off Jasmine's bookshelves." She pulled a book out of her bag and flipped the pages. "Some of this is basic but there's stuff I'd definitely try."

I could not even imagine borrowing my mom's sex-technique books. She gave me a sex talk years ago, and I still hadn't recovered.

Alexis held up a page toward me with a drawing of a man and an extremely flexible woman twisted sort of sideways. "Have you ever tried this one?"

"I haven't tried any of them."

"You mean you haven't done it yet?" She lowered the book.

"No." I pulled back so I was sitting in the backseat.

Alexis twisted in her seat to look at me. "Not with anyone?"

I turned to watch the cars passing us on the left. "Not with anyone."

"Wow." She turned back to face front. "Even Lauryn lost hers last summer." Alexis turned to Lauryn. "Tell the story!"

"That's pretty much it," Lauryn said.

Alexis shook Lauryn's elbow. "Come on, let me tell her some details."

"Stop shaking me. You can tell more, but don't be all dramatic."

Alexis made a serious face and spoke in a monotone. "Beach vacation. Hot guy. She left before things got complicated." She paused. "Is that non-dramatic enough?"

"Perfect," Lauryn said as she changed lanes.

Alexis turned to look at me and continued in her normal voice, "And he was *very* attentive to her, if you know what I mean."

I sort of knew what she meant.

Lauryn smiled and even blushed a little.

There were a million questions I wanted to ask her. *How did she know he was the right one? What did it feel like? Did she feel different now?* But Lauryn didn't seem like she wanted to talk about it and I didn't want to start our trip by annoying her, even though Alexis didn't seem to worry about pushing too much.

"Come on," Alexis said. "Give her a little advice."

"Choose the right guy."

"Agreed," Alexis said. "I've heard stories of the first time not going well at all. You definitely don't want a *wham-bam* guy. I'll do some checking on R. T. and find out how much of a player he is. Don't do anything until I get back to you."

Did she think that I was going to grab a handful of her condoms and jump him the minute we got there?

"We're not chasing guys, remember," Lauryn said. "Whatever happens, happens."

"Let's see," Alexis said. "There are like two hundred guys and about eleven girls signed up for the Outrageous Jam. Something is going to happen."

After five hours of driving to Lauryn's favorite country music, we pulled in to our hotel in western Ohio, got checked in and made the requisite "we're here safely" calls to our parents.

The hotel was small and cheap but it had a pool. Even though it was early evening and the hundred-degree-plus peak heat of the day had passed, humidity hung heavy in the air. We needed a major storm to crack the drought that had followed us from Illinois, but the forecast predicted another record breaker tomorrow.

I opened the curtains to our room and watched all the people in the pool. "Let's go for a quick swim."

"No, we need to get registered," said Lauryn.

Alexis stood in front of the mirror fixing her hair. "I want to check out the scene. We didn't come all the way here to swim by ourselves. We could have done that at home."

We wore shorts and tank tops to keep cool, but there would be no relief without a storm first.

Lauryn closed the door to our room behind us. "If it's like this tomorrow, we'll roast wearing jeans."

I always wore full-length jeans to ride, as did most BMXers. That layer of denim was the last line of defense in case of a bad fall and could save your legs from some nasty road rash, but with this weather I'd be tempted to wear shorts anyway.

We drove to the state fairgrounds where the event was being held and parked in a dusty, packed-dirt parking lot.

I'd been to competitions at the local skate park and seen footage of big contests online, but the Outrageous Jam setup was another universe. Enormous black banners marked off the festival territory, workers pounded ramp pieces into shape, music blared from enormous sky-high speakers, and food vendors were already doing business, cashing in on the competitors and setup crew buying anything edible. The aroma of hot dogs, corn, chicken, and French fries filled the air.

I readjusted my sweaty shirt and scanned the crowd looking for R.T. Even though the events didn't start until tomorrow he might be around, but I didn't see him. Sweat ran down my back. "Let's find a lemonade stand or somewhere with anything cold to drink."

"Ooh, that looks good," Alexis said, standing on her toes.

"Where?" I turned to see. She was looking at three muscular shirtless guys putting together a tabletop ramp.

Lauryn said something, but she was so far ahead of us we couldn't hear. She backtracked into range. "Come on! We need to get registered so we can get out of here."

"Relax, the first event isn't until tomorrow. We've got all night," Alexis said, still watching the workmen.

We found the registration table and stood in the back of the lineup. Over two hundred riders from all over the world were supposed to be here. I didn't recognize anyone. Not that I was plugged in to the big BMX pro scene, but we'd been to some contests before and knew some riders. The guys next to us had a mix of accents that were definitely not Midwestern. Southern, Bostonian, Irish? I wasn't sure, but I loved the sound of them talking and all the people walking around in shirts emblazoned with the names of every team and brand I'd ever heard of. This contest was huge. And I was here! Finally.

I unstuck my shirt from my back even though I knew it would re-stick when I let go.

Lauryn put her hand on her forehead to shield her eyes as she looked past the registration table to the far corner of the grounds where the mega ramp was being built.

"How high is that?" I asked.

"It's thirty-five feet," said a cute guy in an UnnUsual shirt. R.T.'s team! "Not as tall as the big air ramp, but still pretty sweet."

He held out one of two huge full cardboard cups with the VaporTrail energy drink logo on them.

"Want one of these? I got an extra for a friend, but he ditched me and I'd like to have my hand back."

"Sure! Thanks." I reached for the drink. The wet, sticky, wax-coated cardboard cup slipped a little as I took it, so I held it with both hands and took a big swig. I'd never been a big fan of VaporTrail, but the cool sugary liquid was refreshing.

Alexis, Lauryn and I finished the whole drink in under a minute and we chatted with the UnnUsual guy until a guy in an S-Force T-shirt walked up.

"Dude, where's my VaporTrail?"

"I had the choice of holding it until your slow-ass self found your way back or using it as bait to get these three chicks to talk to me, so guess what?"

"Shit," the guy said.

"Sorry," Alexis said. "We'll get you another one."

"It's all right," he told her. "He gets them free since he's sponsored."

"Nice perk," Lauryn said.

We made it to the front of the line, checked in and got our maps and competitor wristbands.

"This is so official," Alexis said, tucking her wristband into her pocket.

Lauryn studied the map.

"They've got park and vert, plus the mega ramp," she said. "I can't believe they're building all this for one weekend and then tearing it down again. I want to go see that ramp."

Guys on bikes wove through the crowd, people with walkie-talkies drove around in golf carts, and pickup trucks laden with equipment forced us to keep moving to the side.

"This is so weird," I said. "I'm used to riding in almost complete obscurity. I can't believe all this setup."

"Oh. My. God," Lauryn said, stopping completely.

The mega ramp towered above us.

"Did you notice it's almost all guys here," Alexis said, looking around to see who else was watching the mega ramp go up. "Isn't it great?"

"There are some girls from MadKapp." I pointed to a group of three girls, with one in a fluorescent-green MK shirt.

"Josie! Josie!" Alexis bounced on her toes, squealing. "R.T. is right there. Don't look. Don't look. Here, we'll move so you can see."

We walked in a circle so I was facing the opposite direction.

He was even more gorgeous in person. His shirtless upper body glistened from the heat, and his skin had already turned a rich tanned brown from the sun even though it was only mid-June.

"You should go say hi," Alexis said.

"Right. I'm going to walk up to his entire team and say hi to R.T. I'd rather get on my bike and drop in on that mega ramp."

"Would you?" asked Lauryn, looking back at the ramp.

"No!"

Alexis blatantly turned to face R.T.'s gang. "I'm liking that blond guy. Who is that?"

The blond guy gave Alexis a huge flirty look, scanning her from head to toe. I started to tell her I had no idea when she left us and headed straight for them. "Come on," she said. "No hesitating."

I forced myself to act as if I felt as confident as Alexis looked. I followed her over, and Lauryn followed me.

Before we reached their group, a handful of kids approached R.T. with their programs to be signed. The other guys moved aside to make room, leaving R.T. and one other guy to the side with the kids.

"There," Alexis turned to me. "Now he's not with his team. Go over there and say hi."

I got to R.T. as he was signing for the last kid. The other guy with R.T. looked up at me and asked, "What's your name?"

"Josie," I told him.

Ho grabbed my program out of my hands and handed it to R.T.

"No, wait." I tried to get the program back, but he'd already started scribbling on it. "I'm *Josie*."

"Yeah, he got it," his friend said.

Did R.T. not recognize me? He'd seen a bunch of my pictures, and there weren't that many girls who rode BMX.

He scrawled "To Josee. Nice 2 meet U," signed his name, shoved the program back at me and backed up to leave.

"R.T.?" If he looked at me, he should figure out who I was.

He glanced up at me, gave me the same smile he'd given the kids and walked off with his friend.

I stood there, waiting for him to turn back and laugh. It had to be a joke. There was no way he didn't make the connection. How many Josies did he know?

Lauryn walked up next to me. "That was a short conversation. What happened?"

"He signed my program. And spelled my name wrong."

Chapter 15

I woke up before our six thirty alarm, showered, and ate by the time Lauryn and Alexis got out of bed.

Lauryn ransacked her luggage and kicked shoes out of her way as she stomped over to the dresser. "How is this room such a mess already? I can't find my socks!"

"Sit. I got them for you," Alexis said.

Lauryn scowled as she grabbed her socks from Alexis and yanked them on.

"Come on," Alexis said. "We're going. Girls vert riders practice from seven forty-five to eight o'clock."

Even though it was only seven thirty, the heat of the day had already started. In the minute it took to leave our air-conditioned room and walk to Alexis's SUV, sweat beaded on my forehead.

"You're lucky you ride early," Alexis said to Lauryn. "We'll be melting by our events this afternoon."

We drove to the fairground and parked in a shady area under a clump of maple trees, then made our way to the practice area.

Girls in MadKapp T-shirts, tank tops, blue helmets, white helmets, and all kinds of bikes whizzed up and down the half-pipe.

I stood, transfixed, watching a girl in a blue helmet try a toothpick stall, balancing on her front-wheel peg on the lip at the top of the ramp. The white-bike girl went next and did a nice footjam, wedging her foot on top of her front bike tire, balancing in total control on the flat area behind the ramp.

"Here." Alexis handed Lauryn her helmet. "Go!"

Lauryn put her helmet on and joined the rest of the girls warming up. At first she just rode up and down, but then she did a can-can, moving her right foot over her bike to the left side while airborne.

"That chick has can-cans dialed!" said a guy standing next to us.

Alexis squeezed my elbow and bounced on her toes.

"Nice," I said. "I hope she does that in the competition."

Lauryn turned to face us and smiled, flashing the Exquisite logo on her mouth guard. We waved and I gave her a thumbs-up.

"Come on," I said to Alexis. "Let's find a spot where we'll be able to see the competition."

Lauryn was third in the lineup. Evie Zafira from MadKapp went first. From the second her ride started, Evie captured the attention of the crowd. Her muscular shoulders strained against her T-shirt and her bike squeaked as she pumped it back and forth to pick up speed, doing bunnyhop one-eighties and building air on each side of the half-pipe. She finished with a flair, flipping upside down and turning midair to land riding back down the ramp.

A girl named Charlotte something from S-Force went next. At least twenty people in S-Force T-shirts roared their encouragement as she dropped down. She did a nice x-up with her handlebars turned and her arms crossed, but then got tangled and wiped out on the way down, adding a huge black skid mark to the scuffed ramp. She stood up, shook it off, and kept riding, but that fall cost her most of her allotted time and she only did one other trick.

In the time it took the first two girls to ride, more and more people crowded into the stands.

The announcer called out, "Now Lauryn Jax of DeerGrove, Illinois."

Alexis zipped her purse open and shut, open and shut, open and shut.

"She'll be fine," I said, putting my hand on Alexis's before she could zip again.

"I know," she said, nodding.

I leaned forward and held my breath, wishing, daring, hoping, praying that Lauryn did well.

She dropped down, picked up momentum and did a nice icepick grind on the top of the opposite ramp, with her rear peg resting on the lip and her front wheel up.

After riding down she did another grind and then rode faster, pumping back and forth in preparation for an air trick.

Come on, Lauryn, I silently willed. She only had sixty seconds to do enough good tricks to impress the judges, but not wipe out and squander precious seconds recovering.

I inhaled sharply and sent "yes!" vibes her way as she rose up the opposite ramp and did a barspin in the air, turning her handlebars around in a full circle before grabbing them again on the way down.

"Nice!" I yelled while clapping and allowing myself to breathe again.

She managed to sneak in a successful x-up right before the air horn sounded, signaling the end of her turn.

I jumped to my feet, applauding and whooping as did half the crowd in the stadium.

"Nice run!" I shouted.

Lauryn looked at us and pumped her fist in the air.

Alexis squeezed my hand and we sat back down to watch the rest of the vert girls.

In the second round, Lauryn tried a five-forty—a full spin plus the extra 180 degrees needed to get back down the ramp. She looked like she had it, but wasn't quite rotated enough and she lost her balance going down. She got back up with no problem but ran out of time.

The other riders did some impressive moves, but I honestly thought Lauryn's first turn had enough tricks in it to put her in the running for a podium finish.

It took forever for the judges to compile the scores and get around to announcing the winners. I closed my eyes and held my breath as the announcer called out the third-place finisher, Charlotte from S-Force, and then second place, "Lauryn Jax of Lakeville, Illinois."

"Aaaahhh!" Alexis and I screamed like maniacs. I sprang out of my seat, and Alexis and I scrambled over people to get to the podium to see Lauryn. I held my phone up to snap photos of her receiving her armload of prize loot—it looked like a shirt, a hat, and a plaque.

First place went to Evie Zafira, which was no surprise.

After Lauryn hopped off the podium carrying her prizes, we made our way through the crowd to congratulate her while the guys poured into the half-pipe, starting their practice runs.

We ended up next to a group of UnnUsual guys, including R.T. and the blond guy Alexis had been talking to yesterday. He nodded to us. "Thinking of dropping in on that ramp?"

"Maybe tomorrow," Alexis said, bridging the gap between us and R.T.'s teammates so we were all one group.

The blond guy stared at me. "You're the wipeout chick from that video."

"It's me." I looked straight at him, refusing to allow R.T. to creep into my peripheral vision.

"That was insane!" A guy in an UnnUsual T-shirt, wearing a knit hat and one-inch-diameter ear gauges held out his phone to take my picture. "Cool. I met someone famous."

Before I could stop myself, I glanced at R.T. and he was looking at me with a weird expression, but he didn't say anything.

"Flynn, R.T., we gotta go," the blond guy said. He wished us luck for later and they left. I glanced at them as they walked away and R.T. was turned back, talking to the blond guy and pointing at me.

"Why didn't R.T. say anything to you?" Alexis asked.

"Don't know. He's kind of weird. What's that blond guy's name?"

"Oliver, and he's mine. You already called R.T."

Lucky me.

My "On Site" event was right after lunch. I could only choke down half of my sandwich, so I checked messages and felt a little better after reading the "good luck, send podium pix" message from Miguel.

We didn't want to lose our parking space or risk getting stuck going back to our hotel so we had everything we needed in the SUV. I used the door as a screen to stand behind as I changed from shorts to jeans and gathered my helmet, mouth guard, and bike. Lauryn's podium finish had me floating so high, even my pastel bike couldn't bring me down.

I joined the other On Site competitors in the warm-up park. We wouldn't know the actual configuration of the park where we'd be competing until later. That was the point of On Site—no one had the advantage of being familiar with the park. The warm-up park included a variety of the typical ramps, rails and obstacles you'd find in most parks, but the competition park would have a different layout.

When a tabletop ramp opened up I pushed for it and went for a turndown. I managed to twist my hips out to the right and straighten my legs to pull my bike to the left, but when I tried turning the handlebars so the wheel "clicked" past the bar of my bike, my hand caught on my thigh. Crap, crap, crap. I was going down. I hit the down-ramp in the wrong place, my bike wrenched sideways and I spun out all the way to the fence.

A chorus of *ohhhs, owwws,* and a "Girl down!" sounded from people watching nearby.

Luckily my jeans saved my legs from what would have been a bad scrape. I lay still for a few heartbeats, inventorying my body to make sure I could move my fingers and toes and that nothing felt badly injured and then I pushed my bike away so I could stand up.

"Whoa. You alright?" I heard a male voice ask as a hand extended down.

The VaporTrail-sponsored guy helped me up.

"I'm good. Thanks." I leaned over to check my bike, but apart from a few scrapes, it looked okay.

"Whoa, are those stars?" the VaporTrail guy asked. "That's the most messed-up paint job I ever saw."

I grabbed my bike and left to find Alexis and Lauryn without letting him finish.

"I couldn't see you," Lauryn said. "What happened?"

"If you hear people talking about the girl on a hideous bike who hit the fence after blowing a turndown, it was me."

"You okay?" she asked.

I inspected my bike for damage. "Yeah. I shouldn't have tried to click that turndown. It's not one of my most solid tricks."

"Forget it," Lauryn said. "Ride hard and make them notice you for the right reasons."

The loudspeakers blared an announcement about closing practice, telling non-competitors to move to the spectator area.

An Outrageous Jam organizer checked my wristband and shuffled me into the competition area.

After gathering all the On Site competitors in a closed-off tent where we couldn't see the configuration of the park, an event official got our attention to re-explain the rules since it was a new event they were testing.

"When you're up, you'll each get thirty seconds to look over the arrangement of the park and come up with a plan before riding. The horn will sound at the end of two minutes and you'll be scored for any trick already in progress, but not for a trick started after the horn. Rides are ranked on originality. If four people do the same move at the same location it will score less. The more locations you hit with the most original moves the higher the score. You need to move quickly and be original."

My riding style wasn't as technically perfect as Lauryn's or as smooth as Alexis's, but I could usually figure out a way to ride on anything. How hard could riding in a reconfigured park be? They only had so many pieces of equipment to move around.

The official read the lineup and my name was last in the girls' category. It would have been better to go first so I could go sit in the stands and watch everyone else. Being last meant I had to wait in the tent and I wouldn't get to see any of the other girls ride. At least I'd get to see the guys. They were riding on the same setup right after the girls, and all the scoring was being done after the guys finished.

When the official turned off the mike, people spread out in the tent.

An elbow jostled me in the ribs.

R.T. was right behind me. "How'd your warm-up go?" he asked.

Now he was going to chat with me as if he hadn't pretended he had no idea who I was? Fine. I could treat him like any random guy I met at a park. "Pretty good. One wipeout."

"You want to wipe now and get it out of the way. What sucks is leaving your best ride in practice."

He looked down at my bike and did a double-take, but before he could say anything, another guy wearing an UnnUsual T-shirt rode up.

"What is that?" he asked looking at my bike.

"Subliminal scoring," I told him. "Before I even start riding, the judges will have already decided I'm original, and it will help my scores."

"Seriously?" he asked.

"You guys practically look like twins," I said, making a point of looking at their identical black bikes with red rims, red UnnUsual T-shirts, and black helmets. "No matter what you do, they're going to get confused and think you're the same. I bet your mouth guards even match."

"Crap," he said.

R.T. grinned. "That's some impressive BS for a girl on an Easter-egg bike."

"Thanks, R.P. Or is it R.D.? I get all you UnnUsual guys mixed up."

"All girls should be in staging area three," the organizer announced.

"Gotta go!" I said.

"Good luck," said R.T. His teammate looked freaked out as they moved away.

I steered my bike to the staging area but stayed in the back, as far as possible from the panicky nervousness radiating off the other competitors.

A buff platinum-blonde in a MadKapp shirt did a series of stretches, showing the flexibility of a circus performer while a girl whose bike had S-Force stickers all over it sat cross-legged with her eyes shut. I zoned out to relax, but it was torture watching the girls leave one by one and hearing cheers and groans from the crowd.

When my name was finally called, I followed the race organizer to the tent door. A buzzer sounded and he led me out for my thirty seconds to see the setup. The park looked more or less normal with a couple of rails, a quarter-pipe ramp, and a tabletop ramp, but what was that in the middle? It looked like a fence post. A wooden fence post. The park I used to ride in with Sean's friends had a row of similar posts that blocked the path from the parking lot to keep people from driving into the park. The posts weren't part of the park, but we used to try tricks on them anyway. Sean sucked at it. I could always do better tricks than he could on those posts. BEEP. The buzzer sounded for my turn to start.

I'd been so fixated on the fence post I hadn't come up with a plan. The tabletop ramp was right in front of me, but there was no way I was trying the turndown again. Back flip? Why not.

Pushing hard, I pictured the spin, gained speed pumping up and down, lifted off, felt it rotate and landed it. Yess! Nice one.

I circled away and realized I should have gone the other direction because I was in a sector of the park with no rails or ramps. I turned sharply and headed straight for the post. It wasn't even as high as the ones I was used to. No problem. I timed it perfectly to get close enough to shift my weight back and rest my front wheel rest on top of the post. Perfect. I leaned forward and swung the rest of my bike around before hopping off. A smattering of applause told me it looked good.

Pumping the pedals hard, I pushed for the quarter-pipe to get in another trick before the horn sounded. That post move had chewed up a lot of time. I hadn't done any grinds, but my back flip was solid and I didn't fall.

Alexis and Lauryn found me after I left the competition area.

"I ran out of time," I said.

"It's okay," Alexis said. "Sight riding is supposed to be really hard."

"What is everyone else doing with that post?" I asked.

"No one else touched it," Lauryn said.

"No one?" I said.

"I think it's to anchor the rain tarp," Lauryn said, not looking at me.

What? So that trick wouldn't even count. Crap. That was bad. If I didn't score well, I wouldn't get into the Ultimate and...

"Josie!" Lauryn waved her hand in front of my face.

"What?"

"Let go of your helmet. I'm trying to help you, but the more I pull on it the tighter you grab it."

"Sorry." I unclenched my hand so Lauryn could carry my helmet. There was no sense in going crazy about my score until I saw the final standings. "How did the other girls do?"

"Hard to say," Lauryn said. "Two of them did the back flip on the tabletop, but one didn't land it."

"Come on, let's go watch the guys," Alexis said, leading us to a spot where we could see.

R.T. was first. He rode as if he'd been practicing in that exact park his entire life. He avoided the post.

Watching the guys usually inspired me and gave me ideas, but each time I saw a trick I knew I could have done, the more restless I felt. Why hadn't I gone up and down both sides like they were doing? Most of the guys were doing pretty much the same run as R.T. with the exception of one guy from Scotland who zigzagged and did odd tricks I couldn't name. People in the crowd criticized him, but I liked his ride because he was unpredictable and fun to watch.

"Oww! Josie! You're kicking me," Alexis said.

"Sorry," I told her and stopped.

When they started announcing the winners, I braced myself.

"I'm not sure I can handle seeing my name dead last on the scoreboard," I said.

"You won't be last," Lauryn said. "There was one girl who wiped out right away and had to be carried off."

"Is she okay?" I asked.

"She's fine. You're going to be fine. Relax," Alexis said.

Right. Perspective. I didn't get hurt. I could recover from being second to last.

We watched the girl with the white S-Force bike, Paige, go up for third and then the flexible blond MadKapp girl, Maya, took second. I figured another one of the MadKapp girls would be first.

I rebalanced my bike against my leg so I could applaud when the announcer named the top girl.

"And in first place, Josie Peters of Oakton, Illinois."

Chapter 16

My body stiffened and someone squeezed my arm.

"Josie go!" Alexis pushed me. "It's you."

"No," I said. "It's a joke."

"It's no joke," Lauryn said, pointing to the screen.

JOSIE PETERS glowed in orange letters on the electronic scoreboard.

I'd fantasized about winning before, but usually I pictured myself pulling off a big trick at the end of my ride and hearing applause right away. My legs shook as I climbed onto the podium. Maya moved aside to give me room to step on her second-place platform, and Paige gave me a high five from her third-place perch. Before today I would have thought these girls were way out of my league, but here I was, one of them!

"She looks happy," one of the photographers said, and I could feel the huge grin that had spread across my face. I shook hands with the other podium finishers. So this was what winning felt like. I could get used to it.

I thanked the guy who handed me my prize loot: a hat and T-shirt like Lauryn had, plus a big plaque and a hoodie. Camera flashes went off in all directions. I hoped no one could tell I was shaking. I kept smiling even while I climbed down and stood where they told us to wait so we could pose with the top three guy finishers.

The VaporTrail guy, Zach, placed third, R.T. was second, and the Scottish guy, Clyde, took first.

We all posed for a group picture with me and Clyde front and center.

"Squeeze in, closer. No gaps!" The official photographer squished us in for the group photo.

All of us were less than fresh after riding and standing around in hundred-plus-degree heat wearing jeans, but Clyde definitely needed to be first to have a shower. I couldn't decide which smell on him was more offensive: the beer or the sweat or maybe it was something he ate but oh my God I thought I would pass out from the fumes by the time the photos were over.

When we were finally given the okay to move, I bolted away from Clyde but he followed me, rambling about being number one and trading trick tips.

"Hey!" Lauryn walked up with my bike.

Alexis held up her phone. "Let me get a picture of you with your bike and plaque."

I posed in front of a big Outrageous BMX Jam banner while she snapped the photo.

"Oooh, be right back." Alexis put her camera away, ran a hand through her hair, and wandered off.

"Where's Alexis going?" I asked

"Something caught her eye," Lauryn said.

"Something?"

"Tall, blond."

"I get the picture," I said.

"I'll put your bike back in the SUV," she said. "Meet you back here, okay?" Lauryn left and I talked to a reporter from *BMX Real Deal* magazine plus a bunch of other people covering the event. I did my best to smile and make quick, interesting comments, but the interviews were almost more draining than the ride. When the last question finished and the cameras moved away, I took a deep breath and looked for Lauryn.

"Hey, fence post!" R.T. walked up with his bike.

What was with him? Every time he saw me alone he was all chummy.

"Hey," I answered back, hoping that *fence post* wasn't going to be my new name.

"So you're the only rocket scientist who strategized right for the scoring."

I wanted to be mad at him, but his smile pulled me in and I couldn't help but smile back. I was beginning to stare so I brushed some imaginary dirt off my hands and tried to remember what he'd just said… something about strategizing… "I didn't strategize; I saw the post and decided to use it."

"Yeah right. You beat everyone." He rolled his bike back and forth by his side. "Any ideas about what they'll throw at us next time? A moat? Live chickens?"

"Why should I tell you?"

A group of guys ran behind him, jostling his bike. R.T. stumbled sideways and I put a hand on his shoulder as if to help steady him, even though I knew he wouldn't fall. It was an excuse to touch him. Holy crap, he was solid. All muscle. I left my hand there longer than necessary, forcing myself to let go before it became too obvious.

He said something and I thought about kissing him. Power, finesse, unexpected moves. If he kissed like he rode…

"Hello?"

He figured out I hadn't heard anything he said.

"Sorry, what?" I refocused my attention on his eyes.

"I said maybe it's a farm thing. I'm not used to fences."

"Aren't some of your teammates from Texas? Aren't they ranchers? Maybe they can help you overcome your fear of fence posts."

"Right. We'll see what happens next time. Later." He flashed me a quick grin before jogging off with his bike in the direction of a group of his teammates.

Alexis ran up to me after R.T. left. "Hey, I saw R.T. go up to you. He seems interested!"

Lauryn found us and we walked together back toward the SUV.

"R.T. was less interested the more I talked."

"What did you say to him?" Lauryn asked.

"I might have said something about him being afraid of fence posts."

"Josie!" Alexis shoved my shoulder and then unlocked the SUV.

"What?" I opened the back door to search for my shorts.

"His ego is probably a little bruised," Alexis said.

"No one cares if my ego gets bruised." I got in the backseat and wriggled out of my jeans. "He was all over me being wipeout girl. It's not like I was gloating about how many more points I scored than he did." I pulled my shorts on and got out.

"Thirty-two," Lauryn said.

I looked over at her and smiled, "But who's counting?"

Alexis was doing the last event, the Sudden Death Park Jam. Everyone would ride for thirty seconds in a rotation, and whoever fell was out. The event would keep going for twelve minutes and then finish the last rotation. Everyone would ride in two heats and the best score would count.

I didn't love the idea of park jam. Since it favored staying on your bike at all costs, people usually rode conservatively on the first heat and then maybe tried some harder tricks the second time. I preferred lots of new tricks and wipeouts.

Alexis didn't have a lot of technically difficult tricks, but her smooth style was truly a thing of beauty in contrast to the thrashing and crashing of other riders. She flowed from obstacle to obstacle, barely causing a creak, making the whole ride look seamless. Any move she made was executed with perfect symmetry. When her legs went out they were completely straight, perfectly balanced, and her toes were pointed. Her years of gymnastics training were paying off big-time, and the photographers loved her look. Each time she moved from one side to the next, the photographers went crazy, snapping more photos of her than they had of anyone.

When she finished, breathless, she turned, centered herself, pulled out her mouth guard, and smiled for a final flurry of photos. She couldn't have posed better if they'd directed her.

Alexis knew how to put on a performance and this was the perfect place for it.

"She probably won't score well, but that's not what she cares about," Lauryn said as we watched Alexis turn and smile.

We went to the podium to hear the winners announced, and as we expected Alexis wasn't in the top three, but she was pleased with her race and had built a following of photographers who wanted to know where she'd be riding next. Normally I would have been put off by all the posing and hamming it up for the camera, but Alexis was using them to steal back some of the spotlight from the guys. She was either an egomaniac or a genius.

When Alexis was done, we picked up some food and took it back to the hotel.

Lauryn crumpled her cheeseburger wrapper into a ball. "We should see if any of the video is online yet and go over our rides."

"We're getting ready for tonight's party. I already know what we're wearing," Alexis said.

Lauryn chucked the wrapper-ball into the garbage. "I'm not spending the night watching you chase guys."

"I won't be chasing anyone. They'll be chasing us. You're going and you're going to look good."

I wouldn't call myself a prude, but the miniskirt Alexis wanted me to borrow would have had me flashing people all night, and I refused to even consider wearing it.

"I'm wearing pants," I told her as I peeled off the scrap of fabric she called a skirt. "I hate carrying a purse."

"Look," she said holding out a vibrant blue dress. "This has a little pocket sewn into the side seam so you can carry money, ID, and even a mini lip gloss with no lumps." She put the dress in my hands. "Try it."

"ID? I need ID? My ID says I'm seventeen."

"Here, I have one for you." She dug through her purse.

"You got me a fake ID?"

"It's not fake. It's borrowed. Mine is fake. It says I'm twenty-one so I can buy drinks."

"Where'd you get that?" Lauryn asked.

"Don't worry about it," Alexis answered. "Memorize yours, Josie, but it looks like you, so you'll be fine. You have to be eighteen to get in, but they don't hassle girls much."

I studied the ID and the picture did sort of look like me, and the girl's basic info was right: brown eyes, five feet, four inches tall. It should pass.

"What's your sign?" Alexis asked me.

"Huh?"

"Astrological. You've had the same birthday for *eighteen* years, right?"

"Umm." My look-alike's birthday was September. "Virgo."

"Right. You'll be fine."

Alexis went in the bathroom to do whatever it was she did to get her hair all spiky, and Lauryn and I sat on the beds, ready to go.

"This should be fun, don't you think?" I asked her.

"Depends on your definition of fun. Fun for Alexis is being surrounded by people paying attention to her."

"And for you? What would make it fun?" I asked.

"There are a couple of people I met at other contests. If I can find them and get caught up, that would be fun."

After several seconds of dead air she asked me, "You?"

"I want to enjoy the scene. Dance, hang out, forget about scoring and contests for a while." I also wanted to see R.T., but I didn't want to admit that to Lauryn.

Alexis emerged from the bathroom with her hair in all its spiked glory. "Okay, let's go."

At the fairground, a space about the size of a football field was partitioned off. Ten-foot-high plastic fencing blocked our view of the inside, but music blasted and the fencing bowed in places as people pushed against it, making the party area look alive, pulsing with energy. Black cables snaked from under the fencing, connecting to power generators to feed the amplifiers, refrigerators, and huge lights that illuminated the area.

As Alexis predicted, the bouncer only superficially glanced at my ID before stamping a big X on the back of my hand to indicate I was under twenty-one and letting me in.

Once we were inside, Alexis said, "I'm getting a drink. Want me to get something for either of you? All you have to do is get a soda in one of those red cups, dump it out and pour the drink in the red cup."

"No. I'm good," I said.

"Me too," Lauryn told her. "You go ahead. We'll meet you over there."

Lauryn and I walked toward the counter that only sold nonalcoholic drinks.

We barely had space to move because so many people were clustered around the tables. I stood on my toes to check the area by the DJ, but only a few people were making a feeble attempt at dancing to music I didn't recognize, and that didn't inspire me to dance.

"There's R.T." Alexis pushed me in his direction. "Go over there."

I moved back where I was, next to Lauryn, and planted my feet so I wouldn't move if I was pushed again. "Forget it. He's kind of an idiot. I want someone else."

"You better be sure. Even though there are twenty guys for every girl here, half those girls are after R.T. You can't wait around."

"I thought we weren't chasing guys," Lauryn said.

Alexis put her hands on her hips. "We're not, but if you stand there you're going to get leftovers."

"I'm okay with that," Lauryn said. "If you get fixated on one guy, he'll become a distraction. If you dance with whoever, you can relax and have fun. Right Josie?"

Before I could answer, Alexis said, "Oh no. You're not going to dance with whoever. You're going to choose a guy in the next ten seconds or I'll choose one for you."

Lauryn protested, but Alexis turned her to look at what she called "good prospects."

Paige, the S-Force girl who was third in the On Site, smiled at me and walked over. "Hey, post girl."

I laughed, even though I didn't want to be called post girl. Lauryn looked relieved to have a break from guy shopping.

"I think it sucks the way some people were talking about your win as lucky. You know if a guy had leapfrogged that post there would be a picture of it on the cover of *BMX Real Deal* and they would have named the move after him."

"The Josie Jump! I love it!" Alexis said.

"It works for me," Paige said. "We should all start doing Josie Jumps from now on and beat the guys at their own game."

"Why is BMX their game?" Lauryn asked.

"It's not," I said, wishing we could change the subject. "Hey, Lauryn, how about that guy?" I asked, motioning toward a muscular guy hauling an empty keg away. "He looks like your type."

Lauryn shot me a death glare.

"Can't we get along?" Alexis asked. "The guys want us here. We want to be here. What's the problem? Ooooh. Speaking of, I gotta go."

Alexis took off, and Paige and Lauryn got into a discussion of sponsorship options.

Paige was in the middle of telling us what she knew about MadKapp when she stopped mid-sentence and stared behind me.

Paige and Lauryn stopped talking and looked over my shoulder.

"What?" I turned to see what they were looking at.

R.T. was directly behind me.

I turned back without saying anything.

He put his hand on my shoulder and leaned in. "Can I talk to you for a minute? Over there?"

I looked at Lauryn and she shrugged.

"I guess." I left with R.T. and we wove between the people lined up at the nonalcoholic drink counter until he stopped next to a recycling bin. A nearby generator hummed like a truck idling. It was a remote place to talk, but not exactly romantic.

"Look, about earlier," he stammered.

"The part where you pretended you didn't know me and signed my program with my name spelled wrong and treated me like a groupie?"

"Yeah, that."

He ran a hand through his hair, then shook his head so it fell back the way it was. "I... uhh. It's not you. It's... I didn't want my brother to know I knew you."

I waited for more of an explanation. "Because..."

"It's kind of a long story, but it's because of me not you."

"Okay, whatever." That was hardly worth wandering over here for.

I half-turned to leave. "Is that it?"

"No... I mean... You look great. That's my favorite color."

"I thought my coral prom dress was your favorite color."

"I never saw your prom dress."

"I thought we were done with the *I don't remember Josie* game."

"Seriously, I never saw your dress."

"You commented on it on my HeadSpace wall."

He shook his head no.

"Give me your phone." I reached toward him with my hand out. I was tired of these games. "I'll log in and show you."

I pulled up the photo and the comment stream.

He scrolled through it and cursed in Spanish.

"Give me a minute." He called someone and talked in rapid Spanish, switching from talking to yelling to what sounded like swearing. After he hung up and put his phone away, he looked at me.

"This is going to make me look like an even bigger asshole, but it was my sister who posted all that."

"Your sister?"

"My family helps me with a lot of online stuff. My brother is supposed to handle approving and liking stuff on HeadSpace, but he's not supposed to write anything, and apparently, without me knowing about it, he gave my password to my little sister and had her managing it."

"Your *little* sister? How little?"

. "Maricela is ten."

"So I've been having a conversation with your ten-year-old sister?" I was an idiot. I should have known it wasn't him. The conversations hadn't matched at all.

"So that's why you were posting one thing on my wall and then texting me a totally different conversation on my phone. Or was that your mom?"

"No that was me."

"And the comments on my wipeout video? Your grandfather?"

"No that was me. The rest is all me." He looked to his right, swore under his breath, and turned to face me "I have to go. I am *really* sorry."

Without waiting for me to respond he ran off, leaving me with the hum of the generator.

Two guys who resembled R.T. and had to be brothers or cousins walked by. "He was here. I know I saw him."

"Head toward that blonde," the other one said, indicating Paige. I trailed behind them, taking advantage of the path they cleared through the crowd.

They paused by Paige and Lauryn, looked around, and moved away. Lauryn was right. Guys were distractions. I needed to forget about R.T. I was the creator of the Josie Jump, not a pawn in R.T.'s games. I'd choose someone at random or dance with whoever passed by.

Lauryn and I left before Alexis and went back to our room. Lauryn passed out almost immediately, but I couldn't fall asleep and I heard Alexis come in at two in the morning.

"What did we miss?" I whispered.

"They finally kicked the DJ out and got some good music playing. Oh, and I see what you mean about wanting to pick

someone other than R.T. He's so flirty. It's like, too much."
She peeled off her dress and put on a camisole.

I sat up a little in my bed. "Flirty? How?"

"Handsy, whispering about how we should go somewhere
quieter... that kind of stuff."

Handsy? He was handsy with her? He hadn't been handsy
with me.

Lauryn threw a pillow at Alexis. "Can you guys please shut
up already?"

Alexis made a face at me, clicked the light off, and settled
into bed.

If Alexis was his type, then I definitely wasn't. Good. Fine.
Whatever. I closed my eyes and tried to force myself to think
of anything but R.T.

Chapter 17

I stood on the first-place spot of the Ultimate winners' podium. The cheering crowd started banging louder and louder. Someone was knocking on our motel-room door.

I turned to see Lauryn stumble over and look through the peephole.

She opened the door a crack. "Yeah?"

"Is Josie there?" A male voice.

"Hold on." Lauryn left the door open a couple of inches and turned to me. "It's R.T."

"What?" I rolled out of the bed, pulled on a pair of shorts, smoothed down the raggedy T-shirt I'd slept in and went to the door.

Holy crap, it actually was R.T. leaning against the railing by the walkway. He wasn't smiling, and his eyes were hidden behind sunglasses.

A tiny voice in my head reminded me that I'd sworn to forget about him. Another voice said that was before I had any idea he'd show up at my door asking for me.

I opened the door wider and squinted into the sunlight.

"Morning," he said. "I know it's early, but could you go to breakfast?"

"Now?"

He nodded. "Right now. Put shoes on. Let's go."

"One sec." I closed the door and turned back into the room. My heart was pounding as if I were facing a mega ramp. I stumbled around, trying not to make too much noise. After pulling off my sleeping shirt, I threw on a bra and whatever T-shirt was on top of the clothes mountain on the dresser. A shower would have been nice, but it would have to wait. I pulled a comb through my hair, splashed my face with water, and brushed my teeth.

None of my shoes were in sight so I slid on a pair of Alexis's purple, sequined flip-flops, whispered to Lauryn that I was going to breakfast, and left.

I couldn't believe I was going to breakfast with R.T. Maybe he wanted to apologize some more.

We crossed a four-lane highway that was too noisy to allow any conversation and then we walked into a truck-stop diner. A pudgy man in a booth by the window who was talking on a hands-free phone waved to us.

That couldn't be his dad. They looked nothing alike. "Who is that?" I asked.

"My coach."

"We're eating with your coach?"

What was happening? I thought it was me and R.T. The so-called coach didn't look like an athlete. He looked like one of my dad's friends who thought an occasional golf game was a workout.

R.T. opened the door for me. "Yeah, he saw you yesterday and asked if anyone knew you."

So it wasn't R.T. who wanted to see me.

I slid into the booth opposite the man, and R.T. sat next to me.

The coach didn't look up as he made notes while talking. "That's right. Fifty. I'm aware of that. Yes. Consider it done." He clicked his phone off but left the earpiece in.

After writing more notes and turning a page in his notebook, he looked up and held out his hand. "I'm Harold Robbins. No relation to the writer, guru, or actor."

I had no idea what he meant so I smiled and shook his hand. He stifled a smirk when he saw my shirt and looked back up as the waitress arrived.

Crap. I was wearing Alexis's "Delicious" T-shirt. Why couldn't I have grabbed one of Lauryn's or my shirts instead?

"So you're the On Site innovator." Coach Robbins opened his menu. "Ever trained with a team?"

"No."

"We need a female for the relay. I don't know if you heard, but our regular girl hurt her ankle yesterday."

I nodded yes.

"The relay is new. Some brainiac decided to make it mandatory to have one female on each team. It seems like more hassle than it's worth, but I told the guys we'd try it this summer. If we wind up with another princess refusing to ride because of a bruise and have nothing to show for it than wasted training time, then this will be the end of it."

He sipped his coffee and then put the cup down. "So what do you say?"

Was he asking if I thought it was a dumb idea, or if all girls were princesses? Was I supposed to be convincing him he should have girls on his team?

"I'm not sure I follow," I said.

R.T. laughed. "I like, just woke her up."

Coach Robbins plastered a polite smile on his face, inhaled, and then said slowly, "Would you like to train with UnnUsual to possibly be our mandatory female?"

"Sure." My voice cracked and I cleared my throat. "Yes."

"See?" R.T. told his coach. "It's all good."

The waitress reappeared with a coffeepot, and although I didn't normally drink coffee, I didn't stop her from filling my cup.

"Order whatever you want. Consider it a welcome breakfast," the coach said.

R.T. ordered the long-haul eggstravaganza, his coach ordered poached eggs with no toast, and I ordered blueberry pancakes.

"You see, that's the difference right there. Guys need to build muscle while girls just want to fit in their shorty shorts." Robbins shook his head.

"Pancakes aren't exactly diet food," I said.

R.T. poured sugar in his coffee while Robbins scrolled through screens on his phone, not bothering to acknowledge my comment.

"You'll need to be at Explosion a day early," Coach Robbins told me. "You're not officially a sponsored member of the team, so you won't have sponsor benefits but you will benefit from the coaching and the experience and exposure. Any questions?"

If sponsor benefits meant free stuff, I would have liked some, but I wasn't going to push my luck.

"Can I still compete as an individual in On Site?"

"Yes. The rules are set up so the girls can ride as much as possible. Having an all-guy team is now politically incorrect. Makes no sense with ninety percent or more of the riders being male, but what do I know?"

I was tempted to point out the cancellation of the girls' class in the Ultimate to prove him wrong about girls getting too much help and support, but I kept my mouth full of pancakes.

Coach Robbins told us he was still working on the practice schedule, and he and R.T. talked about where they were going between the Outrageous Jam and Explosion. Robbins finished his breakfast so fast I'd barely eaten half my pancakes, and I hadn't been talking at all.

"Take your time." He dropped some money on the table and stood up with his phone and laptop bag. "I've got to get going, but I'll send you the schedule."

After the coach walked away, R.T. kicked me under the table. "So?"

"So just like that he wants me to ride with you?"

"He's probably got a couple of girls in mind and he'll see if you come unglued in the training."

"Unglued?"

"Don't worry. Robbins is kind of a tool. He's a corporate guy who wants us to win so he gets a bonus. He doesn't know shit about BMX, but the other guys on the team are good. We help each other out and push each other. Robbins is good at filling out paperwork and getting us primo park time and free stuff."

Training with the team sounded great. Plus, R.T. had told his coach he "knew" me, so that had to mean something. Maybe he'd put in a good word for me, too. I smiled as I dug into the pancakes.

"You good?" R.T. asked.

"Huh?" I said, looking up, my mouth full of pancakes.

"I've got to go." He stood up and put his sunglasses on. "I'll see you around."

See me around? I tried to swallow, but the pancakes caught in my throat. By the time I forced them down, R.T. was gone. I watched as he left the restaurant, not even pausing to look back.

That was it. I was NOT going to get caught up in his games. I'd be all business. An opportunity to train with a coach and ride with a team was huge. I didn't need any distractions from R.T. Torres. I didn't care how good-looking he was.

I repeated that to myself over and over as I finished my breakfast by myself.

By the time I left the table I was almost convinced I could train with UnnUsual and not care what R.T. said or didn't say to me.

Chapter 18

When I got back to the room, Alexis squealed when she saw her purple flip-flops on my feet. "I've been looking everywhere for those!"

"Sorry. I put on whatever I could find."

"So, breakfast, huh?" Alexis looked at me with a raised eyebrow.

"With his coach," I said.

Lauryn zipped her suitcase closed. "Harold Robbins?"

"And?" Alexis prompted.

"Tell us on the way home. We have to be out of here in ten minutes or we pay for another day." Lauryn threw my suitcase on the bed and stuffed handfuls of my clothes in.

We both helped Alexis get her stuff out of the bathroom so we made the checkout cutoff.

When we were on the road headed home, I told them the whole story, including Coach Robbins wanting me on the team and not wanting me on the team at the same time.

"So you'll be training with UnnUsual," Lauryn said. "When's your first practice?"

"I need to be in Milwaukee a day early."

"We'll make sure you're there," Alexis said. "This is perfect. With you on the team, I'll have an *in* with Oliver. Look." She showed me the UnnUsual website on her phone and clicked through all the guys' pictures. Turner was the one with dreadlocks who was often with R.T. and I recognized Flynn because of his black hat and ear gauges. I still thought R.T. was the best-looking one, even though I didn't want to think about him any more.

"The girl who was riding with them isn't even here," I said, clicking around the site. She wasn't mentioned anywhere. "Robbins didn't seem thrilled to have girls on the team."

"Don't worry about Robbins," Lauryn told me. "When he sees what you can do he'll forget you're a girl."

Alexis showed me all the updates she'd done to Exquisite, posting Lauryn's and my results plus a bunch of new pictures. "And I bugged that *BMX Real Deal* guy about not putting more girls on their site, so he gave me some of his extra footage and said I could put clips of us on Exquisite."

We alternated drivers so I was the one to pull into my driveway. When I turned off the engine, Alexis insisted she had to go to the bathroom, and Lauryn said she'd go too, so we all went in the house together. I pushed the front door open and dropped my suitcase in the hall.

A huge "Josie is #1" banner stretched across the back wall of the living room.

"Woohoo!" Cheers erupted and people spilled out from behind chairs and the couch.

"Oh my God!" I took a step back and bumped into Alexis behind me.

Leo and Sandra from the bike shop and two of Sean's friends stood in my living room with my family.

My dad gave me a huge hug and pulled me into the middle of the room. "Congratulations."

"How slow were you guys driving?" Troy asked. "We expected you an hour ago."

My mom put down her camera for a second and pulled me close. "We're so proud of you, honey!"

This was all for me? Whenever a banner had covered the wall it had Troy's name on it.

My mom released her hug, but I held on and squeezed my eyes shut for a second longer. When I moved back, I was facing a video camera.

Miguel!

"You should see your face!" he said.

"How are you here?"

"How could I miss the party for your first big win?" He held his left hand up to high-five me, and Sean's friends approached and mumbled their congratulations.

"It might never happen again, so we better celebrate now." Troy was bursting out of a tight shirt as usual, and maybe I was getting used to the lean BMX guys, but he looked a little chubby to me.

Alexis prodded me with her elbow. "Josie has something to announce."

Everyone stopped talking and Miguel aimed his video camera straight at me.

"The coach from UnnUsual asked me to train with them for the next race."

Cheers and whoops erupted again, and my mom gave me another hug. "I'm not sure exactly what that means," she said. "But if you're happy, I'm happy."

"It means riding with professionals and getting coaching."

"And being around R.T. all summer," Alexis added.

I made bug eyes at her to shut up. My former crush on R.T. didn't need to be announced to the whole room or captured on video. I wished Gianna could have magically been there. She was the one I wanted to talk to about R.T.

"You're hitting the big time!" Miguel said.

"I'm training with them. I'm not officially sponsored by anyone but Spoked."

"Told you we were holding you back." Miguel lowered the camera for a second and grinned at me. I wanted to pull him aside and find out what was going on with him, but my dad started shouting from the backyard.

"Food is ready outside!"

Sean's friends headed straight for the barbecue with everyone else following.

I sat by Miguel at the table and chairs set up in the trough of the half-pipe. "Do you know why Sean's friends are here?"

"Your mom showed up at the park this morning and invited everyone."

"She didn't!"

"Yeah. I guess we all look alike to her."

Oh my God. Did she invite Sean and Mindy? Maybe they were broken up by now. I hadn't thought about Sean at all the whole time I'd been gone. Hopefully I wouldn't run into him while I was home.

I was lucky there weren't some random weirdos at my house eating bratwurst. I'd met these friends of Sean's, but didn't know their real names. They'd always been called Z-Dog and NoFro. I assumed the Z-Dog guy's real name started with a Z, and the NoFro guy apparently used to have a mop of curly white-blond hair which he now kept military short. "I'm surprised they came. Do they even know my name?"

"You think that would prevent them from showing up where there's free food? We also want to see the footage that Alexis got of the contest."

"Video from her phone?"

"She said she got something professional from *BMX Real Deal* and she'd show it later."

"She told you that?"

"She set it all up with your mom." Miguel checked his phone, then put it in his pocket.

Gradually everyone got food and sat at the half-pipe table. Troy maneuvered himself in next to Alexis, squeezing Z-Dog and NoFro down, and Lauryn sat with Miguel and me.

My dad stood at the center of the table. "Before we start, I want to say how proud we are of Josie."

"Speech!" Troy bellowed, turning toward me while pounding his fist on the table, "Speech!"

Was he kidding? He'd never made a freaking speech. He was trying to make me look stupid.

No hesitation. No fear. I stood up. Troy wasn't going to ruin this.

"Thanks a lot for being here. I couldn't have done it without your help. Miguel, Lauryn, Alexis."

Troy started waving and pointing to himself. Crap. Why had I started naming people?

"Leo and Sandra, Mom, Dad, and everyone—thanks! Now dig in!"

I sat down quickly before Troy could pull another stunt.

I turned to Miguel and asked, "How was film camp?"

"Good."

Good? Before I could ask him for details, he prompted Lauryn to tell him about the mega ramps at the summer events. They got deep in conversation about every ramp they'd ever ridden or seen or wanted to build.

I half-listened as I ate two bratwursts plus my mom's famous potato salad.

When everyone but Z-Dog and NoFro had more or less finished eating, my mom walked out of the kitchen followed by Troy, carrying a sheet cake decorated with sparklers.

Troy put the cake down in front of me. It had a BMX bike, miniramps, and a little figurine off to the side. I tapped the head of the figurine. "I can't believe you found a BMX cake."

"It was a skateboard cake. I gave them the bike to modify it," my mom said.

"Check it out!" NoFro said, pointing. "Josie's mom sidelined Vinnie Phoenix."

Mini Vinnie Phoenix was crouched down as if he were on his trademark skateboard, but the board was buried in frosting.

"Boarders are banned from this cake, dude," Z-Dog said, laughing.

My mom sliced the cake into various-sized pieces. "Grab a piece and we'll go to the basement to watch Josie's ride."

Troy hesitated with his hand near one of the jumbo pieces before settling on a medium slice. Even though I was stuffed, I took a piece with a hunk of chocolate ramp on it and led the way down to the basement. At the bottom of the stairs I stopped, causing Lauryn to bump into me from behind.

"Hey!"

"Sorry." I moved ahead slowly, no longer sure where to find anything in the once-familiar space. My mom had been busy while I was gone, completely gutting the room, ripping out the walls and tearing up the linoleum floor. All the ratty furniture was gone, replaced by two rows of folding chairs facing the television.

"Don't mind the mess," my mom said. "We should have enough chairs for everyone."

Z-Dog slid into the seat next to Alexis, edging out Troy, who was forced to sit in back.

"We'll just watch your ride," Alexis said, queuing up the video to the right spot.

I had the best seat, front and center. Analyzing a film was always fun. Miguel and I had spent hours watching other riders and ourselves, replaying the moves that looked humanly impossible and breaking down the tricks we wanted to try.

"I can't believe you got this video," I said to Alexis.

She smoothed down the sides of her shirt and winked at me.

At the part of the competition where I hopped on the fence post, Miguel knocked my knee with his. "Nice!"

"That's the winning move right there," Lauryn said.

When my ride ended, Alexis fast-forwarded. "I'm not sure if he gave me the podium part."

"Who is that?" Troy's voice echoed from the back of the room.

Alexis played the video at normal speed. The camera angle zoomed in to frame Oliver with Maya from MadKapp. She posed next to him and leaned in, kissing him for an obscenely long time with way too much tongue, making me acutely aware that I was in my basement with my parents.

Z-Dog whistled, then said, "Oh man, we've *got* to start going to these things."

"I have that top!" Alexis gestured at the screen with the remote.

"There's R.T.," Lauryn said.

My mom sat up straighter. "Which one?"

"There, in the black and red." Alexis backed up the video so we could all see R.T. sitting on his bike with his arms folded, scowling.

"He doesn't look like he had much fun," my mom said.

Lauryn took the remote from Alexis and shut it off. "Josie smoked his score by thirty-two points."

"For that fence move? Man, some judge liked you," Z-Dog said.

Lightning flashed outside in the distance, then a boom sounded.

Lauryn stood up. "We need to get going."

As people filed up the stairs I hung back to help my mom toss plates and cups into a trash bag.

"Josie? You still down there?" I recognized Sandra's voice and I went to the bottom of the stairs.

"Yeah?" I closed the trash bag and ran up.

"I need to meet with you while you're back," she told me. "Call me tomorrow so we can set it up, okay?"

"No problem." I hoped it didn't have more to do with promoting the pastel bike. Maybe I could claim that UnnUsual was making me paint it black so I could have a normal-looking bike again.

I went outside to say goodbye to people as they left. Miguel stood next to me and we both watched as fat drops of rain pelted down an early warning of the downfall that was sure to follow.

"You don't seem as happy anymore. What's up?" he asked.

"The comment about being lucky that a judge scored me high is bugging me."

"Do you care what Z-Dog or whoever thinks? You shouldn't get so hung up on winning and losing anyway. Do your thing."

"What exactly is my thing?"

Another blast of lightning appeared, followed by heavier rain and a thunder crack.

"The instinct that told you to go for the fence post."

Miguel promised we'd get together to get caught up and then ran to his car.

I went inside and stood next to my mom at the sliding glass doors in the back of the kitchen.

"Thanks for the party, Mom. It was a nice surprise."

"It was my pleasure, honey. We're proud of you."

A flash of lightning cracked down with only a few seconds delay before the thunder boomed.

My mom leaned closer to the glass. "It's getting close."

"Do you think you'll be able to go to my next event?" I asked.

"When is it?"

"In two weeks, on the weekend of the sixteenth. It's closer, near Milwaukee. You'd see me ride with UnnUsual." That event was going to be even bigger than the Outrageous Jam. They'd see up close what a big deal it was.

"Two weekends from now won't work. We're taking Troy to Michigan for summer training camp. Maybe the next one."

Even with the party, the Josie banner, and all the fuss, nothing had changed. Whatever Troy did was always more important, more worthwhile, a bigger deal. If I could be fit in around his schedule that was fine, but I still didn't come first.

The Ultimate would be different. It was huge, and since it was in Chicago, my parents would definitely go. Then they'd see.

A loud rumble started low behind the trees.

"Sounds like a big one," my mom said, looking over.

We waited, but didn't see anything.

"Guess it was a dud," I said. "All that noise for nothing."

Miguel went with me to Spoked Wednesday morning. I told him I planned on telling Sandra I had to paint over my bike. "It should be okay if I offer to put a big Spoked sticker on it, right? I can tell her it got scraped up at the Outrageous Jam." It was sort of true. My bike was a little scraped up.

"Do what you have to do and deal with the fallout later. It's usually easier to ask for forgiveness than to beg for permission."

"How much custom-paint business can Leo possibly think he'll bring in because of me?"

Miguel shrugged as he pushed the door to the store open.

A huge poster of me dominated the front display. I was on my Josie bike with the front wheel up on the fence post, and the caption read *Ask for your Spoked custom-painted bike like*

the one Josie Peters rode to win the On Site event at the
Outrageous BMX Jam.

I stood staring at it. "Oh my God."

"Did they blow that up from a cell-phone photo?" Miguel
leaned in to look closer. "It's all grainy."

"If you can make a better one, we'll gladly take it." Sandra
walked out and said hello to us. "Josie, you may be the solution
to my problem."

She led us into the back storage area which was bursting
with bikes and equipment.

I found a space to sit on an unpacked box and Miguel
climbed up to sit on a stepladder. "What's happening in here?
There's enough for two stores."

Sandra took a deep breath and closed her eyes for a few
seconds before answering, "There's a store across town that
would be perfect as a second Spoked location. We had all the
plans and paperwork ready to go." She exhaled slowly and
continued, "Leo was almost on board but now he has cold
feet."

I wasn't sure why she was telling me, but I was curious to
know more. "Why?"

"When he was at the peak of his career a lot of people took
advantage of him, so now he's so careful about not doing that
to anyone else, he's almost too hesitant. He does well because
people trust him. He's good at matching the bike to the person
and only selling them what they need."

I still didn't see what this had to do with me. "How do I fit
into all this?"

"Your proposal for the girls' beginner BMX bike clinic
could be exactly what we need to show him how expanding
our reach fits in to his overall vision of getting more people on
bikes. He can't fit more in here, he needs more space."

Miguel kicked the tower of boxes next to him. "That's for
sure."

Sandra turned to me. "We'll figure out all the details and I'll show him it won't cost him anything up front. I need to make sure we get a good turnout. That's where you come in."

"Me? How?" I hadn't given the girls' clinic much thought, but I still liked the idea.

"What I need from you is a kick-ass promo video of you and your friends riding. If you can put something together, we could use it."

"Then you need me," Miguel said. "I'm Josie's official kick-ass video guy."

We agreed on a weekend for the clinic that fell between the Explosion and Ultimate competitions and Miguel promised to get the video as soon as possible.

I sent a quick text to Lauryn and Alexis telling them the clinic was on.

Miguel and I took off for Lakewood Park. He was definitely rusty, but got a few good runs in before the skateboarders took over.

Before getting in the car, he reached his arms behind his back and held a long stretch. "That felt amazing. It's been too long since I've been on a bike. It's good to be back in it."

"You're back in it?"

"I'm probably going to Explosion and Ultimate with you."

"Seriously!"

"Not to ride. To film."

We settled into a table at our favorite pizza place, and I got him to tell me what was going on.

"I explained to the professor that I want to film BMX riders, and I showed your wipeout video. He was all over it. He told me to go where the action is. He's letting me do my final project as low residency—meaning I can film Explosion and Ultimate here and send it in for grading."

"So you'll be around for the girls' clinic? I have no idea what I'm doing with that. You just saw the whole planning session."

"Sometimes acting like you know what you're doing is close enough to knowing what you're doing to get things done."

"If you say so."

"Plus, you'll have a kick-ass promo video."

"Yeah. Is that done yet?"

Miguel kicked me under the table. "I'm on it, but there's one piece of bad news."

"What?"

"I don't think you can paint over your bike. It's becoming your trademark."

I grabbed the last slice of pizza as punishment for that comment. "So with this whole film thing working out, is that what you're doing next year? Film school?"

"I'm keeping things loose. It's a good way to live, like how Lauryn is going to take a year off and ride and go wherever BMX takes her."

"Who told you that?" Lauryn had told me she was going to Illinois State in the fall. I was sure of it. Alexis and I had even made plans about driving down to Normal to visit on weekends.

"She did. We went out the other night."

"You and Lauryn?"

I wasn't sure why I didn't see it before. They were a perfect match.

"Yeah. We were talking at your barbecue and I wanted to see more of her so I asked her out."

"So? How'd it go?"

He smiled and shrugged and looked at the floor. *He liked her!*

Maybe Lauryn was on to something. If you don't chase around after the flashy guys, someone great like Miguel will come along. But why was she lying to him about not going to school next year?

The road trip had given me a taste of freedom and it made being at home feel incredibly stifling. I couldn't wait until we left again, and in the meantime I was taking advantage of every opportunity to get out of the house, even if it meant driving an hour and fifteen minutes to meet Alexis Friday night at some small live-music place in the middle of nowhere to hear a band play because she had a crush on the lead singer.

I paid the cover charge and found Alexis at a table with Lauryn. "This better not suck." I sat down on a wobbly stool. "What kind of a name is 'Pain Compass,' anyway?"

We didn't have much time to talk before Pain Compass started playing. Their first song was about how girls kept trying to kill the lead singer.

He was cute, and I could see why Alexis had a crush on him, but his lyrics didn't make it sound like he was too eager to have a new girlfriend.

When they stopped for a break after their first set, Alexis went to the stage to talk to the lead singer anyway.

I started to ask Lauryn about Miguel when a girl I recognized from the Outrageous Jam came up and gave Lauryn a huge hug. "Guess what? We found a place! It's perfect."

"Uhh." Lauryn hesitated before introducing me to Krista. She downed the rest of her soda in three enormous gulps and then handed me the empty cup.

"Want to go get me another of these, please?" she asked.

I said sure and turned away, but I took my time leaving so I could hear what Krista said next.

"You're going to love it," she said. "It's got six bedrooms and the rent is super cheap. We can move in on August first. It's in Lowland, which is just outside Chicago."

"Chicago?" I turned back to face them.

"Yes," she answered, giving me a weird look.

Lauryn wouldn't look at me. I didn't want to ask in front of her friend, but how was she going to move to the city in August if she was going to college downstate this fall?

A waitress came by for our drink order so I stayed with Lauryn and her future roommate.

She kept talking about what they'd do and from what I pieced together, I understood that a group of girls who ride BMX were living together in a big house, working minimum-wage jobs to pay rent and finance trips to big events overseas. All they needed was a job that included health insurance and maybe some free food. The priority was on having training time and being able to take off to competitions.

"Give me your first and last month's rent plus security deposit as soon as you can so I can hold your space." She told Lauryn she couldn't wait for her to move in and then said she had to go but they'd talk later.

"Where's that waitress with our drinks?" Lauryn asked. "I'll go see if she forgot."

"Wait!" I said. "You're moving to Chicago in August?"

"Yes." She didn't look me in the eye when she answered, and I knew she didn't want to answer questions, but I wanted to know what she was up to.

"But you're going to Illinois State this fall."

"As far as my parents know, yes."

The waitress arrived with our drinks and Lauryn took longer than necessary to dig up exact change plus a tip.

When we were alone again, I asked, "You're going to let your parents think you're going to college when you're actually living outside the city?"

She finally looked me in the eye before answering. "Lying is going to be easier than arguing."

"Are you kidding me? You'll never pull it off. Won't they drive you to school?"

"I don't have those kinds of parents."

"Won't they want to see some grades at the end of the semester?"

"I'll tell them fake grades. They won't demand to see the actual paper. I've thought this through. My dad travels all the time and my mom works all the time. They'll have no idea. I'll send email and keep my cell, and maybe some fake pictures from someone else's dorm room."

"You seriously think you can pull this off?"

"I barely see them. They won't know. They want to believe I'm in college so I'll play along with the fantasy."

The thought of living outside the city while telling my parents I was going to college downstate was so unreal to me I didn't know what else to say to her. It wasn't at all something I would have expected from Lauryn. Alexis, yes, but Lauryn?

An uncomfortable silence built up between us until she broke it by saying, "I don't disagree that college is a good idea; it's the timing. College will be there a year from now. The opportunity to ride BMX is here now. It isn't something you can always do. I need to keep training and use the contacts I have now. I want to try it for a year and see how it goes. I also have no clue what I'd want to study. Maybe getting out and seeing more of the world will help me decide. Some people take a year off and travel. This is no different."

The band started to trickle back onstage and pick up their instruments.

"Did you tell your parents that?"

"No. To them it's high school, then college. If you have the grades and the money there's no reason not to follow the path, but no one can give me a good reason why delaying a year is bad other than 'you might never go.' What if in that year I realize college isn't for me? Won't I save myself from wasting a lot of time and money? I think the whole 'you've *got* to go to college' thing is crap. It's not for everyone."

Alexis handed the lead singer a scrap of paper that he pocketed before hopping up onstage.

"I guess, but if they're willing to pay for it now..." I sort of agreed with what she said in theory, but I wasn't sure it was a good idea.

"It's my life. I'm eighteen, so technically I can do what I want," she said. "Asking for forgiveness is easier than begging for permission."

"Did Miguel tell you that?" My glass slid out of my hand a little, so I set it down.

She ducked her head and didn't look at me. "He's a great guy."

The lighting was dim, but I was sure I saw a hint of a blush on her cheeks and a little smile.

So it was mutual. Lauryn and Miguel made a great couple, but this was potentially worse than Gianna and Bruce. If Lauryn and Miguel started spending all their free time together, I'd never see either of them.

Alexis ran back gushing about how the lead singer had begged for her number.

Lauryn still had a little smile on her face.

Pain Compass started their set with a song called "Back Off, Groupie Girl." I glanced at Alexis, but she was tapping her foot, moving to the beat, oblivious that it might be directed at her.

Chapter 19

In the three weeks I'd been home I'd received one message from Coach Robbins reminding me of the mandatory practice session a day before the Explosion competition started. I heard nothing from R.T. Not that I expected him to send anything. I wanted the satisfaction of not responding when I saw his name on my phone. And not that I'd been thinking about him that much. I checked a couple of videos of his, but I kept busy training with Miguel and Lauryn. We worked on my tailwhips, and I almost had it, but my timing was still off. I was looking forward to getting some professional input from the UnnUsual guys and adding it to my list of solid tricks.

Miguel finished the promo video of us for the girls' clinic the day before we left for Explosion. He put it online and we all sent messages to everyone we could think of to let them know about it. I even sent a link of the video to Connor, and he gave it a thumbs-up.

Alexis and Lauryn said they had no problem leaving a day early for Milwaukee, but they showed up at my house an hour late.

As soon as I got in the SUV, I could tell they'd been arguing.

Alexis looked at me in the rearview mirror. "Do you know about this crazy plan of hers to pretend to go to college?"

"Yeah." I clicked my seat belt and settled into the backseat.

"Don't you think she should tell her parents?" Alexis sped up as she maneuvered onto the interstate. "It's going to be impossible for me to keep it from Jasmine. She knows when I'm not telling her something."

Lauryn watched the side mirror as Alexis changed lanes. "You better find a way to make it possible. Or I have a whole lot of stuff I'm sure she'd be very interested in hearing."

"Josie, tell her!" Alexis weaved into an open space behind a sports car and settled in to cruising speed.

I'd never met Lauryn's parents. "I can't say." I sort of agreed with Alexis, but I wanted to be on Lauryn's side. "What about the money? Won't they be paying tuition bills?"

"They'll give me a set amount for each semester. I'll put it in the bank." Lauryn answered as if she'd had this conversation a million times.

"You won't touch it?" I asked.

"No. I'll save it in case they do cut me off when they find out. I'll use it to pay for a year of college if that's what I decide to do, and either get back on their good side or come up with the rest of the money myself."

Alexis glanced at her. "Are you sure you can't tell them?"

"If I qualify for the Ultimate, and if I do well, then I'll consider telling them, okay? Please drop it."

Alexis didn't bring up Lauryn's plans again, but they kept sniping at each other. The air-conditioning was too high, the music was too country, the windows hadn't been washed properly at the last gas stop. I finally gave up and listened to music to drown them out. I hadn't slept well the night before and was not in the mood to referee.

I managed to fall asleep and wasn't sure how long I'd been out when my headphones popped out of my ears as my body slammed forward against the seat-belt harness.

"What the?" I pushed against the back of Alexis's seat.

"You're making me nervous." Alexis shrieked.

Lauryn looked at me over her shoulder. "Sorry to wake you."

"What happened?" I sat up straight and looked out the window. We were parked in front of Jimmy's Bait 'N More, a ramshackle white clapboard building. The sun was already going down. How late was it?

"We're lost," Lauryn said.

Alexis turned off the engine and checked her hair in the mirror behind the visor. "We're not lost. We're a little off track."

"How can we be lost? It's a straight shot up I-94 from Chicago to Milwaukee." I remembered seeing the wooden "Wisconsin Welcomes You" sign in the shape of Wisconsin when we crossed the state line. I checked the time. Ten o'clock. We should have been there already.

Alexis flipped the sun visor back up. "There was construction and the GPS kept saying 'turn around now, turn around now,' so I shut it off, but I'm not sure what happened because there aren't any more detour signs."

"I told you what happened," Lauryn said as she unbuckled her seatbelt. "I told you exactly where you went the wrong way and ignored the detour sign. Now we've got interference from something and the GPS won't work."

"You did not. You've been bitchy this whole trip. Go buy some PMS meds while I ask for directions."

I unbuckled my seat belt and opened the door as Lauryn jumped out and slammed her door.

Alexis stepped down and beeped the locks. "What is your problem?"

"You. What if we had to be there on time and you screwed it up? Josie has a real chance to be on a team. If we act like a bunch of brainless fan-girls who can't even drive in a straight line, no one is going to take us seriously."

Whoa. Where was all this coming from, and why was I in the middle of it? I sort of agreed with Lauryn's points, but I wasn't ready to get in a huge fight over it.

Alexis stuffed her keys in her purse. "This trip is supposed to be fun. Why are you so uptight?"

Lauryn threw her hands in the air. "It was never fun to wait around for you. Just because you don't care about getting sponsored, don't sabotage it for us."

I left them in their face-off. "I'll go in and ask for directions, okay?"

Apart from two pickup trucks with beat-up Wisconsin plates, the parking area was empty. I wasn't looking forward to going into Jimmy's bait shop and telling them we couldn't find Milwaukee. Pulling in to a small town in Wisconsin in a vehicle with Illinois license plates was likely to get us directions back to Illinois.

"I'm bringing in my laptop," Alexis said, unlocking the SUV and pulling her pink bag out of the trunk.

Lauryn rolled her eyes. "Oh, yeah. I'm sure Jimmy's is all set up for wifi."

The guy behind the counter had every inch of skin covered in tattoos of reptiles ready to attack, their bodies snaking up his arms to wide-open jaws with flickering tongues inked onto his neck.

"Three pretty ladies. Look at that!" He and his friend both laughed, and his friend made a low growling noise.

This was not the kind of place to ask about wifi or directions or to engage in eye contact. We clustered together and each grabbed factory-sealed snacks before easing our way to the map rack.

"You pretty ladies lost?"

"Nope. Just replacing one we lost." I grabbed a detailed road map of Elk County and we went to the counter.

"Where y'all headed to?"

"Mi—" Alexis started to answer but Lauryn talked over her. "Friend's place." Her tone didn't invite a conversation.

We paid and piled back in the SUV as fast as we could.

"Ohmigod. Ohmigod. Ohmigod. Did you see that guy's tattoos?" Alexis asked.

Lauryn clicked the door lock. "Let's get out of here before we get thrown in a dungeon."

"Drive," I said. "Head east. Try the GPS again. We'll either hit the highway or Lake Michigan."

Once I took over navigation we managed to get back on the interstate and settled in to our motel by midnight. When I called my mom to check in, I explained our lateness as "we hit a little construction." No need to worry her.

Thursday morning, Lauryn was still pissed that we got in too late to check out the Explosion competition area the night before and she was losing patience waiting for Alexis.

"I want to see your tailwhip by the end of the day," she told me as we stood by the door, ready to go.

"Yeah, me too."

Alexis called from the bathroom that she was ready.

"Finally." Lauryn grabbed the door handle.

"Wait." Alexis grabbed my arm and pulled me to turn and face her. "What are you wearing?"

"What?" I looked down at my cargo shorts and tank top. "It's supposed to be over a hundred today. It's too hot for jeans."

"No, no, no." She rifled through her luggage and pulled out a pair of shorts and a camisole. "Here."

I took them from her and held them up. The shorts were barely bigger than my underwear, and the camisole was cropped to hit several inches above the waist. "What is this?"

"For your audition with UnnUsual."

"It's a practice, and I'll be riding, not swimming."

"They don't care how you ride. Your job is to be eye candy."

She had to be wrong. There were other girls, like Alexis, who would have been much better choices if what they wanted was eye candy.

"I'm not walking next to you if you wear that," Lauryn said.

Alexis stood with her hands on her hips. "Guys are visual. Trust me on this."

If my strategy was to distract them so they couldn't ride straight, her logic might work, but wearing shorty shorts and a mini top would make me feel ridiculous, plus I didn't exactly have the triple-D chest it would take to be a real distraction. I threw the outfit back in her suitcase. "Not happening."

"Do you want to be on the team or not?"

"She'll get on the team, but we need to *go*. I've only been waiting to see the Mezzo Mondo ramp all summer." Lauryn opened the door to go outside and a blast of heat hit us.

"Is it a hundred already?" I asked.

"Feels like it." Lauryn put her sunglasses on and walked toward the SUV.

Alexis held the door open an inch. "Last chance for the outfit guaranteed to make the cut."

I leaned past her and pulled the door shut.

Before we even got to the gate for the Explosion parking area, the Mezzo Mondo ramp came into view, looming over everything else in the competition area.

I leaned forward between Lauryn and Alexis's seats so I could see better. "How high is that?"

"Forty feet." Lauryn unbuckled her seatbelt and had her door open before Alexis turned the SUV engine off.

"Hold on." Alexis grabbed Lauryn's elbow and steered her toward the registration table. "We need to get signed in."

As soon as we had our wristbands, Lauryn took off for the ramp. Even from the registration table I could see the entire thing. From the side it looked like a lopsided "W" with the four-story-high roll-in ramp on the left, then a second ramp leading to a thirty-foot gap, then a half-pipe with a landing deck at the top.

I knew Lauryn wanted to keep examining the Mezzo Mondo, but I needed to get to the UnnUsual practice so I told her and Alexis I'd meet them later for lunch.

"No, we'll come walk you over there," Lauryn said. "I need to get something to drink. I'm dying."

In the practice park, the UnnUsual guys were already riding, and the other girl was there in an outfit even worse than the one Alexis had suggested.

"See!" Alexis elbowed me. "I told you."

"Is that a tube top?" Lauryn said, shielding her eyes to look.

"There's no way that's going to stay up," I said. Strapless tops barely stayed up if you stood perfectly still. It was going to drop the second she started riding.

"There's adhesive you can use so it stays put," Alexis told us.

"Glue the top to your chest?" I looked at Alexis, then back at the girl. She still wasn't riding. "Are you insane?"

"She's moving," Lauryn said as the girl finally went to the top of the ramp. A guy in a black helmet with a big T logo and an all-black bike with red rims cut her off and dropped in before she had a chance.

"That was R.T.," I said. What was going on? Were they looking for eye candy or someone who could ride?

"He doesn't seem distracted. Get over there and work on your tailwhip. Don't let anyone cut you off." Lauryn handed me my helmet and I got on my bike.

"I'll message you where to meet us later," Alexis said.

I rode around the park to get warmed up and then watched the action on the quarter-pipe ramp and tabletop setup. R.T. dropped down the ramp, rode up to the tabletop and did a double-back. Turner cut in right after and did a double, then Oliver and Flynn both went, doing perfect double back flips. Okaaay. So these guys were more than pretty good, they were really good. I could learn a lot riding with them.

I rode to the quarter-pipe and as I got on deck I caught a glimpse of black dreadlocks sticking out of a red helmet. Turner was trying to get in position. I might not be able to do a double back flip, but I did know how to make sure no one cut me off. Adrenaline poured into my bloodstream, fueling my competitive side. I blocked him from getting in front and dropped first. Pedaling fast, I picked up enough speed to hit the ramp hard and launch my back flip. My rotation was tight. I nailed the landing and felt a huge wave of relief as I rode away. I did it!

The guy with the ear gauges, Flynn, came up to me. "Nice back flip. Have you tried doubles?"

"Not yet. I'm working on tailwhips. I'm close, but not consistent."

"O! Do a tailwhip!"

Oliver, the one with the blond curls, nodded and took off. When he got to the top of the tabletop ramp, he kicked his bike with his back foot so it spun around behind him, then caught it with his front foot while putting his other foot over the frame and on the pedal. He was back on his bike in no time, making it look way easier than it was. His position was perfect. That's what I needed to get down. If I could get that nailed in this session I'd be happy.

Robbins called us over so we took off our helmets and left the bikes on the ground. He explained how the relay worked, reading from a clipboard in a monotone. "For the MixUp competition, each team of four has eight minutes on the park, with one person riding at a time for a minimum of thirty seconds and maximum of three minutes." He paused and took an extra-long breath before continuing, as if the instructions were so cumbersome he barely had enough air to read them all. "If a rider is early, the next person has to wait. If a rider is late, the next rider's clock starts running."

"You two, up front." Robbins put me and the other girl at the front of the line. "Everyone is going to do a boxtop spinner."

A what? We didn't always call the tricks by the official name, but I usually knew what announcers at events were talking about. I'd never heard of a boxtop spinner.

I watched as the other girl went first, figuring I'd do whatever she did. She went up the ramp and then wiped out, but her top stayed on. She must have glued it. Coach Robbins shook his head.

That was definitely not what I wanted to do. Think! I put my foot down on the pedal and then pulled to the side and crouched down as if something were wrong with my bike.

R.T. came over.

"Something wrong?" he asked, leaning in to look at the cranks.

"What is a boxtop spinner?" I whispered.

He shifted back on his heels and shook his head. "Robbins can never remember the names for anything so he makes shit up. He means a 180 g-turn. See, Turner's doing it."

Turner went up the ramp, did a nose wheelie on the flat tabletop, spun his bike around and rode back down. It was a pretty basic trick for these guys. Even I could do a 180 g-turn.

I rode at medium speed and leveled out my feet when I got on top of the ramp. I pictured the move as I leaned toward my handlebars and shifted my weight forward, then turned my head and lifted the back wheel up so I could whip it around in the 180. When the back wheel came down, I rolled down the ramp backward in a fakie. No problem.

We stayed in that lineup, and even when I didn't know the names I could see what we were supposed to do. The other girl didn't wipe out again, and was able to get some pretty impressive air. She was a decent rider.

After a couple of rotations, Robbins sent R.T. and Flynn to the quarter-pipe and tabletop setup for drills and sent Oliver, Turner and the tube-top girl to the rails.

When he got to me, he told me to do a barhop, a feeble grind, and a manual to the bottom of the ramp "And get back as fast as you can." I did as he asked and then tried my tailwhip at the end. I almost had it, but under-rotated a little.

I looked to see Robbins's reaction to my almost-tailwhip, but he was making notes.

I rode over and stopped next to him. "Want me to do it again?"

"No. That's fine," he said without looking up.

It was now or never. I took a deep breath. "I've been working on my tailwhip and I've almost got it. Maybe I could work with one of the guys and figure out what I'm doing wrong?"

"No, that's fine," he said again, and I realized he was talking on his hands-free phone. How could he coach if he was on the phone? We only had the practice area for an hour.

I stayed in front of him so he'd have to see me eventually.

Finally he looked at me and covered the phone microphone with his hand. "You're done. You can go."

I flinched as if he'd pushed me backward. Go? That was it? I was off the team already?

He'd only asked me to do a couple of lame tricks, and he'd hardly watched. The other girl was still at the rails with Oliver and Turner. They weren't even riding. So I guess I failed the eye-candy test.

My tailwhip would have improved if I'd stayed with Lauryn all morning and worked on it instead of wasting my time here in this fake tryout. Whatever. I took off my helmet and left it dangling on my handlebars as I rode away.

After getting a drink I checked my phone and saw a message from Sandra telling me she already had ten girls signed up for the clinic. I sent a quick answer, not mentioning that I was off the UnnUsual team. A message from Lauryn appeared, telling me where to find her. I followed the directions and left the Explosion event area. Ten blocks and two turns later I found Lauryn with Krista and four of the other girls in an underpass with lots of smooth concrete.

I rode down next to Lauryn. "It's ten degrees cooler under here. How'd you find this place?"

"Krista." She tilted her head in the direction of her secret soon-to-be roommate.

Krista pulled out her mouth guard. "Usually it's half full of highway runoff water here, but with the drought this summer it's been the perfect place to ride."

I said hi to Charlotte and Paige. Krista introduced me to Geo, short for Georgiana from the MadKapp team and explained what they were doing. "It's a follow the leader thing. One person does a trick, then the next person has to do the same thing, and if she pulls it off she can add something."

Nothing had a name. A lot of it was invented on the spot and was unique to the configuration of the space. I loved this kind of riding. Getting to ride in different spots made road-tripping fun.

Lauryn nudged my foot with her toe. "How'd it go? Got that tailwhip down?"

"Didn't even touch it. I did a couple lame tricks and he told me to go. It kind of sucked, but whatever. I'll do the On Site and qualify for Ultimate myself like I planned all along. It doesn't matter."

"Maybe it's them," Krista said. "They are UnnUsual."

"Maybe you need to join team 'don't have my head up my arse,'" Geo said.

"Yeah, maybe," I said, laughing.

Paige pointed down the street. "Speaking of head up their arse."

Three of the UnnUsual guys headed toward us with R.T. leading the way, followed by Flynn and a shirtless Oliver.

Why did they have to follow me? It was bad enough I didn't make their team, now I'd exposed Krista's secret riding spot.

When they got close, Krista asked, "How'd you find us?"

"We asked people if they saw where the chick on the Easter-egg bike went." Oliver wiped his forehead with his T-shirt and then chucked it on a pile of water bottles, phones, and backpacks. "It's pretty noticeable."

I took my turn after Geo, adding a fakie rollback to the three tricks already in the rotation. When I rode over to where everyone else was, R.T. asked, "Why'd you take off so fast from practice?"

"I wasn't going to hang around like some groupie. I wanted to ride."

"Want in?" Evie asked the guys. She pointed at Lauryn, who was starting her ride. "Do whatever she does and then add to it."

"Go ahead, Flynn." Oliver said.

Lauryn did a McCircle, picking up good rolling speed so she could get her feet on the pegs on the left side of her bike, then moving to straddle the front wheel, facing backward with her feet on the front wheel pegs. She used her right foot to scuff the front wheel and keep the bike moving, then swung herself back around and got back on the bike.

Flynn went next, but he didn't get his leg over the bar for the last part of the trick and wiped.

R.T. and Oliver practically fell over laughing. "What's up with that?" Oliver choked out between snorts.

"I don't see you over here." Flynn picked his bike up and wheeled it over. "These chicks are triple-jointed."

Oliver rode over to take a turn.

R.T. nudged my elbow. "Seriously, why'd you take off?"

We both watched as Oliver did the trick Flynn missed.

"He sent me away and kept the tube-top girl. I'm out. Why would I stay around?"

Oliver did the McCircle and added a nice flatland cherry picker, putting one foot on his back tire and the other under the seat so he could repeatedly hop the whole bike on the back wheel.

"That means he doesn't think you need more training. You *want* to be sent away. The people he thinks suck get stuck there drilling endlessly."

He didn't mention the other girl. "Really?" I looked for Lauryn and saw her helping Geo replicate Oliver's trick.

"You're up." Krista nodded to R.T.

He did the entire trick sequence, then rode down about twenty feet away and hopped his front wheel up on a rock and held it, then rode back. "Modified Josie Jump."

"Nice," I said.

Oliver and Flynn ran over, pushing each other to be in front. "T—who reeks worse, me or Flynn?"

"You guys both reek. How about putting your shirt back on, Oliver?"

He picked up the shirt he had chucked earlier. "Why do I have two? Oh yeah, one of these is yours, Oz."

I caught the shirt he threw at me. "Oz?"

"When Robbins couldn't remember your name he called you Oz," R.T. explained. "Over the rainbow? Your bike? It took us a while to figure out what he meant."

I held up the 2XL dust-covered black shirt with a red UnnUsual logo. "Why would this enormous T-shirt be mine?"

"Oliver hogs all the smalls," Flynn said. "He thinks it shows off his muscles."

"Shut up, Scarecrow."

"Make me, Tin Man."

"What's this for?" I asked R.T.

"You need to wear it tomorrow," R.T. said. You're in the lineup."

"No, I'm not."

"Check your text messages. Robbins made me track you down to make sure you got it."

I checked my phone and saw the message. Turner was first, Flynn was second, I was third, and R.T. was last.

I was officially UnnUsual.

Chapter 20

All night I had weird dreams about competing in odd outfits, including a fringed dress that got all tangled up in my bike chain. I woke up early covered in sweat, so I took a cool shower to try to clear my head, but it didn't work. I desperately wanted to talk to Miguel. He was supposed to meet us later that night, but I wanted to talk to him right away. I'd texted him yesterday about making the UnnUsual team plus all the wardrobe and lack of riding angst.

I wrapped myself in a towel, crept next to the beds to grab my phone, then went back to the bathroom and sat on the edge of the bathtub while I sent Miguel a message telling him I wished he was there.

He wrote back right away. "*You know what I'd say. You can do it. I'll be there soon. Hang in there.*"

"*Any idea when you'll be in tonight?*"

He took a minute to answer back. *Around ten thirty, then I'm going to hang out with Lauryn. She said you'll probably go out with Alexis so I'll see you when you get in. Midnight? Not too late— you're competing tomorrow <grin>.*

Right. Him and Lauryn. I was happy in theory. I'd be happier if somehow there could be two Miguels.

Even though I was officially UnnUsual, I didn't feel like I could call any of those guys to talk.

I could try Connor, but he was probably busy, and I didn't want to bug him. I sat holding the phone in my hands until light knocking sounded on the bathroom door.

I opened it a few inches.

"Can I come in?" Lauryn whispered.

I opened the door more and she sat down on the toilet lid. "Are you as freaked out as I am?"

"Yeah, a little." I tightened my towel so it wouldn't fall off.

"We should head over early. I can't deal with Alexis's drama this morning. Let's let her sleep in and catch up with us later. I'll write her a note."

I agreed and quietly got my stuff together. I felt a little bad about sneaking out, but it was a relief to not listen to Alexis's nonstop chatter and be harassing her to hurry up. I needed to get out of that room and get some air.

Lauryn and I rode over to the competition area. We'd been warned about parking. About two blocks away we saw why. Cars were already jammed along both the sides of the road. There were only a few big ramps set up each year, so the Mezzo Mondo attracted a lot of competitors and spectators.

Before we even crossed the boundary of the Explosion event grounds, the Mezzo Mondo Ramp loomed over us, dwarfing everything around it. Even though we'd seen the ramp yesterday, today it looked bigger, more dominating, living up to its reputation.

Only four girls were signed up to ride it. Much as I believed girls were capable of anything guys could do, the Mezzo Mondo Ramp scared the crap out of me. I wasn't sure there was enough training or practice in the world to make me drop in from fifty feet.

Lauryn looked up, and there was no mistaking the panic taking over her usually controlled expression. She looked ready to back out. I had to say something. The right thing. I couldn't lie and say it was no different than the ramps she was used to. We both knew it wasn't true. A fall on this ramp would result in a serious, possibly permanent injury. Why had I agreed to ditch Alexis? She was the one who always knew what to say to Lauryn. If someone didn't say the right thing, right then, Lauryn was likely to back out and not even try, and I knew she'd hate herself and regret it forever.

I gave her a squeeze on the arm. "You can do this."

She nodded, still not talking, but at least she didn't look as panicky as before.

Since the ramp was so high, the competitors had to push their bikes up switchbacks to reach the level of the starting deck. Even though there was still a half hour before the start, the organizers wanted all the competitors to be at the switchbacks, ready to go. I helped Lauryn go through the checklist of gear: body pads, full cage helmet, and mouth guard. "You've got it all. You belong up there."

After making sure Lauryn and her gear got in place, I locked my bike in the waiting area and then scanned the stands looking for a spot to sit.

"Josie!" I turned toward the sound of my name and saw Alexis standing next to the VaporTrail guy who was wearing an S-Force shirt.

She ran to me and shoved her phone in my hands. "Take a picture of me and Zach." She turned away and flounced over to his side.

I took the picture and handed her back her phone. "There. Now can we try to get some sort of seats so we can watch? I want to be able to see."

"You can sit with us," Zach said. "We saved good seats near the top. Here, I'll boost you. It's easier to climb up the back."

For the first few feet it didn't seem too bad to scale the stands, but the higher we climbed the wobblier it felt. By the time I realized what I was doing was really stupid and probably more dangerous than riding, I was closer to the top than the bottom, so I pushed until I got where Zach and Alexis were and popped up next to a group of S-Force guys.

A couple of them scooted over, making a space for us. I quickly realized why they were so eager to put us between them and the next guy. He smelled as if he'd been sleeping, riding, and partying in the same shirt for a week. Great. I tried to breathe through my mouth and ignore the eye-watering stench.

At the top of stands, we had a good view of the whole ramp. It looked like a lopsided W with a gap in the middle. Competitors dropped in the super-steep side from forty feet up, rode down the ramp, shot up a shorter middle ramp in front of the gap, went airborne over the gap, and then landed with more than enough momentum to go up the last quarter-pipe and do a final air trick.

Twenty guys were signed up, but with so few girls attempting the Mezzo Mondo, if Lauryn managed to not wipe out, she was practically guaranteed a spot in the Ultimate.

The first guy was from S-Force. He dropped down and did a nice x-up over the gap, turning his handlebars so that his arms crossed in front of him before straightening out to pull off a huge tailwhip on the quarter-pipe, kicking the bike out in a circle as he held on to the handlebars, getting his feet back into position on the pedals in time to ride back down the ramp. Nice. I burned the image of that tailwhip in my head. If he could do it on Mezzo Mondo, I could do it on a little tabletop ramp.

Stomping, cheering, and screaming erupted in the stands, with all the S-Force guys going ballistic.

The smelly guy shook his head. "His quarter-pipe is solid, but he's going to need more on the gap if he wants to place in the Ultimate."

Alexis elbowed me from the other side. "Isn't Zach cute?" she whispered.

I nodded even though my patience for her talking about how she and other people looked was starting to run out. This was one place where what you did mattered way more than how you looked.

Next up was Oliver from UnnUsual. He hammered down the drop ramp and launched into an amazing 360 turndown over the gap, leaning way over the bike as he completely cranked the wheel and got it back into position before hitting the final quarter-pipe.

"Yes!" I jumped up and yelled for him even though he hadn't been particularly nice to me yesterday. I had to give him credit for being an incredible vert rider.

A guy in a VaporTrail shirt took the next turn. He had a good drop and went airborne over the gap, pulled his bike in for a tuck no-hander, but he didn't level out fast enough and landed on his tailbone on the other side of the ramp.

The guy next to me groaned. "That's going to leave a mark."

The VaporTrail guy stayed down as the medical team rushed over to carry him out on a stretcher. Several video guys moved closer.

"Is he really hurt?" Alexis asked.

"He's conscious," Zach said. "They won't let you stand up until they check you out."

After the medical team left, the rest of the guys took their turns, but no one outdid Oliver. Then it was the girls' turn.

The announcer called out the name of the first girl in the Mezzo Mondo event. "Shae McMasters." I'd seen videos of her riding in Europe. She had some amazing ramp moves.

I scooted forward to see her better, but instead of getting into position, she pulled off her helmet and moved her bike away from the edge.

"We have a scratch for Shae McMasters," the announcer said. "Up next is Lauryn Jax."

"Chickened out." Smelly guy shook his head. "It happens."

I kept my attention focused on Lauryn, sending positive vibes her way. *Come on, come on. Don't back out.* All she had to do was take the first drop. As one of only three girls left she'd place just by trying.

She moved her bike into position, pushed off and went for it.

I kept perfectly still, not even breathing as I watched, willing her to stay up, stay balanced.

"Come on, Lauryn!" Alexis screamed.

The metal corner of the bench dug into my hands as I held on for her landing. Lauryn was perfectly centered but wobbled a little as she hit the bottom of the drop ramp.

"She's got it. She's got it. Come on!" I sent more positive vibes her way as she shot up the middle ramp, launched into the air, and flung one leg out for a no-footer.

At the speed she was going all it would take was a little bobble and an overcorrection or an off-center landing and she'd go down.

I held my breath as she pulled her foot back into position, leveled her bike out and nailed the landing, leading her into the approach for the final quarter-pipe.

I'd seen her do a lot of air tricks on smaller ramp setups, but this time she played it safe, flying up for a few feet of air before coming down and letting her momentum run out.

"Yesss! She did it!" I jumped out of my seat.

Lauryn pumped her right fist in the air and Alexis and I went crazy yelling and stomping as much as was possible crammed in with everyone else who stood from the bleachers to applaud.

"She did it! She'll be competing in the Ultimate."

Smelly guy was on his feet next to me. "High five!" He raised his arm and the stink intensified, so I slapped his hand quickly while trying not to breathe in too much.

We heard the announcer say it officially over the speakers, "That's a one-footer for Lauryn Jax."

The next girl was Evie Zafira. She tapped her helmet twice and took off.

"Holy crap, I think she's going even faster than Lauryn." The adrenaline from watching Lauryn's ride was still making me shaky and I struggled to focus my attention.

Evie went airborne over the gap, moved her right foot off the pedals, and swung her leg over the bar to the left side.

"She's doing a can-can!" I gripped the bench. If she managed to land it, it would be a first for girls in Mezzo Mondo Ramp competition. I sucked in my breath as she approached the down ramp for the second half-pipe and her leg was still over. *Come on, come on.*

Evie pulled her foot back and leveled her bike just in time to land it and do a quick turn on the final quarter-pipe. We stomped and cheered and I swear the noise was louder than it had been for any of the guys.

When she got off her bike, Evie dropped to her knees and put her head in her hands.

"Is she all right?" Alexis asked.

I saw a huge smile on her face. "Yeah, just overwhelmed I think."

The announcer called out the final competitor, Charlotte from S-Force.

Zach snorted. "Our token chick. What a joke. I bet you twenty bucks she wipes."

The guy next to him took the bet.

Poor her. The guys on her own team were betting she'd wipe out. Jerks. I had to remember to tell the girls who came to the clinic to expect this kind of attitude from some guys and not to let it get to them. Learning to ignore stupid comments about girls riding BMX was sometimes harder than working on the tricks.

Charlotte looked solid going down the steep ramp, but then didn't do anything over the gap and just rolled up and down the final quarter-pipe. Her arms visibly shook when she pulled off her helmet at the end of her ride.

Zach threw his hand up in the air. "What was that?"

The guy next to him applauded. "It wasn't a wipeout, so that's twenty bucks you owe me."

The announcement of the final standings was no surprise: Evie first, Lauryn second, and Charlotte third.

Zach said, "That's so unfair. The chicks did totally lame tricks and they all get podium finishes because there's so few of them."

"Maybe you should put a bra on and compete as a girl," the guy on his right said.

"Maybe I should."

The smelly guy next to me cleared his throat. "Actually, those tricks you think are so lame would have won the guys' competition not too long ago. The girls are coming along fast."

Smelly guy was defending girls? I was continually surprised by who was and wasn't supportive. The loudmouths like Zach often made me think no one wanted us there when it wasn't true. So far, Zach and Robbins had been the only ones who didn't seem happy to have us there as competitors.

Zach stood up and headed toward the back of the stands. "I'm out of here."

Alexis stood to follow him.

I grabbed her before she got away and pointed to the steps. "I'm going down that way. See you at the bottom."

She shrugged and took off after Zach.

I walked halfway down the stands then swung around to the side and climbed the rest of the way, avoiding the thickest part of the crowd.

Lauryn was still next to the podium, being interviewed by *BMX Real Deal*.

When I got closer I could hear the interviewer ask her why she wasn't scared to do something so dangerous.

She paused a second before responding. "There's a difference between pushing your comfort zone and riding recklessly."

Now that Lauryn had qualified, I wanted it more than ever.

Alexis found me and we hung back while Lauryn was doing more interviews. Even though it was the judging that counted for winning prize money and getting sponsors, media coverage was important, too. People got into heated online debates over who really won, and claimed that technically difficult tricks weren't scored as high as flashy-but-easy moves.

"Do you think they'll run her picture in the magazine?" Alexis asked.

"Doubt it. Maybe she'll get a mention online." Girls' events rarely got any attention. I was happy to see them interviewing her, though. It was a step in the right direction.

"Look at that," Alexis said, motioning her head toward the far exit.

Zach and the S-Force guys were taking the long way to get out of the Mezzo Mondo event area, heading toward the far exit instead of the one near the podium. Even the S-Force guy who competed was going the long way with his bike. Charlotte was left alone to gather her stuff and carry it out the main exit.

"Harsh." I thought about going up to her and saying at least she'd tried, and she'd done better than the girl who didn't even drop down the ramp, but I didn't know her, and it might make her feel more self-conscious.

Alexis smoothed down nonexistent wrinkles in her shirt. "If she'd wiped out they'd have no problem talking her back up. She let herself get freaked out and they don't want to be around her."

She was right, and that's probably the real reason I stayed away too. I was afraid of catching whatever it was that made her hesitate. A broken bone would heal, but hesitation and doubt were crippling. I couldn't let that happen to me. No matter what, even if I wiped out royally, I was going to give one hundred and ten percent.

If I did well in MixUp, I'd be set on the team. If I screwed up and we lost, I'd be even worse off than Charlotte. I wanted to get over to the park area so I could warm up, but another person stopped Lauryn to talk. I groaned and checked my watch. I still had an hour, but anything could happen.

Alexis took off her sunglasses and checked her hair in the reflection before putting them back on. "Why don't you head over? We'll try to catch you before you ride but if it's too crazy, we'll meet for lunch at that pizza place we saw yesterday, okay?"

"Sure. Great." I ran to get my bike and headed toward the park area. It was about three football fields away, behind the registration area. The main walkways were filling with people so I cut around the perimeter of the event grounds. There was no fence, but the pavement stopped and waist-high fields of hay started. At one point when I hadn't seen anyone for a few minutes, I stopped so I could change into my UnnUsual shirt. It was so big I put it on over my camisole and pulled the cami off from underneath.

The black T-shirt absorbed heat like crazy, so I was sweating before I'd even started to warm up.

The park was still empty, but riders were clustered around waiting for the go-ahead to start the warm-up. The best seats in the stands were already filled with clusters of spectators, with more heading up the stairs, carrying drinks and snacks. I pulled a water bottle out of my backpack and took a big swig. I couldn't even think about eating anything.

The UnnUsual team had a tent set up so I headed their way. R.T. was off to the side with his dad, who was gesturing and talking nonstop. R.T. stood there, not nodding or answering. Flynn waved at me from where he and Oliver stood next to Robbins. When I got there, the loudspeakers blared the announcement "Practice area now open to competitors only." R.T. and Flynn took off. Robbins ran to the fence next to the park and started yelling at Turner, who was already warming up. He didn't seem to see me at all.

"Want me to hold your stuff?" Oliver held out a hand and I gave him my backpack.

"Thanks." I wiped the sweat from my forehead, put on my helmet, and joined the melee in the park area.

I did a few practice runs on the tabletop ramp, the straight rails, and the quarter-pipe. When they announced that we only had five more minutes to warm up, one of the VaporTrail guys cut in front of me and took what should have been my turn on the incline rails.

Jerk. Cutting people off in practice was a strategy some guys used to freak out the competition, but I wasn't going to get sucked in by it. I rode over to where Flynn and Oliver were standing outside the fence. A huge scrape oozed on the back of Oliver's arm.

"Did you do that on the Mezzo Mondo?" I asked.

"Yeah." He pulled the sleeve of his T-shirt up and twisted his neck to look at it. "I have to make sure no one can claim I didn't click it."

I leaned my bike against the fence. "So if your tire is turned in enough to rip the top four layers of skin off, then you know you did it right?"

"Pretty much." He let go of his shirt.

"Over here!" Coach Robbins called, waving us over.

R.T. nodded at me as he joined us. We listened to Robbins review the features of the park where we'd already practiced yesterday.

"Remember, eight minutes max. Everyone has to be out there for at least thirty seconds, so no hotdogging. If you take too long, we'll run out of time to get everyone out there. I want to finish strong with R.T."

He told Turner, Flynn and R.T. which tricks he wanted them to do. "And whatever you're comfortable with," he told me.

"Josie has a solid feeble grind to 360," Flynn said.

He must have seen me do it in my warm-up I glanced over at him and he gave me a thumbs-up.

"Fine." Robbins was busy reading a text message on his phone and didn't look up.

I'd show him when it mattered. There's no way he'd be checking messages during the competition. Hopefully I could make him see me as a rider first and a girl second.

We went to get our bikes and move into the staging area since UnnUsual was third. The teams were supposed to stay in a group and then move up in the order we'd ride, but since everyone wanted to watch no one was staying where they were supposed to.

S-Force went first. Their lead guy rode with impressive style on the quarter-pipe, lifting up into a backflip, turning midair and heading back down on the tabletop ramp without ever touching the deck for a sweet flair. Then the same girl who had the shaky Mezzo Mondo Ramp ride took off to go second. I was almost afraid to watch, but she pulled it together once she got going and did a 180 disaster switchback. Zach went third and did solid tricks but stayed out so long the last guy only had ten seconds to ride, disqualifying S-Force.

"No score after dialing that flair?" Flynn said. "They got robbed."

The VaporTrail team went next, with the guys doing okay tricks, but not even as good as what I'd seen them do in practice, and the girl on their team went last, with just over a minute to ride, leaving her enough time to do one tailwhip. Could everyone do that trick but me?

Even though their overall score was low, they had at least scored, which meant they were in first.

Robbins gathered us together quickly before it was our turn to go. "Those were our only two real competitors. You guys should be able to beat that top score with no problem. First place is ours. He held up a fist for us bump, but with five of us it was kind of awkward.

We headed toward the on-deck area and someone jostled my arm. R.T. was on his bike next to me. "Nervous?" he asked.

"A little." I forced myself to smile and look less anxious.

"You'll do great. Just like yesterday."

"Thanks. Good luck to you, too."

I could hear R.T.'s dad yelling at him, trying to get his attention, but R.T. acted like nothing was happening.

Turner took off for the tabletop ramp and spun his bike one and a half times in the air for a five-forty, did a double back flip and some rail grinds, but had already gone over two minutes before he rode in and Flynn went out.

After pulling out his mouth guard, Turner told Robbins, "By the time you build momentum for the tabletop you barely have time to do anything."

Robbins was bobbing his head up and down checking his stopwatch as he watched Flynn. "He's going too long. Josie, keep yours to thirty seconds max."

"But I need to get to the ledge to do my feeble grind."

"Forget it. Stick close and come right back. Ride clean, nothing fancy. Your job is to be on the clock. I don't care if you have to ride out there, sit still and watch the clock tick away thirty seconds. Don't DQ and don't cut into R.T.'s time, got it?"

Watch the clock? That was never the top thing in my head. Usually it was don't over rotate or don't forget to keep your elbows tucked. With only thirty seconds I'd barley be able to make it to the rails. I started to argue, but I shut my mouth. I was on a team now. For the team to win, I had to let R.T. have as much time as possible.

"Got it?" Robbins repeated, louder.

"Yeah, got it." I shoved my mouth guard in and got in position.

Flynn rode in and I took off at top speed straight for the incline rail. At the perfect moment I hopped up and landed my front peg on the rail while shifting the back wheel to the other side so my bike was at a thirty-degree angle over the rail for a hangover toothpick grind. I held my balance the whole way down the rail until I popped off and landed textbook perfect. It felt good and I was tempted to make a run for the quarter-pipe to try my feeble stall. A glance at the clock told me my thirty seconds were almost up so I did what Robbins said and sped straight back to cross the line at exactly thirty-one seconds so R.T. could take off.

"Perfect." Robbins nodded after I rode in. "Excellent."

R.T. rode fast to the tabletop, launched up the ramp, lifted his feet off the pedals, kicked his legs back and started to straighten his arms, but never got fully into a superman before he lost his balance and botched the landing.

"Pull it together," Turner shouted.

After scrambling back on his bike, R.T. pounded up the quarter-pipe, grabbed his seat with one hand and turned his bars ninety degrees with the other in what should have been a toboggan, but his timing was off and he didn't get his front wheel angled down so the trick didn't look great. He pulled it off, barely, losing all of his momentum. He managed to squeeze in a quick no-hander over the tabletop before riding back just under the buzzer.

Robbins dropped his head and slumped his shoulders.

Turner kicked the fence. "What the hell, man? Josie could have done better than that."

I took a step back, next to Flynn. "Turner is even more upset than Robbins."

"That's nothing." Flynn dropped his voice so only I could hear him. "I wouldn't want to be R.T. Torres right now. Or ever, actually. His dad's going to explode."

R.T. threw off his helmet as Turner approached him. "T., man, what's that about? You flaked on us."

"I hit it wrong."

I saw R.T's dad in the stands with the rest of Team Torres. "His dad doesn't seem that upset."

Flynn looked at the ground. "Quiet is the worst. He'll unload on R.T. later."

I watched R.T. keep his back to the stands as he took a drink of water with his eyes closed.

"Is it that bad?" I asked.

"Depends how you see things." Flynn tilted his head and looked at me. "His dad is either supportive or abusive depending on your perspective."

"Abusive?"

"Not physical, although if it were me, I'd rather be punched in the face occasionally than hounded twenty-four seven." He shrugged. "We each have our thing."

We watched as a team with Krista on it went next. Krista got to ride longer than I did, but not by much. She managed a few good tricks and they outscored us and S-Force, bumping us to third. It was almost painful to watch the last two teams go, but one of them scratched and the other didn't score enough points to bump us out of third.

"At least we're on the podium," Flynn said.

"And we're in Ultimate, right?" I knew that the top three MixUp teams here would automatically qualify, but I wanted to hear it out loud.

"We're in."

I was in! I wanted to high-five him, but Turner and R.T. were so pissed off I thought they might kill me. I'd celebrate with Lauryn and Alexis later. And Miguel! I wished he'd been here. At least he'd see me ride in the On Site tomorrow. It would be so cool to qualify on my own as well.

Robbins had recovered from his earlier disappointment and was trying to pep up the team. "Way to go! Way to go! R.T. had a rough start but next time I'm sure he'll be more used to having distractions around." He aimed his last comment directly at me, threw his arm around R.T., and walked away.

"What, I'm a distraction?" I asked.

"For R.T., anything female is a distraction," Turner said.

That was even worse.

"Robbins is such a moron," Flynn said.

"Seriously." Turner shook his head. "He could give a shit as long as we make it to the podium. I guess he'll get his bonus this year."

When the winners were announced and UnnUsual was called to the podium, Flynn pulled me up so I was in front. R.T. stood with his arms folded across his chest, scowling.

Alexis and Lauryn were in the crowd of spectators cheering.

I posed with the UnnUsual guys for what felt like a thousand pictures. Even though R.T. had a bad ride, he had a lineup of people waiting to ask him questions.

One of the film crew interviewers put a microphone in R.T.'s face and asked what happened.

I expected him to mumble something and walk way, but he looked straight at the camera and started talking. "This is a qualifier for the Ultimate. The worst thing you can do is have your best ride here. Now is the time to work out some kinks, test a strategy, and get the wrinkles ironed out."

He sounded ridiculous, almost like Robbins. Did he expect anyone to believe he meant to ride like crap? I couldn't stand to hear any more so I left to get my bike and backpack.

Flynn caught up with me. "You did really well."

I thanked him and kept walking, eager to change out of my sweaty shirt.

"What's up? Are you pissed at R.T.?"

I unzipped my backpack and fished out my camisole. "I spent more time posing for pictures and talking about riding than actually riding."

He laughed. "I hear you. The whole media thing isn't for me. I just want enough money to eat and get to the next competition. It's different for Turner and R.T. They're building empires."

I glanced back at R.T., who was still being filmed, and at Turner, who was also giving the interviewers lots of footage.

"Hey." Flynn bumped my arm. "We going to see you tonight? Party in Oliver's room?"

Alexis would be happy about that. "Sure."

"Gotta go. I'll look for you later."

Was he being friendly or more than friendly? I didn't want to be all Alexis and assume that every guy who talked to me was into me. He was nice, that's all.

I looked back once more and saw R.T.'s dad a few feet away from R.T., waiting for him. I wouldn't want to be R.T. Torres right then, either.

"Celebrate! Live a little." Alexis shook out her freshly washed hair and picked up a hair dryer. "You're in the Ultimate, so relax. Enjoy yourself."

"I still want to do well tomorrow. I'm not staying out all night."

"Leave the lovebirds alone for a while." Alexis grinned and looked over at Lauryn who was sitting at the desk, uploading images to Exquisite. "When's he getting here?"

"Ten thirty." Lauryn and I answered at the same time.

Lauryn looked at me with a slightly guilty expression. "I appreciate this. I know he's your good friend."

"It's fine. I'm not going to be the third wheel." I meant that but at the same time I needed Miguel. He was always good at sorting out problems, and somehow I'd managed to turn qualifying for the Ultimate into a problem. I was happy but *not happy* at the same time. Qualifying by riding for thirty seconds didn't feel like much of an accomplishment. If I could qualify on my own with the On Site tomorrow, then I'd feel good about it.

"Josie, hello!" Alexis waved her hair gel in front of my face. "Now who's taking forever to get ready?"

"Sorry." I opened the closet and looked at the selection of dresses Alexis brought. "I have no idea. Pick something," I told her.

She pulled out a short, red minidress that I normally wouldn't have picked, but I figured if I was going out, why not wear something that demanded attention.

"Fine." I took it off the hanger.

Lauryn looked at the dress, looked at me, and shook her head.

When Alexis and I were both ready, we stood side by side in front of the main mirror in the room.

Alexis handed her camera to Lauryn. "Get a picture and post it."

Lauryn obliged without putting much effort into the shot.

Alexis and I left and headed down the outdoor walkway toward Turner and Oliver's room on the other side of the motel. A loud whistle sounded from the parking lot. A black sporty car idled behind a group of men who looked like they were well into their thirties and definitely not part of the BMX scene.

Alexis turned to face them. "They want us to come down."

"They'd want anything with a pulse." I pulled her away. "Come on."

I rushed to get away from the "Hey, baby, where you goin'?" calls, only slowing when we'd turned the corner away from the parking lot.

Music blasted from the room at the end.

"Sounds like it's already going." Alexis re-fluffed her hair.

More than half of the lights were burnt out along the walkway and we had to step carefully to avoid dark stains of suspect origin.

"Ohmigod, it reeks here. I'm glad we're on the other side," Alexis maneuvered around a particularly vile stain.

I followed, forcing myself to breathe through my mouth. "No wonder this place is so cheap."

We finally got to the party room and banged hard on the door so they could hear over the noise. Alexis positioned herself in front of the peep hole.

Turner opened the door wearing jeans and no shirt. "We've been trying to call you. Aren't you in room 367?"

"No. 357," I said. Why?"

He let us in.

Flynn, Zach, and an S-Force guy were sitting on the bed playing a video game. No one else was around.

Were we early?

"Hey." Flynn nodded in our direction.

"What happened to the party?" Alexis asked.

Turner pulled a T-shirt off a hanger and put it on. "Turns out PuppetStone is playing in Cedarton. Everyone drove up. I'm leaving now if you guys want to go."

"I'm in," Alexis said. "Josie?"

"Uhhhh." I was dressed to go out and couldn't go back to the room, but driving to Cedarton? It was an hour each way at least. This totally sucked.

"We can get you a ride back early," Turner said.

"No, it's okay. I don't really like PuppetStone."

"Yeah, that's what we said." Flynn nodded, still playing his game. "Want to play Zombie Attack 3000? We can add a player."

Hanging out with Flynn might have been okay, but not Zach, plus I was a little overdressed to be sitting around their room playing games.

"Thanks, but I'm not into computer games. I'll see you tomorrow."

I left the room with Turner and Alexis.

"Here," Alexis gave me the keys to her SUV. "Maybe you can find a coffee shop or something that's open."

"Thanks." I put the keys in my purse. "Have fun."

I was literally all dressed up with nowhere to go. I started walking back toward our room, then stopped on the stairwell and sat for a minute to check my messages. Gianna had sent a quick update about how summer was flying by and she was having so much fun. I skimmed it until I got to the end and sent a quick reply back telling her a little bit about how the competitions were going and that I was happy for her.

I had a surprise message from Connor. I hadn't seen him since Bruce's graduation party. He was home for a week and wanted to know if I was around. I wrote back telling him I'd be back soon. Nothing from Miguel. He was probably here. I could check the parking lot for his car. And then what?

He and Lauryn would understand if I explained everything to them. I mean, they couldn't fault me for not staying away all night by myself, could they?

"Whatcha doin'?"

R.T. Torres was in front of me with an ice bucket in his arms and a young girl, maybe ten or eleven years old, next to him.

I held up my phone. "What part don't you get?"

The girl grinned.

R.T. looked down at me. "Yeah, I can see you're texting. Why are you sitting on the stairs all dressed up?"

I put my phone down. "The party I thought was happening isn't happening, I don't want to go hear PuppetStone, and the room I'm sharing is otherwise occupied for the next hour and a half."

The little girl shifted the two soda cans in her arms. "Come on, I'm freezing."

R.T. took one of the cans, then turned back to me. "You can't sit out here dressed like that. Hang out with us until it's time to go back."

Hang out with R.T.? "Is this your sister?"

The girl said something to R.T. in Spanish that didn't exactly sound like she thought it was a good idea. He put a hand on her shoulder and squeezed. "This is Maricela. Josie is on my team, remember?"

Maricela glared at R.T.

So this was my HeadSpace friend. She already looked miserable, so I didn't bring it up.

"You two can outvote me and decide to watch chick flicks," he told her.

I grinned at Maricela, but she wouldn't look at me.

Watching movies with R.T. and his angry sister was kind of weird, but it was better than sitting in the stairwell or driving around in the SUV all night.

"Okay." I stood up and straightened my dress.

"Grab a drink." R.T. gestured to his left with his elbow. "The machine's right there."

I got a ginger ale and followed them into their room. When R.T. shut the door Maricela slammed her drink on the table and put her hands on her hips. "No girls in the room!"

"You're a girl," R.T. said.

The room was perfectly neat. Everything was put away or folded, and even the shoes on the floor were lined up.

"Is this room just yours?"

"Me and two of my brothers," R.T. said.

Three guys shared this room? Our room was a disaster area by comparison.

Maricela exhaled sharply, blowing her bangs off her forehead. "No girls in sexy red dresses in the room."

"Here." R.T. chucked a VaporTrail sweatshirt at me. "Come on." He grabbed the ice bucket and slid open the doors to the balcony.

I followed him outside.

He leaned into the room from outside. "There. Now we're technically not in the room. Happy?" He slid the door shut and sat down.

"So you're babysitting?"

He snorted. "Yeah, right. She's my warden. I'm under house arrest after that ride today. She's in charge of making sure I don't go out."

"Can she stop you?"

"Oh yeah." He stuck his left hand in the ice bucket.

"Are you injured?" I opened my ginger ale and took a sip.

"Yeah."

I thought about what Flynn said about R.T's dad. "From the MixUp?"

"Yeah." He dunked his hand lower, submersing it past the wrist.

Okay so he didn't want to talk about how he hurt his hand. At this rate the hour and a half was going to go by insanely slow.

I glanced around and he put his feet up on one of the chairs we weren't using. He had on red shoes with a black design I'd never seen. "I like those shoes."

"Me, too."

"What are they?"

"A friend of mine designed them. He's trying to get his company off the ground and asked me to wear them at competitions."

"You weren't wearing them earlier."

"I know." He fanned his feet open to show the shoes from both sides.

"Why not? They're great."

"My dad wants me to get a sponsorship from Gote. He wants me wearing their shoes."

"Is it working?"

R.T. laughed. "No."

"So wear your friend's stuff."

R.T. deepened his voice and said in a monotone, "BMX isn't a game. It's a serious business."

I couldn't tell if he meant that or if it was something his dad told him all the time. "Why do you do it if it isn't fun?"

"Remember when we tracked you down in the underpass?"

"Yeah."

"That was the first time I've had any fun riding in like, forever."

"Seriously?" I looked at him, but he was staring off into the distance.

"It was fun when I was like eight. Then I started winning." He turned and looked at me. "You don't want to hear all this."

I checked my watch. "We've still got an hour."

He leaned back in his chair and resettled his hand in the ice bucket. "I won a local competition and came home with something like a T-shirt and fifty bucks and you would have thought I won the lottery. My parents thought it was the greatest thing in the world. They started planning their lives around competitions, driving me everywhere, letting me out of anything so I could go practice."

"Nice." I sipped my ginger ale and put the can down. "I wish my parents were that impressed by a win. To them BMX isn't a real sport. Baseball and football are real sports. This is a hobby. I'd love for my parents to tell me to not bother doing dishes or whatever and go practice. I'd be really good!"

R.T. took his hand out of the ice bucket and flexed it. "Yeah, all that practice definitely helped. I kept winning, and my family got more into it. Then my brother started helping with logistics, and my dad focused on sponsorships."

"Team Torres," I said. "How do they have the time to travel with you everywhere?"

"Because it's all they do." He flicked a bug off the table. "My dad was used to running a big department and bossing a bunch of people around, but when his company moved he took early retirement and focused all that bossiness on me."

"But seriously, what could he do if you wore the shoes?"

"I'd hear about how I'm letting down the whole family, I have to be responsible, blah blah blah."

"Do you make that much money?"

He laughed. "No. Whatever I make barely covers the next competition. We're living off what my dad socked away. Which just makes it worse."

"So you'll risk landing on your head doing a double-back, but you're afraid of getting a lecture from your dad."

"I know it sounds stupid."

It did sound stupid, but I didn't want to push him too much or make him stop talking. "Don't any of your brothers ride?"

R.T. shook his head "Nah. I think they saw what happened to me and avoided it. Maricela is a natural, though. No fear."

"Really?"

"Yeah. I can't wait until she's old enough to take the lead with Team Torres."

"You think that will happen?"

"She'll make it happen."

Knocking sounded on the sliding glass door. Maricela pointed to her watch, then at me.

"Guess it's time for me to go." I pulled out my phone. "I'll send a quick text so they can't say I didn't warn them." I waited a few seconds after sending, but got no answer. I hoped Lauryn and Miguel had enough alone time.

R.T. followed me inside the room and I started to unzip the hoodie.

"Keep it for a while. You probably don't want to be wearing that dress around here right now. This is one of the crappiest places we've ever stayed."

R.T. turned to Maricela. "I'll be back in five minutes. I'm going to walk Josie to her room. Don't let anyone in. Okay?"

Loud music blared from one of the rooms as we walked by. R.T. put his hand on the small of my back "Watch that glass."

He kicked the shards to the side and his hand shifted so it was on my hip.

I was hyperaware of his hand and I felt like I was teetering back and forth in the heels I'd borrowed from Alexis.

We turned the corner to my room and I spotted Miguel's car in the lot. "I'm down that hall."

R.T.'s hand gripped my hip a little tighter and he turned me to face him.

I opened my mouth to say something and he put a finger on my lips and smiled.

Was he going to kiss me? Was I going to kiss him? I let my eyes close and leaned in.

"Josie!"

The door to my room flew open and Miguel ran out.

R.T. and I split apart and the moment was gone. He squeezed my hip and let go. "See you later."

"Yeah, thanks."

He disappeared around the corner and I turned to face Miguel.

"Were you just kissing R.T. Torres?"

Chapter 21

I woke up energized and completely alert an hour before the eight a.m. alarm was set to go off. It was going to be my day. I could feel it. I dressed quietly, grabbed my backpack, wrote a note for Lauryn, Miguel, and Alexis and wheeled my bike out. I'd endured endless teasing about me and R.T. the night before, and I needed some time to myself to focus on riding.

After finding a bagel and some juice for breakfast, I rode to the competition area to prepare. I stopped in the space where they'd torn down the Mezzo Mondo ramp from yesterday and leaned my bike against a tree. The On Site competition park was blocked off with big sheets of white canvas stretched between poles that were three times my height. Even though I couldn't see the park setup, it was sure to have rails, a ramp or two, a tabletop, and hopefully a good ledge. This time I had a strategy. I'd find a ledge to do my feeble grind to 360 and take it from there.

Today it was only me, no UnnUsual, and no Robbins calling the shots. All I had to do was place in the top ten and I'd be in the girls' competition at the Ultimate. As soon as the officials let us into the warm-up area, I rode in. Paige and Maya were there, plus a bunch of other girls I didn't recognize.

R.T. was with his dad and brother on the opposite side of the park. Two fingers were bandaged on his left hand, and he was wearing the Gote shoes, not the ones his friend made. R.T. looked up, but if he saw me he didn't react. He was focused.

That's what I needed to be, too. No distractions. I ran through all my tricks in my head, feeling them, picturing them, knowing I could do them.

"Josie!" Miguel called me from behind the fence that separated the competitors' area from spectators.

Lauryn walked closer. "We got your note. Give me your backpack. I sent Alexis to get seats in the stands so she wouldn't clutter your head with chatter."

"Thanks." I got my pack from where I'd stashed it and handed it over.

"You ready?" Miguel asked from behind his camera.

"I think so."

Lauryn held up her fist. "See you at the podium."

"See you." I bumped her fist, then turned back to wait with the other competitors.

The guys went first, and R.T. was fifth in the lineup. Just like before, all the competitors were kept in the corral so we couldn't see the park configuration until right before we each rode. We could hear cheering and applause, but there was no way to know who was winning.

As the last two guys lined up, I got in position to go first in the girls' competition.

I was ready.

When the organizer let me through to see the park I scanned the setup and planned what I could do on each piece, mapping out a route. I'd trained so much mentally that I instantly came up with two or three ideas for each area. The only weird thing was what looked like a quarter-pipe with a slot in the middle and a curved bridge over it. But by the time the buzzer sounded I had a solid plan.

I took off quickly and hopped up on the ledge with my right back peg for a feeble grind, then instead of hopping off, I turned to the left, pulled up hard with my legs and swung my bike off the ledge in a full 360, landing clean. Hah! Eat that, Robbins!

Focus, I needed to focus. And remember to breathe.

I rode up the tabletop ramp, turned back, and went up the half-pipe. It felt like precious seconds were ticking away, but I needed the right speed and momentum. No shortcuts. Just as I'd planned.

When I came down the half-pipe I went for it, pedaling hard to hit the tabletop ramp at full speed. As the ramp angled me, I fully committed to flip, shifting my weight back as my front tire lifted. I forced myself to hold on through that millisecond where it felt like I might land on my head, before I could feel myself coiling into a fast spin. I pulled tight, waiting for the right timing, then released so my bike leveled out and landed on the flat area on top of the ramp.

Without hesitating, I got into position to do the tailwhip. I was going for it. I rode out, turned and headed straight back for the tabletop. I can do this. I can do this. When I hit the sweet spot on the ramp I kicked my back wheel with my right foot and curled my legs under me as I moved the handlebars in a circle to force the back end to swing around me. When my bike passed the 180 point I knew I had it. I held my legs out of the way of the tube then slammed my feet on the pedals to catch the bike. Yess!

Breathe. Breathe. I needed to hold it together and get on that crazy bridge thing linking the two quarter-pipes. I went up one side and did a 360 on top of the bridge. The buzzer sounded as I landed. A perfect ride. I'd done everything I wanted to do and hadn't wasted a second.

I scanned the crowd looking for Miguel, Lauryn and Alexis, but didn't see them.

After downing two enormous cups of orange VaporTrail, I went to find a place in the stands to watch the rest of the girls.

"Josie!" R.T. waved me up to a spot in the top row next to him. I climbed up, apologizing as I squeezed my feet between people and leaned on their shoulders to get to the top.

I sat down with my right leg pressed against his left.

His hair was plastered at odd angles all over his head from being sweaty under his helmet. Mine probably didn't look any better.

It felt oddly familiar and comfortable to be next to him. "How did you do?"

"Not bad, considering I only have one and a half hands. You looked good out there."

Paige went next, dialing a completely stretched superman over the tabletop. She did a couple of the same tricks as I had, including the stall, but I was pretty sure I held it longer, and she didn't do anything with the slotted ramp bridge.

One of the Texas girls had a bad wipeout on the bridge and mangled her bike, but she got up and insisted that she was okay. Three other girls wiped out on the rails, but the rest had solid rides.

By the time everyone finished, I had no idea who I'd call a winner. Some people had amazing style, while others rode with perfect technique and others were unpredictable and fun to watch. It was going to come down to the judging.

The guys' scores were announced first.

R.T. looked over to his left where his family was sitting in the stands. His dad was staring at the scoreboard. As the tenth through fourth places were called, R.T. applauded, but he was mumbling to himself. Was it a mantra? A prayer? I didn't want to disturb him so I kept quiet. Come on. Let him be top three.

When R.T.'s name was called out and flashed in third place, he looked up and closed his eyes. The tension melted out of his body and he squeezed my shoulder as he stood up, then headed down the stands. People moved out of his way, making space and clapping him on the back and shaking his hand as he made his way to the podium.

Team Torres was on their feet, all watching R.T., except Maricela who was watching me watch them. She gave me a tiny half smile.

When it was time for the girls' scores to be announced I looked at Lauryn, Miguel, and Alexis in the stands. Alexis pointed to me and gave a thumbs-up. Lauryn's eyes were on the scoreboard and Miguel panned his camera, taking in the scene.

I listened and watched as the tenth through sixth place winners were announced, almost relieved to not hear my name. I wanted to be top five. Even if I hadn't won, top five would be incredible.

Fifth place went to Maya and fourth place went to Paige. When the announcer got to the top three, he slowed down. "In third place is Dylan McNeil from Shorewood." I forced short shallow breaths as my body stiffened.

Second place went to a local girl I'd never heard of, and as we waited for the number one name I gripped the metal bench hard, feeling the edge cutting into my hands.

"The winner of the girls On Site is Carmelisa Benton of Austin, Texas!"

A bad, twisty knot turned tighter and tighter in my stomach.

Breathe. I had to breathe. I tried to force air into my lungs.

The people next to me were on their feet cheering.

Clap. Had to clap. I put my hands together. No way could I stand with my stomach completely clenched. More air. I needed more air.

Carmelisa took her place on the podium with the other girls.

"You dialed that tailwhip. I don't care what the judges said." Miguel tucked his camera under his arm and helped me load my bike into the SUV.

"Thanks." I adjusted the back wheel so the back door would close.

Lauryn helped stow my helmet and gear. "I thought you'd be number one again."

I bit my lip. So had I.

"Come on." Miguel closed the trunk door. "We better get to the park so I don't miss a minute of Alexis's ride. She gave me strict instructions about how to frame her."

We hurried to the Sudden Death Park competition area and Miguel took off to find a good vantage spot for filming.

Lauryn and I wove our way up into the stands and found enough space for both of us plus room for Miguel to squeeze in once he finished filming Alexis.

Lauryn sat and adjusted her sunglasses. "What's going on in your head? I can hear the wheels spinning."

I considered lying, but decided to admit the truth. "I'm bummed about not making it solo for the Ultimate."

"But you'll ride with UnnUsual for the MixUp. You're with a sponsor already. That's what most people want to get after riding in the Ultimate."

"I know, but with them I'm the token girl and they only let me ride for thirty seconds. I wanted to qualify on my own."

Lauryn nodded. "I get it. I mean, I only qualified for Ultimate because no other girls would even drop on the ramp." She shrugged. "It's still going to be cool to be there."

"I know."

The announcer called out the girls' lineup, with Alexis riding sixth.

Alexis wasn't going to qualify for Ultimate no matter what happened in today's competition, but she didn't look like she cared. She was wearing a new Exquisite T-shirt she made while we were home. She'd done the letters in rhinestones that practically illuminated her.

The first girl took off and the others followed one by one. You couldn't say Sudden Death was dull. The tricks were a little tame, especially compared to Lauryn's mega ramp event, but it was still fun to watch, especially because I knew or had at least met a bunch of the competitors. Alexis took off in a blur of sparkle.

"I hope that she isn't a blinding reflection in Miguel's video," I said

Lauryn started to laugh, but Alexis spun out on a corner, hitting a nearby post.

"Is she okay?" I stood and shielded my eyes with my hands, straining to see.

"She's holding her leg." Lauryn took off down the stands and I followed close behind.

We made our way over to where she was on the ground, where the medical team was examining her.

"It could be broken," they told us.

Alexis was looking to the side, not at her leg.

"Alexis?" Lauryn got down next to the paramedic who had removed her helmet.

"How bad is it?" Alexis asked.

"It might be broken," the paramedic told her. "You definitely need x-rays."

"Did I rip my shirt?" she asked.

Lauryn stood back to allow room for the stretcher. "I can't believe she's worrying about her shirt."

"Could be denial. Or pain meds." I hoped her shirt was in worse shape than her leg.

Chapter 22

By the time we had Alexis out of the hospital with her x-rays, crutches and diagnosis of a badly-sprained-but-not-broken foot, we left four hours later than we'd originally planned so I didn't get home until well after midnight.

Five messages were waiting for me in the morning. Gianna was home and wanted me to go to Connor's parents' surprise anniversary party with her Wednesday. Lauryn had set up a proposed training schedule, Miguel replied to the training message, Flynn asked about Alexis, and Sandra asked me to call her about the girls' clinic. I was busier than I'd been during school.

I'd started to call Gianna when Troy burst into my room, flopped on my bed and covered himself with a pillow.

"Hide me!"

"What? Get out of my bed."

He never came in my room unless it was under direct orders from my parents, but I hadn't heard them at all this morning.

"Troy, get out of my bed." I didn't want his smelly self getting my bed dirty.

"You have to help me."

"Help you what? Move the pillow. I can hardly hear you."

He kept the pillow on his head but moved it so it didn't block his mouth.

"Smash the car, get addicted to drugs. Do something and do it fast."

"What?" I moved to the bed and pulled the pillow off his face. "What are you talking about?"

"I need mom and dad to get off my ass. You have to do something major to get them more interested in you than me."

Ha. I'd been trying to do that my whole life.

"So the weekend didn't go well?" I asked.

"I played like shit. The other guys are way better and it was all a million times worse because mom and dad were there hovering like it was my first day of little league."

"Why did you play bad?"

"I don't know. Nerves? I'm not so stupid, you know. I'll probably never even get close to the major leagues. I get it. I'm the loser who talks about how he peaked in high school."

"No one called you a loser."

"Mom and dad are definitely worried I'm on the road to loserdom."

"I doubt it was that bad." I couldn't believe I was the one giving him a pep talk.

"Troy?" My mom's voice called down the hall.

He grabbed one of my throw pillows and covered his face.

"Troy, honey, I've lined up some coaches for you to talk to. Come have breakfast."

Troy groaned and pulled the pillow tighter to his face.

I kicked him. "He'll be right there, Mom."

Troy moved the pillow off his face and looked around as if he'd just realized where he was. "This room is so girly." He sat up and put his fingers to his lips to simulate smoking a joint.

"Start now." He chucked a pillow at me and walked out, leaving my door open behind him.

Both my parents were in the kitchen eating breakfast when I got there. "Good morning, honey. How is Alexis?" my mom asked.

"Nothing broken, but she's on crutches for a while."

My mom shook her head. "I'll be happy when you're done with all this."

Done? "All this what?" I put two slices of bread in the toaster.

"This dangerous riding."

"Statistically, I'm more likely to be killed in a car wreck."

"Josie, that's not helpful." My dad pulled out a chair for me. "Tell us all about your podium finish with that team."

I told them the highlights and stressed the part about UnnUsual paying my entrance fee to the Ultimate. I was going to need waivers signed soon and I couldn't give my parents any reason to chicken out. At least money wasn't an issue. "I'm hoping they'll let me ride more next time so I can do more tricks."

Troy snorted. "Let's see, they can let one of the guys on their team do a kick-ass trick or let you do a lame-ass trick. Let's see... let's see..." He fake-rubbed his chin as if he were thinking it over.

If Troy wanted my help, this wasn't the way to get me on his good side. Jerk. "My tricks aren't lame-ass."

"Can we all watch our language, please?" My mom gave Troy and me each her mom-look. "I'm sure Josie is doing her best."

Doing my best? That sounded like something you told an uncoordinated toddler.

My dad nodded in agreement. "If you want to play ball with this team, you need to play by their rules."

Play ball? I didn't want to play ball.

"That's something both of you need to think about." My dad pointed at me and then Troy before leaving the kitchen.

My mom took a plate of cottage cheese and a fruit cup out of the refrigerator and put it down in front of Troy. "You need to get a move on. I set up an appointment for you to meet a private coach. We leave in twenty minutes." She put her dishes in the dishwasher and left the room.

"Why are you eating that?" I asked.

"What part of her being laser-focused on me didn't you get? Dad is leaving and she's keeping busy by hovering over me, starting with getting me to drop a few pounds. She took body scans of all the other players and decided I didn't measure up."

"She didn't scan anyone."

"With her laser psycho-mom eyes. I can't take much more." He picked up the fruit cup and dumped the contents in his mouth in one shot.

"I *could* use her help with the girls' clinic this weekend." The promo video Miguel put together was working, and twenty girls were already signed up.

Troy wiped fruit juice off his chin. "Yes, YES!"

"But she'll take over and boss me around. No, forget it." I licked peanut butter that spilled from my toast off my finger.

"Come on. I'll do anything. Name it."

"You and four of your friends need to help out all day Saturday and do whatever I say."

Troy started to answer, but I held up a hand. "*And* you need to get mom on board with me competing in the Ultimate."

"Who's competing in the Ultimate?"

"Me. We just had this conversation."

"I didn't know you qualified."

"Remember when you said UnnUsual wouldn't let me ride more because of my lame-ass trick? What did you think I was talking about?"

"That is actually kind of cool." Troy leaned back and looked at me. "I'll get three friends for Saturday."

"Fine. Three, but they have to be there all day."

"Fine. Deal?" He held his hand out for me to shake.

He'd agreed too easily. Was there a catch? Troy wasn't a genius, but he could be devious. If there was a catch, I couldn't see it, and I desperately needed volunteers for Saturday. I was stuck.

"Deal." I shook his hand and tried not to read too much into the grin spreading across his face as he left the table.

I almost instantly regretted it when I told my mom I could use her help with the BMX clinic. She threw herself into it obsessively, staying up until two in the morning on the computer, creating a color-coded map of the park with activity zones and times indicated. I would have preferred to keep things a little looser, but she was completely into it.

Troy reminded me that it would be good for her to spend time with Alexis and Lauryn. "Seeing your friends volunteering is perfect, that way she'll stop thinking of them as daredevils and instead see them as nice young girls."

Nice young girls. That's what she always said about Gianna.

I was looking forward to going to Connor's with Gianna that night, if only to escape the endless questions and tweaks to the schedule my mom kept proposing. Unfortunately, her new phone had text capabilities so she could stay in touch with my dad easier. Her text typos were causing some odd auto-corrections, but I forced myself not to laugh. This whole mother-daughter bonding thing was so fragile it could shatter at the smallest provocation.

I used to walk in Gianna's house without knocking, but I hadn't done that for ages so I texted from the front steps. *I'm outside.*

She wrote back, *Door's open.*

Her house looked exactly the same. I ran upstairs, three steps at a time and went into Gianna's room.

She jumped up and gave me a huge hug.

"I feel like I haven't seen you in ages, but this summer has been so fun. I wish you'd been there with me." She pointed to her closet and told me to pick whatever I wanted.

It was sort of like being with Alexis except Gianna's clothes were much less flashy. "So, give me details."

She sighed. "It's been like a dream come true. You know the kind of summer you always wanted?"

I was sure she meant the kind of summer she always wanted. Being stranded with Bruce and his family sounded like torture to me.

I stripped off my shirt and shorts so I could put on a dress.

"What have you been wearing?" Gianna started laughing so hard she couldn't talk for a few seconds until she got herself under control. "You have the worst tan ever! You should have told me. We could have done some self tan or something to even it out."

Gianna was evenly roasted all over, and the white dress she picked showed it off perfectly. My forearms and face were dark, but my legs and stomach and chest were still white.

"It's okay. Keep telling me about this dream summer of yours." I put on a halter-style indigo print dress that would at least not accentuate my crazy tan.

Gianna put the finishing touches on her makeup. "It was so nice. If the sun was out, we went to the beach, then we'd walk into town."

"You and Bruce?"

"Sometimes, but I've been hanging out with his sisters. I feel like part of their family, like they're my sisters. One of them is teaching me to crochet, and his mom is showing me her secret recipes."

Cooking and crocheting? Was she kidding?

"I know it probably sounds lame to you since you're on this extreme sports thing, but I feel relaxed for the first time ever. It's like being with them, I can be me."

So the real her was a crocheting, cooking wife in training? I opened my mouth and shut it again.

Gianna turned in her chair to face me. "Oh, and I forgot to mention, we did it."

"Did what?"

"*It!*" She bugged her eyes.

"*It* it? You and Bruce?" I watched her face and she nodded more vigorously in answer to each question.

Somehow I always thought I'd be first, before Gianna. But of course she and Bruce had been going out for a year already. I should have been surprised they waited this long.

"You're telling me this after all the cooking and crocheting?"

"Sorry. I forgot."

"Forgot? So it wasn't exactly fireworks?"

She stretched her legs out and wiggled her toes. "Well, at first not quite what I was hoping for but then..." She looked down at the floor and I could see a blush under her tan.

"Are you guys sneaking into each other's rooms at night? If your mom knew you two were all hot and heavy, she'd have a fit."

"She made me go on that five-year pill before I left. Oh, and speaking of hot and heavy, I saw Sean."

Speaking of reasons why I was alone and still a virgin. I sat down on her bed and readjusted the strap on my right sandal to loosen it.

"He was with Mindy."

So they were still together.

The buckle slipped and I mistakenly made it tighter instead of looser.

That was how many months for him and Mindy? Three. The same as I'd been with him.

"I wasn't sure I should mention it."

I undid the buckle and adjusted it again.

"Josie, say something."

"It's fine. I don't care."

"Why don't you care? Who is he?"

"Who?" I stood and rocked back and forth on the sandals to make sure they felt okay.

"Whoever it is who makes you not care about Sean and Mindy."

"Oh." I looked at my right ankle as I rotated it. The strap hit me kind of funny on that side.

"Did you...?" Gianna stood and moved closer to me.

"Me? No. We almost kissed."

"Almost? How do you almost kiss?"

I told her about R.T. and how uneven he was and how rarely he was alone because his family was always around.

Gianna's phone buzzed with a message from Connor reminding us to be there in twenty minutes.

"We better get going. I don't even want to guess about what he might have planned as a punishment for being late." Gianna stuffed her phone into a tiny purse and snapped it shut.

We got there on time and managed to find Bruce in the sea of adults who filled Connor's backyard. I wasn't sure I'd even know who to invite to a party for my parents, but Connor had managed to find at least sixty people. A man in khaki pants and a yellow golf shirt ran around telling everyone to quiet down and get in place, then less than a minute later Conner led his parents into the backyard.

His mom looked like she was going to pass out and actually had to sit down. Connor's dad stood next to her with a hand on her shoulder and shook his head at Connor. "We thought you might do something this summer, but this is truly a surprise."

Connor's parents each told their version of how they met over thirty ago. Thirty years. They were my age when they met. What if my future husband was someone I already knew? Who would I choose?

I kept thinking about it while I chatted with Gianna and Bruce and met all Bruce's sisters. Apart from the fact that Gianna had dark hair, eyes, and skin, she didn't look anything like Bruce's family, but they did seem to truly like her and accept her. She was in. Her thirty-year countdown was probably in progress.

I felt a tug on my arm.

Connor was behind me, pulling me toward him. "I want to show you something."

I followed him to the opposite side of the lawn, almost jogging to keep up with him. When he finally slowed and faced me, I asked, "What is it?"

"What?"

"The thing you wanted to show me."

"Oh, just that it's much less irritating to be away from Bruce and the rest of my cousins if you want to have a conversation. Thanks for coming. I've tried to steer my mom over here to meet you but she's still kind of shell-shocked."

"She was pretty surprised." I looked over at his mom, who was still sitting down.

"I know. That's why I didn't have everyone jump out. I think it might have pushed her over the edge."

"So is this why you're home? I thought your summer was booked solid." Connor had no tan. He definitely hadn't been on a beach vacation.

"I lied to everyone. I left a gap this week for this specific purpose but I didn't want there to be any leaks, so the only one who knew was me. Sorry for the deception."

"No harm. How are your camps going?"

"With the constraints of the school system lifted I can finally learn something, but it's impossible to pack it all into one summer. I'm going to run out of time to do everything I want to do."

"This summer?"

"Before I die. Assuming I live to eighty-three." Connor looked over his shoulder, and then smiled in a fake way. "Can you laugh at what I'm saying and then lean in and act girly flirty?"

I smiled. "Girly flirty?"

"You know, a little giggle, a hair toss. I'm trying to convince my parents I don't need school to be social and I've given them the sort of impression that you and I are more than pals. I'll owe you big."

I stood on my toes, pulled him close, and leaned in so I could whisper, "I'll do girly flirty but I need your help this Saturday." I pulled back and looked up at him.

He fake-laughed. "You must really need help." He pulled his pocket PC out. "Saturday... Checking that I'll be awake."

"During the afternoon," I told him.

He kept scrolling "Hold on, okay I may need to disappear for twenty minutes here and there, but I've blocked off noon to five for you."

"It shouldn't take that long but I'll send you details." I explained about the girls' clinic. "It's actually getting a little out of control and my mom has kind of taken over, but I need her to sign waivers, so I need to be on her good side. Don't overdo the boyfriend thing in front of her."

One of the guests stopped Connor and told him what a lovely party it was. Somehow we'd linked elbows.

"So what's with your parents and socialization?" I asked him.

"I'm trying to convince them to let me homeschool myself next year."

"Can you do that?" I unlinked our elbows and faced him.

"Technically no, but there are work-arounds. I need them to do some slight misdirection on the paperwork. So far they aren't going for it."

"Is there any rule you don't try to break?"

"Most rules are for the lazy and unimaginative, set up to make someone else's life easier. Anyway, you should talk." Connor grabbed two water bottles from an ice-filled pedestal stand.

"Me? I'm hardly a rule-breaker." I took the opened bottle he handed me.

"You refuse to be bound by the toughest one of all."

"What?"

"Gravity. Flipping upside down on a bike and doing tailwhips."

"You saw me?"

"I do know how to use the internet, yes."

I was flattered. "I prefer to think of it as befriending gravity and momentum. They only pull down the lazy and unimaginative."

"Touché."

"You're paying more attention than my parents." I took a long sip from my water.

"Why does that matter?"

"They don't get what a big deal the Ultimate is."

"And what would you change if they did?"

"What do you mean?" I finished the last of my water and then put the cap on the empty bottle.

"If you went home tonight and they presented you with an official, notarized certificate declaring that they acknowledge your athleticism and accomplishment in qualifying to compete in the Ultimate, what would you do differently tomorrow?"

"I don't know. I guess I'd feel different."

"Try acting as if you have that certificate."

I didn't answer. Sometimes Connor made no sense.

"It's the best way to get your family to see who you want to be instead of who they want you to be. You can't waffle between pleasing them and yourself. Smash the mold they have for you to smithereens and move on. They'll adjust. What they should want is for you to be happy, right?"

His pocket buzzed. "I have to go. It's my nap time."

"Nap?"

"I've been toying with ways to be more efficient and get the rest I need without wasting so much time asleep. I'm in a cycle right now of only taking twenty-minute naps every three hours, but I can't miss one or I'm screwed. Cover for me. If anyone asks where I went say I went for ice."

Connor. I still wasn't sure if he was really smart or really crazy.

Gianna was in the cluster of Bruce's sisters, laughing and looking happy. I thought about what Connor had said about doing what I wanted. It was pretty much the advice I'd tried to give R.T. Funny how it was easier to see what other people should do.

By Friday at dinner I wasn't sure I'd make it the remaining eighteen hours and fifteen minutes until the girls' clinic was scheduled to start without losing it around my mom. Troy had been taking full advantage of being under her radar by sneaking out for fast food, but he was meeting that coach she'd found for him every day.

I'd definitely held up my end of our deal. I'd let my mom get way too involved with planning the girls' clinic. I knew she enjoyed logistics, but I didn't realize how particular she was about everything. She had the whole plan in a tabbed binder, and not only were all the zones color-coded, she'd managed to track down coordinating jumbo chalk so we could mark off each area at the park.

Sandra had reserved the blacktop and picnic area at Maple Ridge Park for us. I remembered going to that park as a kid and feeling like I was in the wilderness.

When we pulled in, I realized that although the trees were huge, the park wasn't. The patch of blacktop that used to be for half-court basketball looked as if it hadn't been maintained in years, and the once-gravel parking area had been pulverized into dust that flew up into huge clouds at the slightest provocation. Due to county water restrictions, grass everywhere had turned brown and looked dead. Today wasn't going to be the day it revived. The minute I left the air-conditioned comfort of the car, hot air blasted me and visibly shimmered over the blacktop. We'd have to warn the girls to stay off any tar-repaired cracks. In this heat, those black patches morphed into gooey tire traps eager to pull riders down onto the burning pavement. Luckily, as the sun moved we'd have more shade thanks to the enormous oaks that had grown along the western side.

A row of ten bikes stood lined up in a rack, ready to go and Sandra and Miguel were installing a low temporary ramp over part of the blacktop that had buckled over a tree root.

"What's that?" my mom asked, flipping to the map section of her binder. "There's not supposed to be a ramp there."

Sandra croaked an unintelligible response and pointed to her throat.

Miguel pulled a nail out of his mouth so he could talk. "She lost her voice."

Sandra kept trying to talk and the less noise she made the more panicky she looked.

"Don't worry," I told her. "I'll set up the circuit for the girls to ride here and the registration table over there, okay?"

I took the binder from my mom and sent her to set up the registration area. I quickly re-sketched the setup to accommodate the new ramp.

Connor arrived with a bullhorn and handed it to me. "Instant authority. Try it!"

I held it up and pressed the button. "IS THIS NECESSARY?"

Whoa, that was loud.

"You'd be surprised how often it comes in handy."

I tucked the bullhorn under my arm and gave him my revised sketch plus the pack of jumbo chalk so he could mark off the sectors, even though his official job would be to take photos of all the girls on bikes.

As I was showing Troy where to put the coolers of water and sports drinks, Alexis and Lauryn pulled in. Troy's friends clustered around Alexis, and Lauryn headed for Miguel.

I needed to act fast or all my volunteers would be paired off and unproductive for the rest of the day.

I turned the bullhorn on. "YOU IN THE RED CAP! GREET PEOPLE AS THEY ARRIVE AND DIRECT THEM TO THE REGISTRATION TABLE. YOU AND YOU IN THE WHITE JERSEYS, YOU'RE ON SAFETY DETAIL. PROCEED TO THE ORANGE SECTOR FOR TRAINING."

"Oh my God!" Lauryn pushed her sunglasses on top of her head and looked over my shoulder.

Alexis moved to see what Lauryn was looking at and screamed, "Aaahhh, I love it!"

I turned around to see Miguel securing a stand holding up an enormous banner that must have been at least ten feet tall and four feet wide with the Exquisite logo plus a bunch of pictures of me, Alexis, and Lauryn.

It looked amazing. If I'd seen that banner for someone else I would have been so jealous. I almost couldn't even relate to the pictures of me, like it was someone else.

I moved closer to see better. "When I asked for a sign, I meant like on poster board from the dollar store. What did you do?"

Miguel tightened the lower right corner, then stood and folded his arms. "I have a friend who prints these. You can use it again for other events."

Our sign was bigger than some of the banners used by the real teams. It made us look professional.

Every time I tried to take my eyes off it, I found something else I'd missed. He'd included pictures from our video ride before I wiped out, from the Outrageous BMX Jam with me on the winner's podium, and an awesome shot of Lauryn on the Mezzo Mondo ramp.

"There's more." Miguel opened the door to the backseat of his car, pulled a box out, and handed it to me. Alexis ripped open the top to reveal a stack of glossy eight-by-ten photos of Lauryn on the Mezzo Mondo ramp with her name at the bottom.

Lauryn picked one up, stared at it and looked at Miguel. "You did this?"

"I had some help." He glanced at Connor, who was looking at me.

"Where's mine?" Alexis asked. She dove into Miguel's backseat and ripped into another box.

Connor took an open box from Alexis and showed me my picture. I was on my rainbow bike in front of the scoreboard that showed my name in the number-one position.

Alexis leaned on one crutch, clutching a stack of her pictures. In hers, she was standing next to her bike, and her hair and makeup looked perfect, as if she hadn't been riding at all.

"Looking good, Alexis," Troy said.

"I know." She fished a black marker out of her purse and uncapped it. "Want me to sign one for you?" She scrawled her name huge with big X's and O's and handed it to Troy.

"Where do you want the boxes?" Connor asked. "You should set up a signing table."

"You think people will want these signed?" I asked.

Alexis signed another of hers. "Of course they will."

"Put them by my mom at the registration table. After people are done registering we'll convert it to a *Meet the girls of Exquisite* table."

We barely had time to put the pictures back in their boxes when cars started arriving. Within minutes my mom was swarmed at the registration table and she waved me over. "You've already had twelve walk-ins. If all thirty preregistrations show up, you're going to have a lot of girls."

Over forty girls? That was double what we'd hoped for. I couldn't believe something I'd come up with as part of a scheme to get some free bike parts had expanded into this. My original schedule with girls in two groups wasn't going to work. I'd have to get things running quickly or we were going to go way overtime, so I told Miguel to start taking the girls in groups of ten to explain safety and gear.

When the first group was geared up and ready, Lauryn demonstrated how to do a basic bunnyhop then showed the evolution of harder tricks with a series of bunnyhop 180s and 360s, twisting her body and hopping the bike, coming to a stop in front of the girls. "Don't worry about half-pipes, ledges, rails, or anything advanced for now. The first step is to get comfortable with the basics," she told them.

The girls arranged themselves into a line and took turns doing bunnyhops and flying around the circuit.

Sandra approached me and tried to say something but I couldn't hear her. She whipped out a mini pad of paper and wrote *Awesome!* and underlined it three times. I knew what she meant. I would have loved to have had something like this when I got interested in BMX. I'd learned to ride by sneaking Troy's abandoned bike out of the garage and riding to the alley behind the grocery store in our neighborhood. Before this summer I'd never had a group of girls to ride with.

Applause grew louder and I realized I missed the last girl's ride. I clapped anyway and saw that we'd attracted at least twenty spectators. I'd noticed a few of the parents setting up folding chairs to watch, but some of them had dropped off their kids and left. People from the neighborhood must have been coming over. I wanted to turn to them and say, "*See? See what girls are interested in if you give them a chance? Just because they might fall down doesn't mean they shouldn't do it.*"

I left the demo area to check the other stations and make sure things were running smoothly. My mom waved me over to the registration table and pointed to the stack of forms. "I'm down to the last few sheets. Do you want me to close? You've already got forty-five."

Two more cars pulled in, and I counted at least five more girls.

My mom looked at me. Letting them in would definitely mean we'd run late. I pushed a loose strand of hair off my face and tucked it behind my ear. "Sign them up."

"This isn't following my plan at all." My mom rifled through the printed forms and counted the girls getting out of the cars.

"It's fine," I said. "I'll hand-write forms if we need more."

She relaxed a tiny bit when she saw that she'd have one spare form.

"Hang in there," I told her.

Since we only had ten bikes we had to keep the forty girls who weren't riding entertained. Miguel was a big attraction, doing tricks and answering questions.

"How did you get to be so good?" a girl with long brown ponytails asked him.

"You get better by practicing. I started exactly as you did, with no skills, just me and a bike. If you put in the hours, you'll get better." He pointed to the blacktop. "This is all you need. A bike, some space and the willingness to keep trying."

She tilted her head at him. "Doesn't it hurt when you fall?"

"You get used to it. I fall all the time and now I'm good at it. You learn how to take falls to reduce your chances of getting hurt, plus you'll all wear safety gear, right?"

Some of the girls answered "Yes."

Miguel asked again until all the girls answered yes.

"Some people might try to convince you that since girls aren't as muscular, they can't take falls like the guys, but you shouldn't listen to them. There are some seriously skinny guys out there taking falls. But it does help to add some muscle, so you should train hard."

He looked up and down the row of girls, all hanging on his every word.

"So don't worry about falling, okay? Everyone falls. Right, Josie?" He looked at me. "What's your top piece of advice for the girls?"

The group of girls looked less scared thanks to Miguel's talk. I didn't want to tell them about my wipeouts. "Ride for yourself. Do it because it's fun. I mean, you have to work at the tricks and be willing to fall, but when you land one, it feels great. You feel like you can do anything. Don't let anyone tell you that you can't."

Alexis pulled me aside and begged for a pee break. I filled in for everyone to give them each a break, taking over camera duty for Connor last.

"Josie, there you are." My mom was breathing hard as if she'd been running. "Some of the girls are leaving and they want you, Lauryn, and Alexis to sign their posters. It's already five o' clock."

She shielded her eyes with her hand and looked at the western end of the park, past the parking area. "Troy should be here any minute with pizza. Are those more of your friends?"

Two guys on BMX bikes rode through the grass toward us. One black bike with yellow rims; one black bike with orange rims. Z-Dog and NoFro.

They rode right up to the table.

"Hey Mrs. Peters. Hey Josie." Z-Dog acted as if we'd been hanging out together all summer.

"What are you doing here?" I asked.

"We heard there were free BMX lessons." NoFro stood up, straddled his bike, and surveyed the setup, "Nice turnout."

"There are more people here than at some of the contests I've done," Z-Dog said.

"It's good you stopped by," I said. "I need your help. Can you take over demos so Lauryn and Alexis can sign posters?"

"There's pizza coming," my mom said. "I sent Josie's brother a half hour ago. He should be back any minute."

"I'm in," Z-Dog said.

"Yeah. We sessioned all day. I'm starved." NoFro sat back down. "Where do you want us?"

I put them on bunnyhop detail.

Girls were lined up at the signing table so I took my place and asked the first one in line her name. I signed the poster to her and then did another one for her cousin, her friend, and probably her dog, but I didn't care. Having someone actually line up and wait for me to sign a picture of myself was a pretty good feeling.

"You're going to have to get faster at that," Lauryn said. "You'll be signing a lot with UnnUsual."

Miguel handed me a memory stick. "Before I forget. My footage from Explosion is here if you want to watch it, but there's a lot. It's not edited."

I stuffed it in my pocket. "Thanks for this and the banner and the posters and the filming. I'm going to have to do another epic wipeout to pay you back."

Lauryn looked up from signing a poster. "Don't even joke about that."

"Final count was fifty-four," my mom said.. "The last girls just finished, and Connor said to tell you he had to go, but he'd send you the images as soon as he could."

After the last girls left with their signed posters, Z-Dog and NoFro insisted on having their own copies. I wondered if they'd show them to Sean. I hoped so.

NoFro held up the picture of Lauryn on the Mezzo Mondo ramp. "Nice!"

Miguel moved in closer behind Lauryn and put his hands on her shoulders. "Yeah, she's amazing."

"Has anyone seen my mom?" I wanted to tell her she could go and let us finish cleaning up. I knew she hadn't planned on being here so late and she liked to be home when my dad called.

Z-Dog tried to say something, but his mouth was full of pizza. He pointed to the parking lot.

I found her saying goodbye to one of the moms who had been the last to arrive.

"Making friends?" I asked.

She picked up an empty water bottle from the parking lot. "They drove all the way here from Wooddale. They're already planning to caravan to that Ultimate competition."

She tossed the bottle in the recycling bin. "I want one of those MadKatt T-shirts."

This was a huge improvement over her being completely clueless about BMX. "It's MadKapp, and I'll see what I can do about getting you one."

If I'd managed to sort of turn my mom around, maybe I could do the same with Robbins and get myself more riding time.

Chapter 23

By the time I got everything cleaned up from the bike clinic and made it back home I was so tired, I barely had the energy to shower before passing out.

When I got up Sunday morning, my phone showed a message from R.T. asking how it was going. I answered back that I was spending the day watching film from Explosion.

The house was so quiet I could hear the floorboards creak under my feet. A note sitting on the hallway table explained that my mom had gone shopping. I pictured her coming home with a custom RV for traveling to BMX events. Team Peters. Ha!

I headed into the kitchen and found Troy eating a tiny bowl of cereal at the table.

"I'm confused," he said, spooning cereal in his mouth.

"The longer you leave the milk on, the soggier it gets." I found two slices of bread and popped them in the toaster.

"Ha ha. No, I mean you. Why did you ditch your friends to tag along with those guys?"

"I'm not tagging along with anyone. Alexis and Lauryn ditched me last night."

I went to the refrigerator to get juice and saw Troy's latest diet chart with severely restricted calories. I so wanted to make fun of him, but he'd pummel me.

Milk dribbled down his chin and he wiped it with the back of his hand. "No, I mean you ditched them to join the team you're with now for the competition."

"The guys' team has an actual sponsor." Why was he so suddenly interested? Had Alexis been talking about it?

"So you change, like that?" He snapped his fingers. "What kind of sponsor deal did they give you?"

"A T-shirt and they paid my entrance fee."

"Oooh. That's what, sixty bucks? If someone offers you sixty-five, you'll switch again?" He pushed away from the table and stood up.

The hot toast burned my fingers as I pulled it from the toaster. "What is your problem? That's how it works." I flipped each piece onto a plate and slathered them with peanut butter.

"And you say baseball is a brutal sport." He dropped his bowl in the dishwasher and left.

Brutal? What was he talking about? Maybe the sight of my delicious high-calorie peanut butter toast was making him jealous. I enjoyed every bite, glad I wasn't restricted to a mini bowl of soggy cereal.

Four fast taps sounded on the sliding glass door. I looked over and waved to Miguel to come in.

He barely had the door open before asking, "Is Lauryn here yet?"

"What happened to hi Josie, nice to see you?"

"Sorry. Hi." He slid the door closed behind him. "Can I have some juice?"

I poured banana-mango-orange juice in a tall glass and handed it to him. "That anxious to see her, huh?"

He smiled and then looked down. "Yeah. She's incredible. I hope that next year we can make something work out."

I lingered over my last bite of toast. He liked her, and she liked him. They both knew how the other one felt. It was simple. No games, no trying to decipher subtext of conversation snippets. There was no reason it had to be complicated.

Miguel stood up with his empty juice glass, took my plate, and put both in the dishwasher. He turned around and looked outside. "We're getting rain today. You're lucky the clinic was yesterday."

I moved next to him to look at the sky. "How is that possible? When you got here it was sunny."

"The storm clouds were off in the distance, making their way over. Looks like they're settling in now. I hope Lauryn and Alexis get here before it opens up."

I tried to picture Lauryn letting Miguel shield her with an umbrella, but I couldn't quite see it. Alexis would gladly take refuge to protect whatever she'd done to her hair, that was for sure.

"Josie, hello!" Miguel waved his hand in front of me. "Are you ready?"

"Sorry, yeah, let's go get set up."

We headed down to the basement. When I flicked the light switch the room went dark instead of light. Someone had left the lights on all night.

I flicked the switch again. "Am I a tagalong?"

"What?" Miguel opened the storage closet where we kept the projector screen.

I connected input and output wires to the laptop and projector. "With UnnUsual and R.T. Am I a tagalong?"

He wrestled the projector screen to the front of the room and unrolled it. "Why are you asking me?"

"Because you'll tell me the truth."

The screen tilted to the left. Miguel adjusted the legs to rebalance it. "Why do you want to be on the team?"

I hit power on the projector and started up the laptop. "I guess I want to be like them— successful and confident."

"You are those things, except when you manage to find some guy who eclipses you." Miguel stepped back to look at the now-straight screen. "Sometimes it seems like you do it on purpose. You get scared when you're doing well and you find someone whose shadow you can hide in."

The projected image was too big and too far to the right. "What are you talking about?" I fiddled with the controls to resize and reposition the image.

Miguel flopped on the chair to my left. "I'm no psychologist, but look at your brother. You're comfortable in that space behind him."

"I want to get away from him! Are you insane?" The image was on the screen but looked tilted. I clicked the projector adjustment, but the image distorted worse.

"Part of you wants to get away, but it's a familiar space. Any time you get scared, you go back there by choosing a guy exactly like Troy."

He was wrong. He had to be wrong. I didn't go after guys like Troy, did I? Sean... R.T... They both had Troy-esque qualities.

Miguel elbowed me. "Jos, don't freak out." He slid off the couch and crouched down by the projector. "I don't think you're a tagalong. You're not tagging along if you're doing what you want to be doing. If you had zero interest in BMX and you were doing it because you had a crush on someone, that would tagging along."

He lifted the projector to readjust the support underneath, then put it back down. "You're not tagging along with UnnUsual. They want to win and they need a girl who can ride well, so they chose you."

He stood back. "Looks good to me."

When the doorbell rang, Miguel jumped leaped to the stairs, taking them two at a time.

I hauled myself off the couch and followed. When I got to the front hall, Alexis was already inside next to a tray of iced drinks in plastic cups with straws sticking out.

Lauryn lingered at the doorway, kissing Miguel.

Alexis pointed to the tray. "Have a mocha while it's icy. It will cool you down, although it's about to start pouring outside."

"Isn't that a chick drink?" Miguel asked.

"Well, you are hanging out with the three of us," Alexis told him.

He let go of Lauryn's hand to take two cups. "It's definitely the first time I've sat down with three girls to watch BMX videos. Iced mochas it is." Lauryn took the other two cups and they headed downstairs.

I turned to go to the basement.

"Wait." Alexis shifted on her crutches.

"How's your ankle?"

"Still sore, but way less puffy." Alexis hopped her way to the stairs. "Let's go. Make lots of noise on the stairs so they aren't all over each other when we get down there."

Alexis and I slowly stomped our way down the stairs, announcing our arrival.

Lauryn was perched on Miguel's lap in the chair and Alexis and I settled onto the couch.

The footage was in clips with file names that were letters and numbers, but after three tries I found Lauryn's Mezzo Mondo ride. Miguel made us repeat it over and over until Lauryn stopped him on the fourth go-round.

I hit the stop button. "We need to move on. There's a lot to see."

We watched my On Site ride plus the others and I knew I was supposed to be humble but I thought I was as good if not better than most of the girls who made top ten.

Alexis threw a balled-up napkin at the screen when the number-one girl was announced. "You should have scored way higher."

"Can't say I saw a lot of problems with that ride," Miguel said. "The judges scored some easier tricks higher than yours, but your ride was solid, so do you really care what your number was?"

I clicked stop and queued up the next clip "I care a little. I wanted to ride on my own at the Ultimate." I hit play and we watched my ridiculously short MixUp ride.

"Wait, could you play it again?" Miguel asked. "I blinked and missed it."

"Keep it going," Lauryn said, straightening up a little. "This is the part where R.T. screws up."

I almost couldn't stand watching R.T.'s crappy ride and I stopped it immediately when it finished and moved on to another clip.

"Oooh." Alexis sat forward on the edge of the couch even though the film was a candid, not an event. "If R.T. moves we'll be able to see Oliver. He's right next to that dreadlocks guy. Which one is that, Josie?"

"That's Turner."

"Turn up the volume." Alexis shifted to sit up straighter. "Can we hear what they're saying?"

I cranked up the sound and the Ambiguous Pluto song playing on the loudspeakers got louder, but we could also pick out the conversation.

Turner was easy to hear since he was shouting. "R.T., man—what happened?"

R.T. mumbled, "I didn't have it."

"Is it that chick?"

R.T. wiped sweat off his forehead. "Nah, it's not her."

Turner threw his arms up in the air. "Then what? At least she stayed on her bike. You should tell Robbins to give her some of your time."

"I can't do that."

Oliver's attempt to get Turner and R.T. to stop arguing faded into the music.

The remote clattered on the floor where I dropped it and I squeezed my eyes shut. I didn't want to see or hear any more.

Stupid R.T. Stupid me. I thought we were friends, but what did I expect? Of course he wouldn't give up any of his time. None of them would.

"He's an ass. Ignore him." Lauryn picked up the remote and paused the video.

I pulled in a ragged breath, opened my eyes, and saw the frozen image of R.T., Oliver, and Turner on the screen.

Alexis touched my arm. "Are you okay?"

I pulled my knees in tight and squeezed them to my body. "I'm a joke."

"You ride really well. If they can't see that, it's their problem." Miguel shifted position in the chair.

Alexis shook the remnants of ice in her cup before drinking the last of it. "You're making a big deal out of nothing. I mean, at least you're on a team that might win."

But I wasn't helping them win. Even if Robbins took time away from R.T., he'd give it to Turner or Flynn, not to me. How was I supposed to get better if I never got to ride?

I let go of my knees but kept them bent in front of me as I rubbed my flattened hands across the velvety fabric of the couch. Rough. Smooth. Rough. Smooth. "I'm not sure I want to win by not riding."

"But if you quit UnnUsual you can't compete in Ultimate," Lauryn said.

I stared at my knees. "I know."

"I wouldn't quit," Alexis said.

"Neither would I," Lauryn said. "I'd show them."

Miguel walked around behind the couch and put his hands on my shoulders. "Forget them. Forget us. Do your thing."

Chapter 24

An out-of-control fire raged in a fire pit touching a row of trees growing against the side of a house. Flames took hold in the trees and threatened the wooden siding. I ducked low as I squeezed between the trees and the house to get inside, because I seriously had to pee. Hot, so hot.

I woke up sweating with my feet trapped in the blankets and the urgent need to go to the bathroom. After kicking my feet free, I staggered out of my room.

When I got back in bed, the realness of the dream was still there. Even though I didn't find out what happened, going inside a burning house to pee was probably a bad plan. But what did it mean? Was I being stupid by wanting to quit UnnUsual, or was I unwilling to accept that I was in a bad situation and needed to get out?

That was the problem with the rare dreams I remembered long enough to think about, they were so weird I could pretty much interpret them however I wanted to.

If I had to choose a message, a dream about going in a burning house probably meant I was in trouble. I needed to quit UnnUsual.

I wasn't looking forward to talking to Coach Robbins, but it had to be done. If I was lucky, I'd be able to leave a message. I dialed his cell number.

"Robbins." He answered before it even rang.

"Hi, it's Josie Peters."

Silence.

"I'm the girl who did the MixUp with UnnUsual at Explosion?"

More silence.

I took a breath. "I'm calling to let you know that I won't be able to be part of UnnUsual or compete in the Mixup at the Ultimate."

"Okay."

"Okay."

He hung up.

That may have been one of the most painful conversations of my life. At least it was short. I put my phone down and reviewed the whole exchange to make sure it was real.

I'd never have to talk to Robbins again. An odd, floating sensation washed over my body. I wasn't accustomed to walking away from challenges. It felt weird, like I'd lost something big. Maybe this was what it was like to be on the verge of making a huge mistake.

I looked at the contact list on my phone.

Lauryn was going to be disappointed, disgusted even. Alexis would be pissed about losing her Oliver connection, and Miguel... Even though he said I should do what I wanted, I was pretty sure he hoped I wanted to be on a sponsored team. Knots and cramps dug into my stomach and started fighting for dominance. What had I done?

Usually I knew I was doing something potentially stupid and could bail in time, but this was a done deal. I needed to muster up the energy to tell people, starting with my mom.

Not telling her wasn't an option. She'd made her policy on withholding information clear. If Troy and I didn't tell her what she wanted to know, she'd play detective to find out what was going on. I'd seen it happen. Troy had kept his first girlfriend a secret; our mom had found out and kept his life under a microscope for the next six months.

I could easily lie and say Robbins cut me for some vague reason. Like Lauryn said, it would be easier than arguing, but I'd never been a good liar.

I went downstairs and found my mom sitting at the kitchen table with a half-empty cup of coffee.

"Mom? Can I talk to you about something?"

"Sure."

She shifted her chair so she could look me in the eyes in investigator mode.

No way could I have pulled off a lie.

I took a deep breath and explained about not being happy as part of the UnnUsual team and quitting. I focused on the part about not getting to ride much and glossed over the part about R.T. flat-out refusing to consider offering some of his time.

She sat perfectly still, looking at me.

The silence was agonizing. Did she think I'd ruined my life? Was she going to force me to call Robbins back and tell him I made a mistake and beg to be let back on the team?

I had to hear whatever it was she was going to say. "Well?" I asked.

She shook her head, her expression changing from intense interest to stunned disbelief. "That's it?"

"Pretty much." Did she suspect I'd left out part of the R.T. story?

"Don't do that to me." She leaned back in her chair and closed her eyes. "You scared me. I thought something was seriously wrong."

"You're not mad?"

She looked at me with her investigator face again. "Why would I be mad?"

That question reeked of mom-trap but I couldn't stop myself from answering. "Because I quit something. When Troy tried to quit baseball his freshman year you guys went berserk and gave him endless lectures about sportsmanship and teamwork."

My mom started to say something, stopped, then started again. "You and your brother are completely different people. He can be incredibly undisciplined and lazy, and you are usually way too hard on yourself. From what you told me, it was the team and the coach who weren't living up to your standards, not the other way around."

She took a sip of her coffee and then continued. "What I saw at that clinic was not a lazy girl who doesn't want to work. I saw a highly motivated leader who is only beginning to scratch the surface of her potential. If you think this is what you need to do to be happy, then do it."

She stood and kissed me on the top of my head as if I were a little kid. "I'm meeting some friends for brunch. Make sure your brother doesn't sleep all day."

The rest of her coffee got dumped down the drain and she left me sitting there.

It was funny how she couldn't tell what hurt and what didn't. If I'd come downstairs with an ugly but relatively harmless scrape down my arm she would have made a huge deal.

I wasn't happy. Somehow I felt worse.

There was nothing to eat in the refrigerator. Nothing. No yogurt, no bagels, no bread. No milk for cereal. Nothing. I slammed the door shut.

"Guess I'll find a drive-through for breakfast!" I shouted at the almost-empty house.

I needed air. I'd go out and get a muffin. I dug a fistful of change out of the change bucket, sifted through to make sure I had lots of quarters, and ran upstairs, pounding every step to make sure Troy couldn't sleep in.

While changing into a T-shirt and jeans, I scooped up the change and stuffed it in my pocket, then pulled half of it out to go in the other pocket to even the lumpy look it left.

I had one shoe in my hand when my phone rang. Miguel.

"Josie hey. I was going to—"

"If you're calling to talk me out of quitting UnnUsual, you're too late. I called Robbins this morning." My throat felt tight and I was talking way too fast. "It's done. I can't get into it right now."

I hung up before Miguel could answer and left.

When Connor found me, I was finishing my fourth donut.

"You, with the donuts!" He pointed to me from the doorway. "Put the bag down and keep your hands where I can see them." He slid into the booth across from me. "I need to send one quick message. Everyone is in a panic looking for you." He finished, put his phone away, and sat back. "What happened?"

I told him about calling Robbins and telling my mom and then I started rambling about the tree dream. I knew I was going into too much detail and that it didn't make sense, but it felt good to be telling someone and getting it all out.

When I'd exhausted myself and stopped talking, he slid me a napkin.

"Anything else?"

"I was mean to Miguel."

He nodded. "Anything else?"

"No."

"Okay." He put his palms flat on the table. "Look at me."

I looked him in the eyes.

He held my gaze without blinking. "Three things. No interruptions. Ready?"

"Go ahead."

"First. Get out of this vortex of doom. You made a decision, now it's up to you to make sure it's the right one. Acting like this will make sure it's the wrong one. Get what I'm saying?"

I nodded and slid the remaining half donut to his side of the booth.

"Second. Call Miguel and apologize. He'll help you with whatever you need and so will I, but you need to pull it together and stop worrying about what other people think of you."

I braced myself for his last point.

"Third." He moved in closer, leaning into the table until he was only inches away from my face. "Why didn't you pee on the fire?"

Chapter 25

Lauryn and Alexis were more understanding than I expected about me deciding to quit the team. They conference-called me when I got back from the donut shop.

"You can do Exhibition." Lauryn said. "You should do Exhibition. They need to see that they could have easily had enough individual girls for an open class."

"I'd do Exhibition if I could." Alexis said.

She had a point. At least I could ride.

Lauryn said she'd work out a training plan for both of us and send it to me.

R.T. and Flynn sent me text messages asking if it was true I quit. I told them I wanted to ride more and didn't think I'd get the chance on the team. I told R.T. I'd be looking for him in his friend's shoes at the Ultimate.

A couple of girls from the clinic set up profiles on Exquisite and posted pictures of themselves on bikes. I sent messages to encourage them and told them to let me know how it was going.

In the few weeks we had to train, I spent as much time as possible with Lauryn and Miguel. We used the posted park configuration to map strategies for the rides we could each do to show off our best tricks.

Like I expected, the draw of an event in the city worked on my parents. My mom booked a suite at the Hilton downtown for the weekend of the Ultimate so the whole family could be there. Friday afternoon I'd prepped my bike, packed and repacked everything. We were supposed to get my dad from the airport and go.

Troy had started to pack the car when the house phone rang.

My mom answered, listened for a few seconds and said, "We're just leaving. Oh. Oh no. Okay." She wrote something down and then said, "We'll see you then."

"Was that Dad?" I asked.

"Your father's flight was cancelled. The next one he can get on only arrives Sunday morning."

"Sunday morning?" I needed to go tonight! The first events were tomorrow.

My mom held up her hand. "I know you have to be there early. You and your brother can drive down tomorrow morning in time to watch Lauryn, and then stay one night, and be there ready to ride on Sunday, okay?"

I wanted to go right then but I couldn't think of anything to say that would convince my mom.

Troy was the one who pushed. "We can go now. The rooms are already booked."

"You are not running loose in the city all weekend. I have my misgivings about letting you be there tomorrow alone."

Troy looked like he wanted to say something else, but my mom gave him a look that didn't invite further discussion.

I texted Lauryn, Alexis, and Miguel to let them know I'd only get there Saturday morning. I was so close; I hoped nothing else would go wrong.

At nine o' clock Saturday morning I was ready to go and I hadn't seen Troy yet. Even though the city was only a forty-minute drive, we had to find a spot to park, and I wanted to get going.

"Troy!" I pounded on his door. "Are you awake in there?"

After pushing the door open I took a step back. With the windows blocked, the dark colors, and the stuff piled everywhere, his room looked and smelled like the inside of a gym bag full of old sweaty clothes.

The lump on the bed didn't budge when I threw a ball of socks at it. "Troy! Come on. We need to go soon."

He stayed unmoving, so I crept in and reached over to shake him, but before I could touch him, his arm shot out and trapped me in a headlock.

"Oww. Let go!"

"I thought you said it started at noon."

I clawed at his fingers, but I was twisted in an awkward position over his bed. "The gates open at eleven. I want to be sure I have a good seat to watch Lauryn."

He let go just enough so I could wriggle out. "You think it's going to be a problem to see around the twelve other people who are going to be there?"

"There will be more than twelve."

The crowds in videos from the previous year's combined BMX and skateboard events in Austin were huge. I wasn't sure what to expect for BMX only or specifically BMX girls, but I was pretty sure it would be more than twelve. It had better be more than twelve.

He threw his blankets off and stretched. "I'm up. Make me my breakfast and we'll go."

Although I didn't like being bossed around by him, I did want to get going, so I went to the kitchen to make his protein shake.

"That's nice of you to make breakfast for your brother." My mom looked like she hadn't slept at all.

"He's so slow."

"Be nice. I expect you two to get along. He won't be at home much longer."

Luckily. "I want to get going. Where is he?"

"Don't rush him and don't encourage him to speed. Your father will have a fit if Troy gets one more ticket."

By the time I finished blending his shake and putting it in a to-go cup, he was downstairs with a bag packed. In his Michigan T-shirt with cutoff sleeves and mirrored aviator glasses, Troy wasn't going to blend in with the BMX crowd.

We were finally walking out the door, but my mom kept stalling us with last-minute instructions and was tearing up as if we were both shipping out overseas.

"Mom! We'll see you tomorrow," Troy said, hugging her back. "Relax."

Our car couldn't play digital music files so I'd burned a bunch of CDs with my favorite pre-race music and I popped one in.

Troy immediately ejected it and tuned in a talk-radio show. "I need to hear the commentary on last night's game."

He slurped his shake and occasionally grunted in disbelief as two sportscasters droned on about every nanosecond of the White Sox game.

Trying to drive anywhere near the Lakeshore in the summer was a potential traffic nightmare. Luckily there were no accidents, construction snafus or unexplainable gapers' blocks stopping us, and we pulled into a lot right next to Soldier Field with five minutes before the gates would officially open. We parked facing the water with a clear view of the chop on Lake Michigan and the masts of the anchored boats bobbing up and down. I opened the door before he even had the engine turned off.

Even though we couldn't see anything yet I could hear music blasting from the competition area, a welcome relief from the endless baseball statistics.

Wind whipped my hair around my face so I found a rubber band in my pocket and made a ponytail. I wouldn't want to be on the water today for sure, but the wind was still going to be a factor on the ground. It wasn't a steady wind, either. It was that kind of wind that toyed with you and teased you first blowing in one direction until you turned away, then dying down for a few minutes so you'd lower your guard before it would hit you full force with a gust from behind.

"Good thing BMX isn't a water sport." Troy double-clicked the car-door locks with a beep and we left the lot to head toward the south fields. Sheets of paper, garbage cans, and cardboard boxes skipped across the parking lot to eventually be trapped at the fence lining the edge of the parking area.

"Can you even ride in this?" Troy asked.

"It wouldn't be my preference, but it's doable." Wind would screw you up, but it wasn't as dangerous as riding in the rain. Although the sky was cloudy, it didn't look like we'd get rained out.

As soon as we stepped past the end of the football stadium, the enormous golden U logo of the Ultimate event came into view. The Ultimate banner must have been at least eight stories high with vents so no matter how hard the wind tried to blow it away, it wasn't moving.

The Ultimate had taken over the entire festival lot south of Soldier Field. The lot was three times the length of a football field, with the park area at the southernmost end, the half-pipe on the eastern side closest to Lake Michigan, the stage where the band would play closest to Lake Shore Drive, and sponsor tents set up by the entrance at the northern end.

I couldn't wait to get inside the gates. Not only were VaporTrail, UnnUsual, MadKapp, Relentless, and S-Force there, but so were tons of foreign brands including a Chinese company that made funky pedal grippers I'd only seen in magazines. Their fluorescent-orange tent was easy to spot and they had a corral set up behind their spot where they had demo bikes for people to try their pedals.

I paused for a long moment, letting it all sink in. This was no fringe event held in some remote field in the middle of nowhere. It was big time, and I was there. Even having Troy with me couldn't ruin it. For once it was all about me, not him. I was the athlete and he was the spectator.

"OutDone network is here?" Troy stopped walking and I crashed into the wall of his back.

It was the third time he'd stopped, staring at the cameramen and reporters setting up.

"There will be time between events to go look at everything." I didn't mention that if he'd gotten moving a little faster this morning we would have had more time to check everything out. "I'll go sign in. Competitors get in for free."

Zach was at the registration table with a couple of guys I recognized. He nodded at me as the event organizer attached a red competitor wristband to his right hand. "You can take it off when you ride, but don't lose it. You need it to get in and out of the event area and competitor-only areas."

I gave the woman at the table my name "Josie Peters."

She clicked her computer a few times and frowned. "Event?"

"Exhibition."

She sighed and looked at me over the top of the screen. "You'll get in free tomorrow, but today you're a spectator."

"Really? I thought competitors got in the whole weekend for free."

"If you were in a main event you would. You'll have to pay at the gate with the other spectators. Next, please."

I slunk away from the table and joined Troy in line for the main gate.

"You don't get in free?" he asked.

"Only tomorrow" I did my best to keep my voice even, but I felt the quiver in it. I was not going to let it upset me. I was here.

At least the line was short. The middle-aged couple ahead of us already had their wristbands, but the man kept asking questions about how the preliminaries worked and how many people advanced to the finals.

Troy straightened up and folded his hands under his arms, a move I recognized as one of his favorite ways to show off his biceps.

I turned around and saw a group of five girls in line behind us who looked as if they spent hours doing their hair and putting on makeup.

"Do you think he's here already?" one of them asked.

They all had their eyes glued to the gates where three VaporTrail guys flashed their red wristbands and wheeled their bikes through.

The couple ahead of us finally moved on and Troy paid the cashier for two.

She attached a band to Troy's wrist then asked, "Who is this one for?"

Troy pushed me forward.

"Left hand please."

The fluorescent-yellow band pinched as she secured it to my wrist.

"You can access all main areas, but competitor areas are off-limits."

I took a step, then jumped behind Troy when I saw Oliver and Flynn at the competitor gates with their bikes. Of course they'd show up at the exact time I was getting my stupid spectator band.

Chapter 26

I couldn't believe I was going to be stuck in the stands watching with the parents and kids. It totally sucked they weren't letting more girls compete. An announcement blared, "Ladies' park starts in fifteen minutes." I'd wanted to see Lauryn before she began warming up, but Troy and I weren't even close to the stands yet. I texted Alexis that we were on our way.

Troy stopped in front of me to snap a picture of an inflated two-story VaporTrail can whipping back and forth. "I can't believe how many big-name companies are here."

"Come on!" I prodded Troy to keep him from stopping to talk with every Lycra-clad girl offering free samples. "Alexis says she's sitting in front of the quarter-pipe."

We finally got close enough to see Alexis and her crutches sprawled across the front row of the spectator stands, saving a group of spaces. She'd picked a good spot where we could see the air tricks. The stands were about half full with a steady stream of people arriving. Even though most of them were probably there to reserve their spots for the guys' preliminaries, it was still good to have more people watching the girls.

I stepped onto the metal stairs leading up to the stands and as I grabbed the support rail, the cross braces on the outside of the stands slammed against each other, causing the rail to rattle in my hand. If the wind was causing the stands to shake, I could only imagine what it was doing to bikes or the row of seats at the top.

Alexis picked up her crutches as Troy slid in on one side of her and I sat on the other. She'd changed her nose stud to match her bright blue shirt and even with her ankle wrapped she looked perfect. Leave it to Alexis to get a cute injury, nothing that messed up her face.

"Thanks for saving seats," I said and then raised my voice for Troy's benefit. "It's getting crowded with all the spectators here for the girls' event."

I scanned the girls warming up and found Lauryn easing her way up and down a ramp, not showing much energy or drive.

"How's she doing?" I asked.

"Completely freaked out." Alexis tucked her foot out of the way of people walking by.

"More freaked than Mezzo Mondo?"

"It's the atmosphere and competitors," Alexis said. "Miguel tried to get her to calm down."

"Where is Miguel?" I asked.

"He's set up over there." She pointed to the cordoned-off media area where Miguel stood in front with the other cameramen. "He got a pass from someone who wasn't interested in filming the girls."

It was good that Miguel got in the official media area with the best spots for filming, but bad for us that not everyone would be covering the girls' competition.

The music blasting from the loudspeakers crossfaded into a drumroll to set up an announcement. "And now a special treat before the amateur preliminaries: an invitation-only ladies' park competition at the eleventh Ultimate competition." I helped Alexis to her feet and we shouted and waved our arms to make as much commotion as possible, but there wasn't a huge crowd yet, so the cheering wasn't exactly ear-splitting.

Ladies' park. Why were we ladies? It's not like they called the guys gentlemen. I checked the lineup printed in the program. Five girls, no preliminaries. If they'd split the girls into park and vert or let us have twenty amateurs like the guys, my name would be on that list. I closed my eyes for a second and shook off the what-ifs. At least girls were included. I'd get my chance tomorrow.

One of my favorite songs started, and Alexis pulled me down to sit and watch.

Carmelisa Benton, the girl who won the On Site competition at Explosion, went first. She dropped in, looked like she was going to do a back flip, changed her mind too late and spun out.

Bad start. What was wrong? I'd seen her do back flips before with no problem. Was the Ultimate atmosphere that freaky? I hoped all the girls wouldn't ride badly, or we'd never get more competition slots.

After waving that she was okay, Carmelisa got back up, shook her head, and circled back to set herself up to try again. I held my breath as she managed to rotate the flip, but fell on the landing. She got up, but ran out of time before she could try again.

Dylan McNeil went next and nailed a 360 over the tabletop. She did a couple flatland moves, then finished with a sweet can-can.

"Nice!" I applauded hard, whistling and cheering with the rest of the crowd.

A girl from Indiana who I recognized from the Outrageous Jam wobbled down the ramp, did a slow circle in the park, and never picked up any momentum.

The guy sitting behind me shifted, bumping me in the back. "That's the kind of ride that gets you dumped by a sponsor."

Another male voice answered him. "No shit. It's like sudden death. One bad ride here and you're out."

I snuck a glimpse behind me and the guys were way younger than us, maybe ten or eleven.

Alexis elbowed me. "You're scowling."

"Sorry." It was disappointing to hear them so focused on sponsors. At that age, I was riding to ride. I don't think I even knew what a sponsor was.

Lauryn was up next. I mouthed a silent prayer as I watched her on the start platform.

Alexis shouted, "Come on, Lauryn!"

I hoped she was calm and focused. *Come on, come on, you can do this.*

After dropping down fast, Lauryn picked up plenty of momentum to drive up the tabletop ramp. She hit the top of the coping standing up on her pedals, and then threw her handlebars for a perfect barspin. Yesss! I knew she could do it. If she was riding what we'd planned she should go to the mini staircase next. I sat up straighter so I could see better.

Lauryn approached the stairs at medium speed and launched into a 360 over the steps. Her height looked good and she cleared the steps but I could see that she'd under-rotated it. I didn't breathe as she landed, hoping she'd somehow find a few extra seconds to turn. Her bike came down about twenty degrees off of straight, but she managed to not wipe out by putting a foot down. I exhaled and let go of my death grip on the bench, shaking my hands to get the blood recirculating.

After doing a few grinds, Lauryn charged toward the quarter-pipe in front of us to go for her final trick. I covered my mouth as she launched into the air and kicked her right leg out for a one-footer. Her leg wasn't super-high, but it was pretty clean, and she landed it solid.

"Way to go, Lauryn!" I screamed and clapped furiously as she rode away. She had one of the best runs so far.

Evie Zafira was up last. She dropped down and built momentum heading toward the tabletop ramp. I expected her to do a back flip, but she lowered her shoulder so she turned and flipped at the same time and landed going back down the ramp she just went up. A flair! I bet some guys in this competition didn't have that trick down.

Without pausing, Evie drove hard for the staircase and did a perfect 360 down the steps. She had so much air, she could have done that trick over a staircase three times as steep. Evie rode the way the top guys did, fast and fully committed. Each time she launched into a trick it looked like she'd either kill it or wipe out completely. She hit everything with perfect precision and pulled off a front flip as her last trick. The crowd went crazy, screaming and cheering. Even Troy was on his feet.

While the organizers tallied the scores and pulled the podium out for the top three finishers, the amateur guys poured into the park for their warm-up.

Alexis readjusted her crutches. "Guess we know who will be in first place."

"What do you think about Lauryn?" I asked. "Top three?"

"Definitely."

The music volume lowered and we turned to watch the competitors grouped around the podium.

I closed my eyes when the announcer started talking. "In third place, Lauryn Jax of Lakeville, Illinois."

"Woo-hoo!" I jumped out of my seat, cheering. Alexis hauled herself up and we hugged while she hopped up and down on one leg.

We kept cheering as Dylan McNeil took second and then waited for the announcer to call out first place which, no surprise, went to Evie Zafira.

"And that's the end of the ladies' park competition. Next up, amateurs."

What about Exhibition? Would it have killed him to mention it? Did people even know there would be more of us riding? He made it sound like there were only five girls in the world who rode BMX.

The guy sitting behind me burped. "Do you think VaporTrail will put any of these chicks in the Launch Pad?"

Launch Pad? There was going to be a Launch Pad at Ultimate?

His friend answered, "That Evie chick dialed some nice tricks. She'll probably get in."

Launch Pads were like a best-trick competition, except they liked to pick people who weren't known. Top Launch Pad tricks became legendary. The footage went online and got sent everywhere. Even my parents knew what Launch Pad was. It would be incredible if they featured some BMX girls.

But even if they did, they wouldn't pick girls sitting in the stands.

Chapter 27

"Josie. Earth to Josie." Alexis shook my arm.

"What?"

"You're in a trance."

"I…"

Miguel ran up to us. "Don't move! The stands are filling up. Save those seats, or we'll be standing for guys' park."

"Did you hear that VaporTrail is doing their Launch Pad here?" I asked him.

"Yeah. Everyone's talking about it."

"Any idea who's picking the riders?"

"No one knows, but everyone is trying to figure it out. The VaporTrail guys probably have an idea." Miguel shook his head. "Figures it's in the first competition I decide to miss on purpose."

Crap. I didn't mean to make him feel bad. "How's the video going?"

"Not great. Whoever the genius was who decided everything should be gold isn't into filming. It's throwing off the light on everything. I need to figure out a recalibration before tomorrow or if it's sunny we're not going to see anything."

The loudspeakers blared an announcement about the amateur guys park warm-up finishing.

I bet the Launch Pad guy would be watching and picking guys from amateur and pro prelims. That's what was cool about Launch Pad. It didn't matter if you didn't make it to finals; you still had a shot if you had one good trick.

"Who's in the first heat?' Miguel asked.

Alexis flipped open her program. "I'll put a little star next to all the ones Josie has made out with. Or maybe it would be easier if I mark the ones she hasn't kissed yet."

"What?" Troy glared at me.

"She's kidding." I shoved Alexis. "Tell him you're kidding."

"Relax. I'm teasing."

Was Sean actually competing? I looked at the lineup and there he was in the first heat.

I scanned the guys warming up in the park, looking for a red bike with gray rims. "Do you see Sean out there?" I asked Miguel.

"I don't see him, but maybe he changed his bike."

I realized I hadn't seen Sean in months. He could have changed everything. New bike, new girlfriend...

When Sean's name was called third, I saw that Miguel was right. Sean had changed his bike to black with blue rims. Even though I was still mad at him, I was curious to see what he'd been working on. He did a 360 and a tuck no-hander without much air.

"What was that?" I asked out loud. It was a safe ride, a chicken ride, not even up to the level of what he was doing last summer.

"He'll never make it to finals," Miguel said.

"Or the Launch Pad," I added. Sean's ride would have been okay for him three years ago, but not now.

Most of the amateur guys were pretty competitive, doing double flips, flairs and tailwhips. One guy did a cool variation on a toboggan, but I didn't see anyone who might be from Launch Pad approach him.

When the first heat of pro guys warmed up I scanned the area where the VaporTrail riders were, trying to figure out who the Launch Pad guy was.

"Who are you looking for?" Alexis asked me.

"R.T.," I told her. "His family is across from us." I pointed out Team Torres in the stands. R.T.'s parents and Maricela were there plus about six others in UnnUsual shirts.

"Where's Lauryn?" I asked. She'd left to go to the bathroom a while ago and was going to miss guys' pro park.

"She's getting seats for vert," Miguel said. "I'm going to go help her save them. She said it's filling up already."

When the announcer called out Zach's name I elbowed Alexis and she gave me a look. He did a one-handed x-up, a superman, and pulled off a double tailwhip that made the crowd go crazy. He was sure to advance to the finals. And maybe the Launch Pad.

Next up was R.T. Torres. I hadn't talked to him since Explosion. He was wearing the Gote shoes, not the ones from his friend.

Alexis whispered something to Troy and Troy leaned forward, watching more closely.

R.T. rode out, did a 540 tabletop, an opposite flair, and a downside tailwhip. His ride was solid, but not epic. Should be enough to advance to the finals.

Since it was guys' preliminary, there was no podium, just a list of the top ten who would advance to tomorrow's finals. R.T., Oliver, and Zach made it, but Flynn missed by one spot. I knew how that felt.

Troy and I helped Alexis hobble down the steps, and she stopped to talk to Zach.

"Nice double whip," I told him. "Did you get tapped for Launch Pad?"

Zach smiled. "I did, and he asked me about you."

Me?

"Asked what?"

"If I knew who you were."

"And what did you tell him?" Why could guys never tell the story? It always had to be an interrogation.

"That you were with UnnUsual and you'd be in the MixUp tomorrow."

"But I'm not..."

"ZAAACH!" Before I could tell him I'd be riding in Exhibition, another of the VaporTrail guys bellowed from fifty yards away, waving and whistling.

"Gotta go! Good luck." Zach took off.

Great. The Launch Pad guy would be watching some other girl in MixUp.

Chapter 28

I ran after Zach to tell him I was doing Exhibition instead of MixUp, but he was gone before I could grab him. Pretty much everyone who had been watching the park prelims was heading to the half-pipe to get a seat for vert and the crowd was so thick I was afraid I'd lose Alexis and Troy if I went too far.

Lauryn texted me to hurry up and I did my best to prod Alexis along, but we weren't making good progress. Everyone was passing us because Alexis was so slow.

"Come on, the faster we get there, the sooner we can rest." I paused a step ahead of Alexis as she lurched her way forward, then stopped.

"I can't go any faster." Alexis pulled a crutch out from under her arm and wiped sweat off her chin. Troy took her crutches away and handed them to me, then threw Alexis over his shoulder. She squealed but didn't tell him to put her down.

I started to protest, but Troy was pushing through the crowd much faster, so I followed behind him with the crutches.

When we got to the spots Lauryn and Miguel saved, Troy eased Alexis down onto the bench and sat next to her. I barely managed to squeeze in, and my view was partly obstructed by a big, swinging mechanical arm that held a cage with a cameraman in it.

"That cherry picker will move as soon as they start filming," Miguel said. "That's OutDone network. They scored the sweet spot to get the best coverage."

Media was all over the half-pipe event, and this was only the preliminaries. I knew *BMX Real Deal* was streaming their coverage live, and others were posting it as fast as they could.

This was what I wanted my parents to see tomorrow.

Music started over the loudspeakers while the guys warmed up.

I half-watched the first two amateurs as I tried to spot Zach with the other VaporTrail guys. Miguel was right, the cherry picker with the camera on it did move but it kept moving in and out of my view. I would have been better off watching the streaming coverage at home.

"Look at that guy!" Miguel nudged me and I leaned over to see that the third amateur competitor had climbed up onto the scaffolding holding the big media box. He grabbed his bike and set himself up six feet above the drop-in ramp.

The announcer sounded flustered as he tried to keep his commentary rolling. "Whoa! Our drop-in wasn't high enough for Derek Johns."

I leaned way over Miguel so I could see around the cherry picker arm as Derek plummeted onto the half-pipe, powered up the other side and launched in the air.

He moved so fast I couldn't see which height marker he hit, but it had to be higher than anyone so far.

"Nice! Have you heard of this guy?" I asked.

"Nope."

The rest of his ride was just as crazy, with no tricks I could exactly name. Everything he did had a funky twist to it.

When Derek Johns finished, everyone was on their feet, stomping and whistling.

When we sat back down, Troy asked, "Are you allowed to drop in from the media box?"

"This is BMX, not baseball. Anything goes," I told him.

None of the other amateurs tried to replicate the move.

The announcer called out the top ten who qualified for the finals as the names appeared on the board, but Derek Johns wasn't there.

Loud boos echoed from the stands.

I cupped my hands around my mouth and joined in the protest until an announcement started. "We had a safety-related disqualification for Derek Johns."

Safety? It's not like he threw off his helmet. BMX was definitely risky; but to innovate, you had to try new things.

"This sucks," I said.

"What?" Miguel asked.

"He had the best move today and he won't even be in the finals."

Miguel shrugged. "Competitions are run by corporations. They like rule-followers, herd mentality."

"I bet the pro guys won't try anything as good as Derek."

Lauryn scanned the names in her program. "I wonder if Jimi P. will do his 900."

"Maybe not in this wind," Miguel said.

"I would kill to be able to do a 900." Lauryn watched the pro guys warm up, transfixed.

"You're more than one-third of the way there." Miguel told her.

She still didn't look away. "I put a foot down on that 360."

"Yeah, but in calm air you can do it."

One of the VaporTrail guys did a 540 but the wind was gusting, and a couple of guys who rarely wiped out in competition fell.

After the competition, a dozen girls in gold string-bikini tops and short shorts ran into the trough in the half-pipe and started dancing. Troy applauded, and even Miguel was completely transfixed.

"You've got to be kidding me." Lauryn kicked the stands in front of her. "They have time to let these twelve girls prance around and they couldn't squeeze in ten more girls in the competition?"

I tried to imagine the equivalent happening after a girls' event. Would we have a dozen shirtless guys wander out and start dancing? Probably not. It wasn't that we didn't appreciate visually appealing males. But blatantly parading them out? I couldn't get into it or I'd be too annoyed.

When the gold girls finally pranced away, the announcer officially closed day one of the competition and reminded everyone that they could meet the athletes in the signing tent.

"I never would have picked that lineup for vert finals," I said. "I wonder how many of those guys will do Launch Pad. It may be more interesting than the finals tomorrow."

"Except they won't have the chance to win a three-thousand-dollar travel voucher. You take away the prizes and you might not see some of these guys do an actual ride," Miguel said.

"They'd still perform with the cameras rolling." I stretched my neck to loosen the kink from trying to see around the cherry picker.

Miguel grabbed both my arms. "You're a genius. I'm going to go find that Derek guy and get him on camera."

Chapter 29

After Miguel took off, Lauryn turned to me. "I told Evie I'd go the signing tent to support the girls. You should come with me and meet them."

I agreed. It would be cool to meet Evie and I'd be in proximity of Zach to set the record straight about me not doing MixUp.

Alexis refused to fight her way through any more crowds, so Troy volunteered to stay with her.

When Lauryn and I stepped into the signing tent, R.T. was only a few feet away to my right.

"Come on, let's go this way." I veered to the left and got a few steps away when a hand pulled me away from the crowd. I tried to shake it off, but the grasp got much stronger.

I turned to face R.T. "You don't have to drag me off like a caveman."

He let go of me and I waved to Lauryn that I was okay.

"Actually, I do. You're not answering my calls or texts, and you literally ran the other way when you saw me. What's going on? Did I miss something?"

I took a step backward. "I'm not going to line up for your autograph with all your groupies. I'm busy."

"You don't have ten seconds to talk to me?" He moved closer, making sure I couldn't slip away.

"Ha. That's funny, asking if I have time for you. You're the one who has no time to give me."

"Huh?"

"I heard you on film." If he wanted to have this out right there, then fine. "Turner asked if you'd give up time for me in MixUp, and you said no."

I'd been talking too fast, so I took a breath and continued slower, "I mean, I get it. You want to max your ride, but so do I. I thought we were friends, but you couldn't spare even ten seconds."

He leaned in closer to me. "You know what else friends don't do? They don't jump to conclusions without giving the other person a chance." He looked away for a long pause and then looked back at me. "If you'd kept listening in on my private conversation you would know that I couldn't because I dropped out of the MixUp."

I felt acutely aware of my arms dangling by my sides, so I stuffed my hands in my back pockets.

R.T. continued. "So I could focus on park. I don't like that MixUp event. I hope that's not the reason you dropped."

"I dropped because I want to ride for more than thirty seconds. And partially because I can't say Robbins is my favorite person."

R.T.'s phone buzzed. He closed his eyes for a second. "I have to get it. Don't run off." He clasped my wrist with one hand and pulled his phone out with the other.

"What?" he asked. "I'm still at the... Okay. I know. I know. I know. Okay."

He put his phone back in his pocket and let go of my wrist. "Do you ever feel like your family is smothering you?"

"Actually, I have no idea what that would feel like."

"It's gotten completely out of control. I'm looking forward to tomorrow because this will all be over." He exhaled in a loud sigh.

I tilted my head to look at him. "Hypothetically, if you were doing the MixUp, would you give me a few seconds?"

A big grin spread across his face, but he didn't answer.

"Too bad we can't do pairs like in figure skating." I brushed my hair off my face. "Picture it. Synchro BMX with matching outfits, choreographed to cheesy music."

"When that happens, I'm out of this sport." He laughed. "Don't even bring it up. Someone will do it."

His phone buzzed again. "This is why I never have a girlfriend." He pulled it out of his pocket, checked the caller, and looked at me. "I have to go."

"I'm sorry," I said.

"Me too."

"No. I mean I'm sorry I jumped to conclusions."

"I'm not as much of an asshole as everyone thinks. Good luck tomorrow."

"You too."

I watched as he walked away, answering his phone.

While I stood there, someone body-slammed me from behind, almost knocking me over.

"Watch it!" I turned to see Derek Johns on the ground behind me, red-faced.

"Sorry. Someone clipped me from the side." He stood up and wiped his hands on his jeans.

"Hey, nice move earlier." I said. "Sorry it got you DQ'd."

"Thanks. You're Josie right?"

"Right." How did he know who I was?

"You riding tomorrow?"

"Yeah."

"Show 'em what you got!" He punched me lightly on the shoulder and took off, out of the signing tent.

When I turned to look for Zach at the VaporTrail tent, Sean, Mindy Z-Dog and NoFro were in front of me. It would have been too obvious if I tried to ditch. I had to say something.

"Nice ride," I told Sean.

"It was okay." He shrugged.

"Why didn't you do your lookback? You had it in May."

Mindy tugged on his hand and whispered to him, avoiding looking in my direction.

"Didn't feel it today. See you around." They left, but Z-Dog and NoFro lingered.

Z-Dog shook his head "Pathetic."

"He should have done the lookback," I said.

"Yeah, maybe if he'd practiced a little," NoFro said.

"What?"

Z-Dog kicked the dirt in front of him. "He's hardly been to the park all summer."

"What's he been doing?"

NoFro started to answer. "Sometimes, when a boy is near a girl, he gets a tingly feeling..."

I cut him off. "Never mind. Why didn't you guys ride?"

"It filled up before we could register," Z-Dog told me.

"Are you doing Exhibition?" I asked.

"After vert finals? Forget it. No one wants to watch a bunch of lame wannabes after the pro half-pipe." NoFro checked a message on his phone. "We gotta go. See ya J."

"See ya," I said.

No one would be watching exhibition? He was wrong.

By then the signing tent was jam-packed. I couldn't even see the MadKapp table. I sent a message to Lauryn telling her I was going to grab some food and head back to the hotel. I'd have to meet the MadKapp girls another time.

It took me forever to get through the food lines and back to the hotel room. Before I could flop down on the bed the phone rang.

It was Troy. "About time you're there. Get over to Alexis and Lauryn's room. *Now,* before they kill each other."

Even from the elevator I could hear them yelling in the hall.

Troy let me in and I stood in front of Alexis, who was making most of the noise.

I put my hands up. "Will you guys shut up? You're going to get us kicked out."

"Tell her how ridiculous she is." Lauryn turned to face me.

"What?" I asked. "What happened now?"

"Just because I'm proud of my body." Alexis leaned back on one of the double beds, glaring at Lauryn. "Miss Uptight."

"Proud of her body." Lauryn threw her hands in the air and paced in a tight circle. "Give me a break."

I stopped Lauryn from pacing. "What is going on?"

"That Launch Pad guy is asking girls to ride in bikinis tomorrow, and Miss Exhibitionist here is upset he didn't ask her."

"It's because of those stupid crutches. Otherwise I'd be in."

Bikinis? Was that why he wanted to find me? To ask me to ride in a bikini?

Lauryn put her hands on her hips. "Josie, would you do it? Ride in a bikini?"

"No."

"See." Lauryn leaned down and got in Alexis's face.

Alexis swatted Lauryn away. "Why not?"

"Because it's a good way to get road rash." I sat down in the chair.

"See?" Lauryn sat down on her bed.

Alexis rolled her eyes. "You don't do flips and stuff."

"Then why ride at all if you're just part of the scenery?" I asked. "They can hire models to do that. Why waste actual talented riders? It's insulting."

Lauryn pumped a fist in the air. "Yes. Thank you."

What I said to Lauryn was true. I was insulted, but part of me was also disappointed.

Chapter 30

I woke up before my alarm went off. Troy never came back last night. He was probably with Alexis, and Lauryn was with Miguel. I was alone. I'd skipped the Ambiguous Pluto concert the night before, claiming I wanted to rest for today, but really there was too much swirling in my head and I couldn't face everyone paired up.

My parents should have been en route. I checked my phone for messages, but had no news.

Someone knocked softly on my door.

Lauryn and Miguel waved at me as I looked through the peephole. "Hey! We brought breakfast—egg muffins."

I let them in. "Thanks."

"Did you sleep okay?"

"Not bad."

"You know you don't have to watch the MixUp. Alexis is going to skip it."

"No. I want to watch." I had to watch. "I'll come back for my bike after park finals."

When we got outside, it looked as if the cloudy windy weather from the day before never happened.

"You got the perfect day to ride," Miguel said. "It's going to be hell to film with all this sun bouncing off the gold."

"I bet Jimi P. will do his 900," Lauryn said.

Lauryn and Miguel kept talking about the weather and who would do what trick. I listened but I couldn't contribute anything to the conversation. Who was riding with UnnUsual? What if Robbins let her ride a full minute? Whatever happened, I had to smile and clap and look like I didn't care.

At the park, teams were finishing their warm-ups for the MixUp. R.T. was probably in the stands somewhere, but I didn't look around. I didn't want to see anyone or anyone to see me.

"Where's R.T.?" Lauryn asked.

"He dropped out of MixUp so he could focus on park."

She started to ask more but I cut her off. "I found out yesterday, but I don't want to get into it."

Miguel reached over and squeezed my shoulder. "You're better than this. Don't worry."

The S-Force team went first. Their girl looked young, and was in a shirt about three sizes too big. She rode up and down a tabletop ramp, then back. Her coach clapped her on the back as the next guy went out.

All the teams used the same strategy with the girls. They gave them the minimum time allowed.

Lauryn snorted as the third girl rode out and back without doing anything. "This is so stupid. I'm glad you boycotted. They need to change the rules or dump this stupid event."

"I know," I said. "I want to see girls compete more, but not like this."

The girls were there technically, but they didn't count. It all came down to what the guys did.

When the UnnUsual team was up, I felt my jaw and shoulders tighten.

Flynn went first and had a great run, then Oliver took his turn, and then Carmelisa rode.

Lauryn shielded her eyes with her hand and leaned forward. "Isn't she the one who kept trying the back flip?"

"Yeah."

We watched as she rode out, but instead of heading for the tabletop, she went around it, did a bunnyhop, and then looked up at Robbins who waved her in.

What a waste.

Turner went out last and did a 540, a barspin and a flair.

"That's going to be close," Lauryn said. "Either S-Force or UnnUsual will win."

We watched as the third-place team stepped on the podium. I closed my eyes as they announced S-Force in second place.

UnnUsual won. Flynn high-fived Carmelisa and they all crowded onto the top of the podium. Turner had his arm around her waist. That could have been me.

Heaviness filled my body as I watched them receive their prizes, five hundred dollars each.

As soon as the photographers got their podium pictures, Turner was pulled aside by a Rulebreaker network guy and his cameraman for an interview. Oliver and Flynn were approached by an interviewer for *BMX Real Deal*, and two MadKapp reps went up to my replacement.

"Hey." Lauryn shook my leg. "No regrets, right?"

I couldn't answer her. I'd ruined everything. That could have been me up there... should have been me up there.

I swallowed hard, willing myself to hold it together.

Warm-ups for guys' park finals were announced and guys on bikes poured into the park from all directions.

Miguel showed us a quick replay of his MixUp footage. "I tested out lighting strategy. It's working. Look. No glare."

"Nice." Lauryn kissed him on the cheek and I assured him that whatever he did was working, although I couldn't bring myself to look at the replays.

Troy and Alexis found us and as they were sitting down I saw R.T. drop in to warm up. He did a big-air front flip and a smattering of applause came from the stands below us to our right. Team Torres was in position, with everyone on their feet clapping and cheering like mad.

"Looks like that T.J. guy is on his game today," Troy said.

With the lack of wind today, they were all trying bigger tricks than yesterday.

When the pro guys' competition officially started, a UK guy went first and did a triple whip as his opening trick and didn't back down for the rest of his run.

Miguel let out a low whistle. "No pressure."

Each guy was doing an incredible run and it looked like Oliver was going to pull off a barspin-to-x-up, but he blew it on the landing.

R.T. was second to last and when he went for a front flip turn down, I held my breath as he came out of the flip with his handlebars back in position, then landed it solid and rode off. He did it! I was on my feet with everyone else. If his prelim ride had been stronger he would have been in a better position to win.

Finally, R.T. wound up in second place, behind the UK guy, and none of the other UnnUsual guys made it to the podium.

We only had an hour and a half to get food and get back for vert finals, and I needed to get my bike, so we split up. Lauryn went to get lunch while I went to my room to change.

I put on my Exquisite shirt and slicked my hair into a low ponytail so it would fit under my helmet.

Who was I kidding? My ride wasn't anywhere near the league of what we just watched. I didn't want to make a total fool of myself out there. I should stick to riding in my backyard where it was fun. What was I thinking wanting to ride here? I was going through all this angst, and probably no one would even be at the exhibition event. Z-Dog was right. Riding after vert finals was insane.

I leaned my bike against the bed and sat on the floor.

When Lauryn got to the room, she took a wax-paper-wrapped sandwich from a bag.

"I can't eat," I told her. "I seriously feel sick."

"If in that head of yours you're comparing yourself to the best male park riders in the world, it better be in an 'I'm going to show them and do a kick-ass ride' kind of way, right?"

I silently reached for a sandwich.

She lifted it up over her head, out of my reach. "Right?"

I stood on my toes to grab it.

She lowered it and gave it to me.

"You've got to think like an alpha dog. They're constantly comparing themselves and trying to outdo each other. One sets the bar and the next one grabs it on his way higher."

She tapped her head. "It's all in here."

The guys' vert finals were such a huge draw that it took us forever to make our way to the edge of the park and get my bike checked in for Exhibition.

Music blasted as the guys warmed up, whizzing back and forth on the half-pipe.

I scanned the stands, and for once was happy Troy stood out so much. Lauryn and I wove through the crowds to go up the center aisle and get to our spaces. Our seats weren't as good as yesterday. I could only see part of the half-pipe, but I had a pretty good view of the big replay monitor, so I'd be able to see whatever I missed.

After showing some poor guy stuck cleaning pigeon crap off the ramps, the monitor featured highlights from Saturday and flashed "Look for him at the Launch Pad" on certain guys, including Derek and R.T.

Stupid Launch Pad. I looked away and watched the warm-ups. I recognized Turner and sort of recognized some of the other guys. It was hard to tell in their full-cage helmets.

The calm air made a difference for the vert riders. They were going for big tricks, even after a guy from Portugal spun out on a toboggan.

On Jimi P.'s turn everyone was waiting to see him do his 900. He started with a 720, did a no-hander, and then he went for it. I held my breath as he went up for one, then two rotations and then I got on my feet to see better as he kept going for the third one. When he landed people went insane, jumping up and screaming.

I sat back down and tried to focus on the rest of the competition, but I was getting anxious.

My phone buzzed and I checked to see if my parents were there yet, but my only message was from one of the girls from the clinic, telling me she couldn't wait to watch me ride at Exhibition.

At least someone would be there.

After the winners were announced, with Jimi P. in the top spot on the podium, the crew of dancing girls wheeled a cannon into the trough.

"That's the end of the eleventh Ultimate Games. Enjoy the Ultimate dancers and the rest of the Ultimate sport festival."

No mention of Exhibition.

One of the girls peeled off her T-shirt, loaded it into the cannon and then fired it into the stands. People went crazy, jumping and grabbing for the shirt. With the possibility of getting a free T-shirt, who was going to go to Exhibition? No one.

I stood up to leave. "I have to go get warmed up."

Miguel stood. "We'll go with you."

"Wait! I'm trying." Alexis struggled with her crutches.

"I can go by myself. It'll be faster." I didn't wait for them to discuss who would stay with Alexis or go with me. I wanted to get it over with. I couldn't stand waiting there any longer, seeing all the attention focused on the dancing girls. "I'll see you over there."

Lauryn grabbed me on my way by. "You can do this. Look at me." She held onto my wrist until I looked her in the eyes.

"You're going to go in that exhibition and show them how wrong they are to not let more girls compete. Remember, the only thing guys have that we don't just gets in the way on a bike."

Chapter 31

Troy refused to stay behind and went with me out of the vert stands. He must have been under direct orders to keep me in sight. We walked without saying anything until we got to the far end of the Ultimate grounds where the exhibition was taking place.

"What's that?" Troy pointed to a huge inflatable bouncy castle that had been set up next to the park, along with clowns handing out balloon animals and a face-painting station.

"Great. It's a kiddie area," I said. Exhibition would be little kids and me. Perfect.

The stands by the park were practically deserted except for the trash that littered the ground under the stands. They hadn't cleaned up yet from the guys' park finals.

"You don't have to stay," I told him. "I know Mom told you to keep an eye on me, but I probably won't do anything that could get me injured anyway. Why risk it?"

"Don't think like that." Troy wasn't facing me, and I couldn't see his eyes behind the mirrored lenses of his sunglasses. "Treat this like it's the make-or-break competition of your life. If you ride that way every time it won't matter what scores you get or whatever because you'll know you gave it one hundred and ten percent."

He was right in theory. I should have felt like going out there and pushing past my comfort zone, but I wasn't feeling it.

Pounding footsteps announced someone behind us, and I turned expecting to find Miguel with another pep talk. An older guy in a VaporTrail T-shirt stopped next to me. "Josie?"

"Yes."

"Josie Peters?" He stared at my bike and then looked back up at me. "You've been next to impossible to track down."

"I'm right here." I wiped a sweaty hand on my jeans.

"How would you like to ride in the Launch Pad?"

"I'm not comfortable riding in a bikini, thanks." I started to wheel my bike away.

He put an arm out in front of me. "No, wait. Those were posers with their own unofficial Launch Pad. This is for real."

"Seriously?" I stopped and looked at him.

"Fully clothed." He held his hands up like he was surrendering.

"But I didn't even compete. Why me?"

"We saw you at the Outrageous BMX Jam, and you've got a decent following online. That wipeout video of yours is becoming a classic."

Great. One day I wanted to be known for staying on my bike.

He pulled his phone out and glanced at it. "We need you to get over there right now."

"Now?"

"It starts in a half hour and girls are first."

"I'm doing Exhibition."

"Not if you're doing Launch Pad."

I'd be riding with Derek and R.T. I could text everyone that I changed. They'd rather watch Launch Pad anyway. "Let me check to see where my parents are."

As I pulled out my phone, the Launch Pad guy kept talking. "We've got a new low-calorie energy drink coming out this fall that we're targeting to the teen girl demographic..."

While he yammered I read my only message, from another girl who was in the clinic. *I made my family take me to see you. Good luck!*

How many girls from the clinic were going to be at Exhibition because of me?

The Launch Pad guy was still going on "...getting a female in today's Launch Pad will help strategically widen our bandwith."

Bandwith? Demographics? Why couldn't girls drink regular VaporTrail?

As he kept jabbering about his marketing plans and how I fit in, a few more people filed in and sat in the Exhibition stands. I knew who I wanted to ride for and where.

I straightened my bike and got ready to go. "Sorry. People are counting on me at Exhibition."

"Seriously?" he asked me.

"Seriously. But thanks for the invite."

I got on my bike and put on my helmet. "I've got to go. Warm-ups are starting."

After popping my mouth guard in, I took off for the park. The surface felt smooth under my tires, and the ramps were solid. I rode around picking up speed and didn't feel anything catch or throw me off. I recognized two MadKapp girls, and a couple from the Outrageous Jam, but there were even more I didn't recognize. At least twenty girls were there for Exhibition. Excellent.

When the mini staircase opened up I went for it and did a 360. After I stopped, one of the MadKapp girls nodded at me. "Nice!"

A petite girl on a silver bike did a no-hander and then one of the MadKapp girls did a tailwhip. I realized that Lauryn was partially right. Seeing that girl pull it off made me want to do it too, but not so I could beat her.

Not so I could prove I was better.

Seeing her do it showed me I could do it too.

I was scheduled midway through the girls' lineup. I watched as one of the MadKapp girls did an amazing ride that easily was as good, if not better than some of the guys in preliminaries. I could hear cheering but I didn't bother checking the stands. It didn't matter who was there, if my parents showed up or not. This one was for me and for all the girls watching who'd ever been told they couldn't or shouldn't ride for no good reason.

The announcer called my name and when my music started, I built up momentum and went straight for the tabletop, hit it hard, pulled my knees in and did my back flip, landing it perfectly.

I pulled off a nice barspin, then decided to go for the tailwhip. I kicked the back of my bike out, caught it, but came down a little too fast and spun out. I got back up as fast as I could, but the buzzer sounded the end of my turn.

When I got outside the competition area, a girl with an Australian accent nodded in the direction of the stands. "You've got yourself quite the cheering section there."

In the stands a group of at least thirty people each held a card that together spelled out *JOSIE*, and then when they flipped the cards they showed *ROCKS!*

When they finally pulled down the cards I saw it was mostly girls from the clinic in matching T-shirts. Was that Connor telling them when to flip?

As the announcer named the next girl to ride, a familiar male voice called out, "Josie."

R.T. was behind the fence.

I went to where he was standing. "What are you doing here? You're supposed to be at Launch Pad."

"I know, but I couldn't miss your ride. You almost had that tailwhip."

"Next time," I said.

"Hey will you sign this for me?" He held out an eight-by-ten glossy of me that was different from the ones we had handed out at the clinic.

"Did you steal this from some little girl?" I asked.

"Your mom gave it to me."

I looked toward the stands and saw that my parents were both there.

"Josie? Two of my brothers are heading this way so I have to make this quick."

I turned to face him. "Make what..." He pulled me to him and kissed me, hesitating a little as soon as our lips touched, as if waiting to see if I'd pull away. I kissed him back, and I could feel him smile before he pulled back to look at me.

"You're a dead man." One of his brothers clapped a hand on R.T.'s shoulder.

R.T. ignored him and kept watching me. "It was worth it."

"Come on. You're done here."

R.T. walked away backward, facing me. "There's a BMX Jam in Westdale in October. You should definitely check it out."

His brothers turned him around and practically dragged him away.

When I couldn't see R.T. anymore I brushed my fingers over my lips, willing myself to remember exactly what that kiss felt like.

I watched as the rest of the girls did their Exhibition rides, making a mental note of who had tailwhips down.

When the last rider finished, I was mobbed by the girls from the clinic. They stood out in pastel Spoked T-shirts painted with the same tie-dye effect Leo had done on my bike.

Troy had a pen and pictures ready for me. "You started a friggin' cult."

Some of the girls had brought sisters and friends. I signed for everyone who asked.

"Where did these pictures come from?" I asked.

"Mom arranged it with your photographer friend," Troy said.

My mom and dad waved to me from the stands, but before I could go to them Sandra approached me with a woman I recognized, but couldn't place.

"Josie Peters?"

I knew that voice. She was a reporter from OutDone.

Chapter 32

The OutDone reporter raised her arm in the air and shouted "I've got her."

A camera guy who couldn't have been much older than eighteen ran over and shone a light on us. "I'll need a minute to set up."

She waved him away when he tried to readjust the lights. "If we hurry we can make the cut. Let's go. We're here with Josie Peters a virtual unknown in the world of BMX biking, yet a girl who may well represent the future of the sport. Josie, how did you get all these young girls so interested in trying BMX?

"I told them to have fun."

She did most of the talking but asked me a couple of decent questions. "You wiped out just then in front of everyone. Would you call that fun?"

I shrugged. "Not trying is way worse than wiping out."

She put the microphone down and motioned for the camera guy to stop. "I've got what I need here. I can't believe you didn't film her riding."

The camera guy looked ready to strangle her. "You told me it was a nonevent."

Miguel ran over to me with his camera. "Too bad about the tailspin, but the rest of your ride was perfect. In case you missed any of the others, I got everything."

The OutDone camera guy looked up "You have those girls from start to finish?" He talked into an earpiece. "We have event footage." He pulled Miguel aside and got deep in conversation.

Z-Dog and NoFro came over and congratulated me.

"I can't believe you guys are here instead of at Launch Pad," I said.

Z-Dog looked over to where Alexis was hopping toward me on her crutches. "We're interested in supporting the up and coming..."

I cut him off. "Yeah, it has nothing to do with the fact that this is where all the girls are."

Lauryn walked over with one of the women from MadKapp. "Josie—got a minute?"

She introduced us and the woman told me they wanted me to be an expansion delegate for the team, which meant I'd travel to competitions in advance and do promo events to help grow the sport.

"And you want me?"

"The guys may get big air, but the girls buy more clothes and you're apparently influencing them." She gave me her card, took my number and said we'd work out the details. I hoped those details might include the Westdale Jam in October.

"Josie honey I can barely get through." My mom gave me a huge hug.

"Congratulations." My dad hugged me after my mom let go. "You were wonderful."

"Who did the cards?" I asked.

"That was Connor," my mom said. "He had the girls practice and organized getting them here."

Miguel came over with a huge grin on his face.

"What's with you?" I asked.

"They just paid me a nice chunk of change for that footage. Come on—they want a group shot of everyone."

All the girls got together, and as the cameras snapped, my bad landing didn't matter, UnnUsual and my replacement winning didn't matter. This was what I wanted all along. To see more girls riding for themselves. Not trying to fit in with the guys or look like the guys or impress the guys. Just ride. Like girls.

THE END

Acknowledgements

Thank you to my parents for encouraging me to read anything and everything. Thank you to everyone who didn't laugh (or at least not in my face) when I said I wanted to write a book. Even more thanks to my sister and her family for building me a room of my own in their house. A ton of thanks to E. for refusing to let me make any excuses not to finish writing this book, for simulating bike wipeouts, for disabling internet access on my writing laptop, and for all the tech support. The NaNoWriMo 2009 loss and recovery incident will never be forgotten. Special thanks to my critique group for reading multiple versions of the manuscript and for providing plenty of chocolate to help make the criticism easier to take. More thanks to the Montreal breakfast club for sanity checks, encouragement, and laughs. Thanks to everyone who helped me research BMX.

About the Author

Karen Avivi is never bored. If the weather is nice, it's almost impossible for her to stay inside. Karen has tried surfing, skydiving, scuba diving, stunt classes, archery, winter camping, orienteering, mountaineering, mountain biking, and she even attempted a bike ramp once but it didn't end well. If she's not reading or writing, she's usually planning a new adventure.

Visit www.karenavivi.com to find out when her next book will be released.

###